SMALL TOWN LAWYER

Defending Innocence

Influencing Justice

Interpreting Guilt

Burning Evidence

Peter Kirkland is a pen name created by Relay Publishing for co-authored Legal Thriller projects. Relay Publishing works with incredible teams of writers and editors to collaboratively create the very best stories for our readers.

www.relaypub.com

SMALL TOWN LAWYER - BOOK FOUR

BURNING EVIDENCE

KIRKLAND & HALL

BLURB

In a small town, it's all too easy for secrets to stay buried...

When a young woman dies in a late-night restaurant fire, the owner, Bobby Carter, is charged with arson and murder. The evidence is stacked against him, but something doesn't add up. And his only chance for justice rests on the shoulders of small-town lawyer, Leland Munroe...

Leland's client insists he's innocent. But the local media is quick to demonize Carter, and powerful forces behind the scenes are determined to keep the truth from coming out. Leland must navigate a web of corruption and deceit to expose the real culprit.

Meanwhile, defending a young athlete accused of selling drugs has Leland facing off against a former colleague with an axe to grind. The two cases seem unrelated, but in Basking Rock, things are rarely as straightforward as they appear. Can this quick-witted lawyer outsmart the real killer? Or will he become their next victim...

CONTENTS

SMALL-TOWN LAWYER

Book 4: Burning Evidence

1

MARCH 6, 2022

I remember reading one of those top-ten lists, years ago, that listed out the most painful ways to die. Crucifixion was number one and a boomslang snake bite was number ten. Burning to death came in at number four.

I've no idea why that stuck with me, but it came to mind when I saw the building where the girl had died was coming down. I'd driven past it many times since the fire, but this time the traffic light was red. I stopped. A bulldozer sat on the far side of the rubble, waiting for its operator to return on Monday. Two intact doorways jutted out of piles of fallen bricks, their closed doors protecting no one.

My son, driving behind me so he could continue up to Charleston after the appointment we were heading to, honked his horn. There was nobody behind him urging us on—it was a minor street in a small town—but the light had changed, and he was impatient. He was too young to know you ought to make time for the dead.

We pulled up in front of a large, fine house. The front door and the underside of the porch roof were *haint* blue, the pale aqua shade that some folks believed kept evil spirits away and others painted on their houses just in case. I never bought into it myself, but those shades of blue had become downright ubiquitous around the South and any houses listed for sale were sure to sport a fresh coat of blue.

We went up the front steps. I couldn't remember what color anything had been the last time I'd been here. That must've been thirty-five or forty years ago, and I might not have seen the porch back then at all, since the family that had lived here didn't let my mother and me use the front door. They had us come in through the servants' entrance along with all the other staff.

Before I could ring the doorbell, Chance Carpenter, the realtor I was working with despite his ridiculous name, waved to me and Noah through the beveled glass and let us in.

After the customary chitchat, I smiled and looked around appreciatively at the woodwork Chance was pointing out. I clearly could not afford to buy this place, even though I was doing much better than I had been when I first moved back to my hometown. I wondered whether Chance had gotten some numbers transposed when I told him what my house-purchase budget was.

I also didn't tell him how wrong this home was for me. There was no sense in being rude; it wasn't his fault I hadn't recognized the place when he'd given me the address. I'd never thought of it in terms of an address. When I was a kid it had just been the fanciest of the many houses that my mother cleaned to keep us fed.

Apparently, Chance saw me as the type of man who came home to a beveled-glass front door. The master of a house like this, in a neighborhood full of doctors and lawyers.

I couldn't blame him for that. He wasn't from around here. I'd only met him a week ago.

"The high ceilings give it so much light," he said.

"Sure do." I noticed a smoke detector up there, about twelve feet above the hardwood floor, and said, "I'd hate to have to change the battery on that thing in the middle of the night."

Noah laughed.

"Oh, you won't have to," Chance said. "This whole system here is hardwired. It only goes to the battery backup if the power goes out. I doubt you'd have to change it more than once every ten years."

"That actually is the safest setup," Noah said. "Whatever house you get, you should probably get a hardwired system installed."

I looked at him. "Since when are you an expert in fire alarms?"

His face turned somber. "Oh, it's that arson case. I learned some stuff researching it."

"My goodness," Chance said, matching Noah's serious tone. "Are you working on that—the fire where that poor young lady so unfortunately passed away?"

"No, not that one," he said. "Man, that poor girl. No, this is something I'm helping a professor with."

Noah had graduated in December and was working as a researcher for one of his former teachers while peppering every detective agency in Charleston with resumes, trying to land his first real job.

The fire Chance was asking about had been all over the news, but there hadn't been any finding of foul play. Not yet, anyway.

It had nothing to do with me, apart from happening here in Basking Rock. But I'd stopped trying to lose the habit of having my ears prick up at any hint of tragedy or crime. Seventeen years as a prosecutor in Charleston, South Carolina, and another three doing criminal defense had left marks that would never go away.

I knew useful information sometimes came from unexpected places, so I said to Chance, "That's a hell of a thing, isn't it, that fire. You hear someplace it was arson?"

"Oh, it's just—" He waved one hand, like the idea had floated to him through the air. "I don't know anything personally. It's just, people talk. And she was the same age as my little sister. I saw that on the news. So I think it hit me harder because of that."

We all shook our heads. It was a terrible thing. A pizza shop had gone up in flames in the middle of the night, and the girl who lived in the apartment above it—a beautiful girl, from the pictures, who, if I recalled correctly, was only twenty-two—had been killed.

Chance said, "Anyway, look. I am so sorry, Mr. Munroe, I do not want to waste your time—"

"Not at all. Call me Leland."

"Leland. I will, thank you. So, obviously we're not here to talk about the news and how it makes me feel…" He flashed a smile. "We're here to find you a house, and I brought you to this one, even though it's bigger than what we'd talked about, because I know how deep your Lowcountry roots go, and—"

"Oh, yeah," I said, nodding. "This is a real Lowcountry house, that's for sure."

It was a pale-yellow Victorian, with deep porches across the front and down one side. Strong beams framed the doorways, and every corner was crammed with woodwork so delicate it looked like lace. It had to be more than a hundred years old—the big old oak out front looked at least that age—and both the house and the tree seemed like they'd been built with only two purposes in mind: to look beautiful, and to withstand hurricanes.

Chance led us into the kitchen, which was straight off some cooking show, perfectly curated to look homey and inviting while also letting you know that the remodel had probably cost north of eighty grand. I'd feel like an ass using this kitchen to reheat the pizza or takeout shrimp I ate most nights.

Noah pointed to the far wall and said, "That there's a stove, Dad. Those red knobs are how you turn it on."

"Oh, shut your mouth," I said, laughing.

Chance caught our mood and said, smiling, "Okay, I'm sensing this house doesn't exactly hit the mark?"

"Not unless it comes with a chef," Noah said.

"It's a beautiful home," I said. "And I do have a soft spot for true Southern style. But I'd hate a kitchen like this to go to waste. And anyway, this is a four-bedroom, right?"

"No, it's three. Although, you know what, there probably were four back in the day—the master suite upstairs is stunning, and I'm guessing they got that by combining two of the original bedrooms."

"Uh-huh."

I had a memory of ceiling fans, one in every bedroom, turning slowly, stirring the hot, heavy summer air—there was no air-conditioning back then. I remembered they'd been hard to clean.

"Well," I added, "even so, three is a lot for me, with Noah moving away. I mean, I don't think my Yorkshire terrier needs his own bedroom."

Chance laughed. "I hear you. I knew it might be a little large for you, but since you didn't love that mid-century place yesterday, I thought looking at this one might help us pinpoint your style."

Noah said, "His style is, if there's a coffee maker and a desk, he's good to go."

I said, "And a microwave. I do need *some* luxuries."

As they laughed, I thought how strange it was going to be not having my son around to crack jokes with. I'd been thinking that a lot, and then shaking off the thought. I shook it off again.

As we headed back to the front door, the beveled glass shot rainbows all over the foyer. I wasn't able to enjoy the sight of it much. There'd come a point about twenty years ago, after I'd been through a few trials and heard some stories, when any front door with that much glass in it started looking to me like it had nothing there at all. Anybody with a glove on could just punch right through.

Right now I was representing a kid up in Charleston who'd picked the wrong roommate, one with drug-gang connections. I liked living an hour and twenty minutes away from people like that, but I wasn't sure it was going to be far enough. It definitely wouldn't be far enough if I lived in a fragile bauble like this place.

I silently crossed cute Victorian houses off my list.

"You know what, Chance," I said, "I know there's not that many of them around here, but if you could keep an eye out for a stone house, or a brick one, I do have a little bit of a preference for that."

"Okay, I'll do that. Good to know." As he took us back out onto the porch and turned to lock the door, he said to Noah, "See? Your father does have a style! Everybody does."

"Yes, indeed," I said.

If I'd felt like explaining it, which I didn't, I would've told him my favorite home style was any type of architecture that was resistant to fire, intruders, and bullet holes.

2

MARCH 10, 2022

I was at work, mindlessly finishing the cold dregs of my morning coffee as I prepared for a Monday hearing, when Laura, Roy Hearst's long-time secretary, leaned in my office door and asked, "Is there any way you could jump on a Zoom call with a potential client at eleven? I can try to set something up for tomorrow if you need to focus on the Drayton thing."

Drayton was my client in Charleston, the student who'd gotten himself tangled up with a drug-dealing roommate. Normally, in our office, the name Drayton referred to his father, who ran an insurance agency and was one of Roy's longtime clients. Since returning to Basking Rock, three years ago, as a disgraced former prosecutor, rescuing the sons of Roy's clients from whatever trouble they got themselves into was a much bigger part of my practice than I wanted it to be.

I said, "Any idea why they need to talk right now? Please tell me this isn't another rich boy who got himself a DUI. I just got through about three dozen of those."

She smiled sympathetically. "No, this one's more interesting. Bobby Carter's wife wants to talk to you."

Mr. Carter owned the pizza place that had burned down, where that girl had died. And here he was, or his wife was, calling a criminal defense attorney.

"His wife wants to talk? Not Carter himself?"

"It might be the both of them. She didn't say."

I thought for a second. If Carter didn't own the building—if he just rented space in it for his restaurant—then he wouldn't have nearly as much motivation to torch it as whoever did own it.

"Did you ask if it's their building that burned down? Or if it's not, who the landlord is?"

"I didn't need to. That's one of Clyde Boseman's properties."

"I swear, you must have every land title in town memorized. I take it Boseman's not a client of Roy's?"

"Oh, no. I would've told her you couldn't help, if he was."

"Of course. Sorry."

We both knew I couldn't represent a guy whose case might create a conflict of interest with an existing client of the firm. I was apologizing for any scintilla of doubt in Laura's thoroughness that my question might have conveyed.

"No, it's better to ask," she said. "That way we can double-check each other."

"Uh-huh. It's hard to believe there's a commercial landlord in town who isn't Roy's client."

She smiled. "Yeah, he has managed to land most of them over the years. Anyway, if you're free, click on the calendar invite I sent you

8

for eleven o'clock for, uh…" She put her bifocals on and looked at the pink message pad she was holding. "Marianne. That's it. Marianne Carter. It's funny, I've been following this case, and I'm normally good with names. I don't know why hers just will not stick."

"You've been following it? What have you heard?"

"Oh, everybody's saying he burned it down for the insurance."

"Why's that?"

"Well, I suppose… I mean, even with his record, if he'd had a kitchen fire during the dinner rush, nobody'd think anything of it. But for the place to catch fire in the middle of the night, when nothing's running and nobody's there? Or he thought nobody was there?"

"I can see where that makes some sense. What's his record, though?"

I'd left Basking Rock at eighteen, intent on getting the hell out, so I was not privy to much of anything that had happened here during my seven years of college and law school or the seventeen I'd spent in Charleston as a prosecutor.

"Oh, you didn't see in the *Patriot*?"

"No."

I'd lost the habit of reading our local paper, the *Southeast Patriot*, when I left for college. By the time I returned home, the paper had become Sunday-only, with a website for the rest of the week, but I avoided it. I disliked the owner, Dabney Barnes IV—or "Fourth," as I referred to him when I was among friends—and was not inclined to give him my ear.

"Oh, they mentioned him spending time in jail for check fraud. When he got back from Iraq, there were a few bad years. Petty crime. He sort of fell off a cliff for a while. I was already working for Roy back then, so I heard whatever gossip he brought back from court."

9

"Was it a PTSD thing? From combat?"

"It might've been. And he did eventually turn his life around. But even without the *Patriot*, folks don't forget."

"No, I guess they don't."

I spoke diplomatically, because it sounded like she was including herself among those folks. To my mind, that was one of the worst things about Basking Rock, or probably any small town: you couldn't get away from your past. Folks hung on to you like crabs in a box, clinging to the legs of any of their brethren who tried to escape.

"It's quite a story, when you think about it. Maybe, after it's all figured out, it'll be on *Carolina True Crime*. Have you talked to her lately?"

She meant Shannon Pennington, our local true-crime groupie, who had a podcast that Laura listened to religiously.

"You know what, I haven't. My son follows that show."

"You don't?"

"Oh, I've listened to it once or twice. But I get more than enough true crime right here at work."

"Have you been following this fire at all, though?" she asked. "What do you think?"

Her tone was a little too eager. I couldn't blame her. After the many years she'd spent helping Roy with zoning issues or contracts for the sale of a car dealership, it was no wonder if crime and violence seemed more exciting.

For me, the excitement had gone extinct before my first year as a prosecutor was over. Every crime I dealt with had left a person broken or a family shattered. Criminal charges did the same thing to defendants and their families. I was the cleanup guy, trying to set right what was left.

Still, I didn't want to shoot down her enthusiasm. If she enjoyed her job, that was good for me and my clients. I gave her a smile. "What I think is, I ought to keep my trap shut and hear what Mrs. Carter has to say. Go ahead and let her know I'll take the call."

When Mrs. Carter appeared on my screen, I realized I must have had some assumptions about how the wife of a pizza-shop owner ought to look, because she surprised me. I took her to be around forty. She had nicely styled shoulder-length brown hair, and she was sitting in a well-appointed living room decorated in shades of green and blue, wearing a blazer and a light-colored blouse. On a table in the background was a tiny tree in a pot—maybe some kind of bonsai.

"Good morning, Mrs. Carter."

"Good morning. You can call me Marianne."

If I had to guess what she did in life, I might've thought psychologist, or maybe professor of nursing, something along those lines. Pizza-shop owner, or wife thereof, would not have crossed my mind. Especially not the wife of a pizza guy who had a criminal record.

"I really appreciate your taking my call on such short notice," she said

"It's not a problem. What can I help you with?"

"Well, it's about what happened at my husband's restaurant two weeks ago. That horrifying fire. I've been telling Bobby that he should get some legal advice, but, uh…" She made a steeple with her fingertips and rested her chin against it for a second, thinking.

I let her think. I was trying to figure out who she was. Her voice was smooth and warm, like the kind of radio host you could listen to all day, but there were hints in her accent that told me she wasn't from the South. A mix of familiar and not, like she'd lived here a good long time but had been raised elsewhere.

After a moment, she sighed. "This is just really hard for him. So I finally realized, well, I'm the communicator here, right?" She flashed a pained smile. "I'm the talker, he's the doer. So maybe it should be me who reaches out. And here I am."

"Uh-huh. Well, so I'm clear, is this his restaurant alone, or do you both run it?"

"Oh, it's all his. He owns it, he runs it."

"Okay. That suggests to me that if this does turn into something you need a lawyer like me for, then unless something really unusual is going on, most likely he's the only one of you that would be facing any charges."

"Right, no, it's not myself I'm worried about."

"Okay. So if he's my potential client, I really do need to speak with him. I'm glad you've reached out, and I'm happy for you to fill me in on the facts and your concerns, but I can't actually *do* anything for him without his okay and his participation."

"I understand. What I was thinking, or hoping, is that if you agree that it's time for him to be seeking advice, that would make it easier for me to convince him. So we could set up another Zoom, or... The thing is, I think at this point, with the news coverage, he's a little leery about being seen walking into a law office. It almost looks like a perp walk, you know?"

"I do. So we'll figure that out. Now, what is it that's led you to think he ought to consult a criminal defense attorney?"

She took another thoughtful pause, and then she said, "I *hope* it's not an intuition. I hope it's just anxiety, or a normal response to—to—I mean, knowing that some poor girl died in a fire at your husband's restaurant! Having a tragedy like that happen almost right *next* to you, it… I mean, it throws you. But, Mr. Munroe, even apart from all that, I've had a bad feeling about this right from the start."

"Uh-huh."

I knew the fire inspector must've been on this case like white on rice from about ten seconds after the last flame got put out. I wondered why Mrs. Carter hadn't called sooner.

"Marianne, just so I know what you're dealing with, there's been no charges filed, correct?"

"No. But the fire inspector's been… for lack of a better word, sniffing around. I don't mean that in a bad way—I know that's his job. He talked to Bobby right after it happened, and now he wants to talk to him again."

"All right, I do think you're right to reach out for advice. I'd like to talk with Bobby before he talks to the inspector again."

"I would so appreciate that. Can I just ask that… this is going to sound strange, but could you try to keep your tone as positive as possible? Maybe I don't even need to suggest that." She cocked her head and looked at me. "You seem perceptive enough to pick up on his cues, and you've got that Southern gentility thing going."

"Uh… thank you. And, pardon my curiosity, but are you not from the South yourself?"

"I'm from Connecticut originally. But that was a long time ago."

She didn't seem inclined to go on. I returned to the topic at hand. "So, what you said—how do you mean, a positive tone?"

"Well, what I'm hoping for is something along the lines of this is important, and you're helping him get through it, but it should be fine in the end. As opposed to *this is a huge problem he needs to address now*. That's all."

"Huh," I said. "That's an interesting request."

Interesting was my go-to word when I meant *weird* but didn't want to offend. Something in her smile and her level gaze told me she wasn't fooled by my diplomacy.

"I know it sounds odd, Mr. Munroe. So let me give you some context. My husband is a combat veteran. He came home from Iraq with... just, the works. Memories of roadside bombs, friends dying in front of him—long story short, untreated PTSD. He's made admirable progress, in terms of reaching a point where he doesn't react to every little thing like it's a threat to life and limb. But the issue is that when there really *is* a serious problem, it's..."

She moved her hands up and down like the two sides of a scale.

"I hear you," I said. "You don't want to push him too far."

"Yeah, you *really* don't. It's... Can I ask, how familiar are you with PTSD?"

"Formally? Not much at all."

Informally, I suspected losing my wife, nearly losing my son, and having my life threatened more than once by criminals I'd crossed might suffice to get me diagnosed myself if I ever saw a doctor. But I preferred the remedy I'd come up with, which consisted of morbid humor and a state-of-the-art home security system.

"Think of it like this," she said. "You have a front yard, Mr. Munroe? Or a backyard?"

"I've got a few feet of grass on either side of my house, yes."

She laughed. "Okay, so, you walk outside, you can walk pretty much anywhere on that grass. All over your yard, wherever you want. Right?"

"Uh-huh."

"Well, Bobby can't. His yard, so to speak, is full of sinkholes and quicksand. He's reached a point where he at least knows where those things are, though. He knows where he can walk safely and where he can't, and he knows that if something startles him, he's got to hold still and just breathe…"

She closed her eyes and demonstrated, complete with hand gestures, a deep breath in and out. As her hand floated up past her collarbone, the pendant she was wearing glinted in the light. It looked to be a yin-yang symbol in silver and gold. Or platinum and gold, if I was correctly gauging her position in life.

"Right?" she said. "Hold still and breathe until you calm back down. Don't jump, because who knows where you'll land."

I realized I'd been breathing deep right along with her. I snapped out of it and said, "I see. Yeah, this must be a hell of a thing for a man like him to go through."

"Yeah, it is. And for the past couple of weeks, he's been… holding still. That's why we haven't reached out to a lawyer before now."

"Uh-huh. Well, hopefully the investigation will play out and finish up without much more stress. But, fair warning, if it doesn't, if the fire inspector thinks your husband did something wrong here, then things could get *real* hard. Now, I've never represented a client with PTSD like what you're describing, but if there are strategies or… I don't know, medications, whatever it is that helps, you might want to reach out to his doctor to make sure all that's in place and ready to go."

"I'm already on that," she said, nodding. "But thank you."

"Okay. And we might want to think about... I'm looking way down the line here, and again, hopefully it won't come to this. But if he did end up needing an actual criminal defense, we might want to think about what's disclosed to his doctor and how that might play out in court."

"Oh." Her eyebrows screwed up like that created a complication. "Well, in the past six or seven years, he's gotten off all the meds he was taking. So there's no actual doctor anymore. It's just me."

"You're in healthcare?"

"I'm a licensed hypnotherapist."

"I see." I kept my expression neutral. I didn't say "interesting," since she'd already seen through my politeness, straight to what I usually meant by that word.

I sensed a faint chip on her shoulder—my profession required a license, too, but I never called myself a "licensed lawyer." My job title didn't need the added legitimacy, but I couldn't blame her for feeling like hers did. I wondered how a hypnotherapist wife would play to a Basking Rock jury.

If she got them all breathing in and out at the same pace as her, like she'd done to me a minute ago, and they got the sense she was pulling their strings, it wouldn't be good.

3

MARCH 14, 2022

I t was 8:30 a.m. and sunny when Terri and I parked near the squat modern building in North Charleston where pretrial hearings in criminal cases were held. Terri was my private investigator—we'd known each other since we were kids—and she'd suggested she come with me to Jacob Drayton's hearing that morning. This proceeding was where the State had to convince a judge that they had probable cause to charge Jacob with felony drug possession with intent to distribute. The prosecution had to present its evidence and walk the judge through the police investigation. Terri, who was not just a PI but also an ex-cop, wanted to hear what they said.

When we got out of the car, she said, "Oh, my goodness, it is gorgeous out," and tossed her coat back onto her seat. She tilted her face up into the sunlight—the sky had been cloudy for most of the trip —and said, "Look at *that*. There's nothing like springtime."

I wasn't looking at the blue sky. I was looking at her. She was wearing a butter-yellow skirt suit that contrasted beautifully with her dark skin, and she was smiling with her eyes closed, taking in the warmth.

I stopped looking. We were good friends, and we'd even gone to dinner a time or two, but she worked for me. So far I hadn't figured out a way to take things any further without being a creep or impacting our working relationship.

I said, "Heck of a nice day," and she opened her eyes, smirking at me.

"That all you've got to say?"

I just shrugged, unsure what else I could say, and we headed for the entrance.

Jacob was meeting us there, but as we strolled up to the security line, I didn't see him. I did see two former colleagues of mine. One of them, Jake Rawls, gave me a friendly nod. I nodded back and went over to shake hands with him, exclaiming how long it had been—we'd lost touch when I left the solicitor's office more than three years earlier—and introduced Terri.

As the two of them chatted, I reached out for a handshake with the other guy, Cody Varner. He gave me a cold glance and kept his hands in his pockets.

Rawls whipped out his phone to show us photos of his son's high school graduation the previous summer. I suspected part of the reason he was showing us the pictures was that his wife was Black, and since Terri was, too, he wanted to let her know he was one of the good guys.

Varner faced the front of the line, as if we weren't there.

He was about fifteen years younger than me. Before I'd left the solicitor's office—that is, before I was generously allowed to resign to avoid being fired—I'd been mentoring him. We got lunch together at least once a week. He was my protégé, or, as I'd heard some folks put it less kindly, my Mini-Me. I'd obviously never let on to him about the improprieties I was guilty of, and when the axe finally fell, I was so mortified that I just packed my office things in a box one night and left without any goodbyes.

Terri and Rawls were talking about the lovely spring weather as Rawls slid his belt off to walk through the metal detector. Varner still hadn't said a word. I couldn't blame him. It must've been hard to get his footing again, in terms of office politics, when everyone saw him as being under the wing of the guy whose ethical lapses got him canned.

The problem for me now was not that we weren't friends anymore. The problem was that he'd been assigned to prosecute Jacob Drayton's case.

The courtroom was packed. Monday morning hearings were in cattle-call format: everyone got there before nine and waited, sometimes for two or three hours, for their case to be called. Not a soul was wearing a mask, including me. COVID was over, as far as South Carolina was concerned, and I'd seen some judges get snippy with the few lawyers who still took precautions. I pretty much tried not to think about it. There were only so many risks I had the mental space to worry about.

Before going to our seats, I stopped Varner with a quick hello. "Good to see you," I said. "I hope y'all are well."

"Yep. Fine." He didn't ask how I was.

"I was wondering when you'd get me those crime-scene photos." I'd sent him a discovery request a while back.

"You'll get them," he said, and turned away. His tone told me I'd get them when he damn well felt like it, unless I wanted to go to the trouble of running to the court to tattle on him. I was hoping to avoid that, because judges hated it when attorneys couldn't resolve our petty squabbles by ourselves. It gave them a poor opinion of counsel for both sides, but—again, the world being what it was—that often played out worse for the defense than the State.

Varner headed off with Rawls toward the front pew on the left, where the attorneys from the solicitor's office always waited until proceedings began. I figured they were prosecuting most or all of the cases whose hearings were happening today.

As we took our spots at the back, Terri said, "No sign of Jacob yet? Maybe he changed his mind about coming."

"I hope not."

Defendants didn't have to attend their preliminary hearings, but I normally preferred my clients to come—though I had to warn them that we would almost certainly lose. Judges just about always found that the prosecution had probable cause. Apart from a rare stroke of luck like a key witness not showing up, at this stage of the game we were pretty much doomed. The main point of the exercise was to find out what we'd be up against at trial.

My phone vibrated in my pocket, and I glanced at it. "Oh, he's here. Huh. Says his dad can't make it." I showed Terri the text Jacob had just sent.

She nodded grimly. "His dad can't make it for a lot of things."

We'd already learned that Jacob was not his father's favorite son.

I typed an answer telling him how to get from the security line where he was waiting to the courtroom we were in. As I put my phone away, I said, "Well, at least this judge is going to like him, I think. For whatever that's worth."

The schedule taped to the door had said that the judge assigned to today's hearings was Warrington. He was a white-haired, old-school, preppy type. In his chambers—which I'd been in many times in the nearly two decades I'd worked in Charleston—his USC varsity jacket, which had to be fifty years old, hung in a place of honor on his antique oak coat rack. He'd love the fact that my client was a champion target shooter with Olympic aspirations. Few details could be less relevant to today's proceedings, but I was going to find a way to work that one in.

An hour and forty minutes later, the bailiff finally called out, "State of South Carolina versus Jacob Ellis Drayton." I stood and gestured to Jacob, and we walked up to the defense table. Jacob was dressed like I'd told him to dress, in a navy suit and a discreetly patterned bow tie, looking every inch the good Southern boy. He politely stepped aside to let a heavy older lawyer with what looked like an even heavier briefcase get past us. That lawyer, like every defense counsel so far this morning, had moved to have the case against his client dismissed, and lost.

Judge Warrington was not a fan of the defense bar. As we got to our table, I could see him pushing his glasses up his nose and peering at me like he was sure he knew me but couldn't recall why. It must've been four years since I'd last been in front of him, and he'd never seen me on this side of the courtroom before.

"Your Honor," I said, "may it please the Court, Leland Munroe, counsel for the defendant, Jacob Drayton."

Warrington's bushy white eyebrows went up. "Morning, Mr. Munroe," he said. "It's been a while."

"Yes, Your Honor, it has."

He looked over to the prosecution side, where Rawls and Varner had been sitting all morning. Varner gave him the nod that meant they were ready to proceed.

"All right," Warrington said. "I understand Mr. Drayton is charged with possession with intent to distribute. Is the State ready to move forward?"

"Yes, Your Honor." Varner stood up. Without notes, looking the judge in the eye, he said, "On behalf of the citizens of the State of South Carolina, we're here to talk about the fact that this young man, Jacob Drayton, despite having every advantage and opportunity in life, chose to walk the path of indulgence and greed by trafficking marijuana. Thanks to a tip from a concerned citizen who was acquainted with both Mr. Drayton and the other tenant, a search warrant was issued on January 28 of this year, 2022, and upon executing the warrant, Charleston city police officers recovered ten pounds and four ounces of marijuana from Mr. Drayton's bedroom."

He looked at Jacob and gave a faint shake of the head, conveying profound disappointment at the opportunities Jacob had squandered.

Turning back to Warrington, he repeated, "Ten pounds… and four ounces… of marijuana."

Under the South Carolina statute, ten pounds was a critical threshold: anything that weight and up got a mandatory prison sentence. Had it been nine pounds fifteen ounces, it would still be a felony, but with Jacob's good-kid credentials and lack of any priors, he'd get probation.

Varner said, "We believe the evidence will show probable cause to charge Mr. Drayton with felony trafficking in marijuana, as set forth at Title 44, Chapter 53, section 370. And that's our purpose for being here today."

He paused. Everyone was quiet, listening. Varner still looked like a kid to me, but his courtroom presence had gotten much stronger since the last time I'd seen him.

"With that, Your Honor," he continued, "absent any remarks from defense counsel at this point, we call Detective Richard Milton from the City of Charleston Police Department to the witness stand."

Judge Warrington looked at me. Knowing his preferences, I said, "No remarks, Your Honor."

Detective Milton was a big, sturdy, serious-looking guy. Varner walked him through his name, title, and background in drug enforcement. He was the lead investigator in the case, and he'd been in charge at the scene when Jacob's apartment was searched.

Then came the part that's never on TV. The step-by-step trip through police paperwork is of high interest to lawyers and judges, because it shows that the investigation was conducted properly and establishes the chain of custody for the narcotics that were seized. From the moment the drugs were found in Jacob's apartment, every officer or lab tech who touched them—whether to transport them, store them, test them, weigh them, or even move them from one shelf to another —had to be documented. If a single link in that chain was missing or compromised, Varner wouldn't be able to prove that the drugs in evidence were what was seized from the apartment. I could move to have the evidence excluded, and the case would evaporate.

So for me, Varner, and Judge Warrington, the twenty minutes or so that Milton spent going through that paperwork and testifying as to what it said were twenty minutes of nail-biting tension.

For anybody else, it was about as interesting as listening to a man read the phone book out loud.

When it was over, Varner said, "So, Detective Milton, to sum all that up, can you state for the court what it was that was found when your team searched the suspect's apartment?"

"Objection." I stood up. "Your Honor, I appreciate the fact that there's no jury here today that Mr. Varner's statements could confuse, but we do still need to be clear about the facts. He's characterized the premises as Mr. Drayton's apartment, but I'd like to make a record of the fact that the apartment is leased to a Mr. Kyle Parr, who as far as I know is still living there now while awaiting trial on drug charges, and that Mr. Drayton only started subletting Mr. Parr's spare room about a month before the search we're talking about here."

"That's correct, Your Honor," Varner said. "I'm happy to clarify that."

Judge Warrington said, "His roommate's also facing drug charges?"

"Simple possession, Your Honor," Varner said, "but yes."

The roommate had been charged with a misdemeanor for a joint found in his nightstand drawer. Nearly half of the fifty states had decriminalized possession of small amounts of marijuana for personal use, or even straight-up legalized it, but South Carolina wasn't one of them.

"Oh, okay," Warrington said. "First offense?"

"I would have to check on that, Your Honor. That case was assigned to a colleague of mine."

Terri's research had told me it was Parr's third offense, but this was not the moment for me to play that card. I stayed quiet.

"There's no need for you to check on the roommate at this stage," Warrington told him. "If it's important, I'm sure Mr. Munroe will let us know."

Varner laughed.

In most of the states where simple possession was still a crime, their conversation wouldn't have made any sense. If a person was awaiting trial, that meant he had to be a repeat offender, since otherwise the punishment was nothing but a small fine. But South Carolina was more traditional on that point, too: first-offense simple possession could still get you thirty days in jail.

The reason that mattered was because Jacob had told me his erstwhile roommate made his living selling weed to college students. According to Jacob, Parr kept some inventory on hand, and when the cops had come knocking with their warrant, Parr must've stashed it in Jacob's room. To make that story plausible, I needed to bring the judge's attention to what little solid evidence there was of Parr's misdeeds. I had just laid the groundwork for that.

Varner knew what I was up to, so his next move was to distance Parr from the drugs Jacob was charged with possessing.

"Your Honor," he said, "for the record, I like to be very precise, so in this case I personally wouldn't use the term 'roommate.' It's a two-bedroom apartment, with the bedrooms on, essentially, opposite ends. The common areas are in the middle."

"Okay, thank you," Warrington said. Then he looked at me and said, "When did you say your client took up residence there? A month before? So, right after Christmas?"

"That's correct, Your Honor." I mentally thanked him for this opportunity. "Mr. Drayton spent the fall semester in Germany, training with a coach he'd met when he won a bronze medal in the ISSF, that's the International Shooting Sport Federation, Junior World Championships a few years back. He was training there because he hopes to represent the United States of America at the 2024 Olympics in Paris. And then he returned here to the Lowcountry to spend Christmas with his family and finish his business degree at the College of Charleston."

I could feel Varner glaring at me. My little speech was one step short of showing the courtroom a video of Jacob mounting the medals podium in slow motion to the tune of the heroic theme from *Chariots of Fire*.

"Shooting championships?" Warrington said. "As in, target shooting?"

"Yes, Your Honor. I believe his medal was in, uh, the fifty-meter rifle event?" I turned to Jacob, who nodded. "Yes, that's what it was, Your Honor. And he hopes to compete in the same event, among others, at the next Olympics."

"My goodness." Warrington looked at Jacob with interest, as if he was seeing him for the first time. Then he said, "Okay, well, thanks for clarifying. Let's move on."

Varner said, "Before I proceed, Your Honor, I'd like to request a stipulation. We've discussed that there were two people living in the apartment, but, Mr. Munroe, would you stipulate to the fact that the bedroom where the drugs were found was the bedroom of your client, defendant Jacob Drayton?"

There was no way around that, but I didn't want to give it away for free. "Assuming we can also stipulate that he was renting the room from the main tenant, a Mr. Kyle Parr, then I'll stip to that, yes."

"Uh… yes. Thank you. And would you stipulate to the fact that his bedroom had a lock on the door?"

"Yes." Milton had just testified that the door was locked when the officers began their search, and he'd shown a photo where the keyhole on the doorknob was visible.

"Thank you again. Okay, Detective Milton, my apologies for that interruption. I believe my last question was about what you found in Mr. Drayton's bedroom. When you proceeded into the bedroom of this young man here, who's seated at the defense table, what did you see?"

"I saw a desk over by the window, and on that desk I observed a cardboard box, which appeared to be—I wouldn't say open, but not sealed. Not taped shut or anything."

"Okay, and what did you then do?"

"Well, being as how the warrant authorized a search for marijuana, I determined that the box appeared to be of a size that could contain marijuana, meaning it was an appropriate place to search."

"Appropriate in the sense that, in your understanding, it was within the scope of the warrant?"

"Yes."

"And did you then search it?"

"Not immediately. Before disturbing it, I called Detective Hoffenmeier over to take a photograph."

"And do you recognize this photograph?" Varner handed him a printed photo.

"Yes. That's the one Detective Hoffenmeier took."

"And would you mind holding it up where His Honor and Mr. Munroe can see it?"

In the picture, someone's hand was holding a measuring tape next to the box. It was eighteen inches high and looked about twenty-four long. Varner went step by step, eliciting testimony and more snapshots. The box, when opened, was stuffed to the brim with ziplock baggies that each looked to contain about an ounce of weed. We then followed the photo trail back to the police station, where the box was weighed with and without its contents, and then the baggies of weed were lined up, labeled with numbered tags—there were 164 sandwich bags—and photographed again. Milton walked us through more photos to show several of the baggies being weighed, and he testified that the paperwork showed the same process had been followed for all of them.

I noticed something. The five photos of sandwich bags on the scale all showed identical weights: the digital readout for each one said 30.05 grams. I figured that meant 28.35 grams of weed—one ounce—plus a typical 1.7-gram plastic bag.

That brought two thoughts to mind. First, it seemed awfully precise for a college kid who was allegedly selling casually to his friends. You needed a good scale to make packages like that—a digital kitchen scale was what most dealers used—and Varner hadn't put on any evidence that Jacob had one. He didn't need any such evidence to get a conviction, but the lack of it would make it easier for me to raise doubts about whether these drugs really belonged to Jacob.

After writing "scale?" on my legal pad, I scribbled another note to myself to check the police department's math. With over a hundred baggies that allegedly totaled ten pounds and four ounces of marijuana, any mistakes—even something as small as failing to separately weigh each plastic bag; after all, not all brands were the same weight —could get us under the ten-pound threshold.

That mattered, but it wasn't enough. Any felony conviction, even without prison time, would leave Jacob unable to legally possess a gun. His Olympic dreams would be over.

And he didn't have much else. Unlike his older brother, he wasn't a strong student, and he was no good at any sport other than shooting. He also didn't have the affable, back-slappy personality that made his brother come across as a good salesman and the heir apparent to their father's company.

To keep what he did have going for him, Jacob needed me to get this case dismissed or the evidence thrown out. Or, as a worst-case scenario, he needed it pled down to a misdemeanor. He'd told me he'd prefer a misdemeanor with a little time in jail over a felony with probation. No other option would leave his life as he knew it intact.

So I had to fight this at every step. Even at today's proceeding, when the applicable rules left us pretty much doomed.

When it was my turn to question the witness, I said, "Detective Milton, can you tell me what time your team arrived at the premises on January 28 of this year?"

"As I recall, we arrived at the building at approximately ten minutes before three, and we'd reached the front door by 2:54 p.m."

"And whereabouts did you folks park?"

"On the street."

"Bouquet Street or the side street?"

"Bouquet Street."

"And how many cars did you bring?"

"Three."

"Were they unmarked vehicles or police cruisers?"

"This was a normal warrant, not an undercover operation."

"Which is to say, you drove over there in police cruisers? The standard black-and-white kind, with the lights on top?"

"Yes."

"And at three in the afternoon it was broad daylight, correct?"

"Daylight, yes."

"So, broad daylight, and you parked right out front in clearly marked police cruisers. Correct?"

"Yes."

I didn't ask about sirens, because I knew he never would've put sirens on for a search warrant trip.

"And based on the times you've testified to," I said, "it took you about three or four minutes to get to the front door of the subject's apartment?"

"Approximately, yes."

"And did you or one of your officers then ring the doorbell or knock on the door?"

"Not the doorbell, no. This was a knock-and-announce warrant, and Officer Montgomery knocked while the rest of the team stood back."

"Why not the doorbell?"

"In that building the doorbells are down below, in the lobby. To avoid the risk of flight, it's our policy not to alert the residents until we're right outside the door."

"You mean apart from alerting them by parking right out front in police cruisers?"

Before Varner could object, I said, "I'll withdraw that question." Asking it had made the point I was trying to make; I didn't need an answer.

I continued. "Okay, I'm going to jump ahead in time here for a second. I understand somebody eventually came and opened the door of the apartment. Was it Mr. Drayton, over there at the defense table?"

I knew it wasn't, but Judge Warrington did not.

"No, it wasn't him."

"It wasn't him. In fact, you didn't see Mr. Drayton at all that day, did you."

Milton glared at me, but he had to acknowledge that was true.

I said, "Because he wasn't home, correct?"

"At that exact time, no, he was not."

"That exact time being the entire three hours and twenty-eight minutes, according to the report, that your team spent at the building?"

"That's correct."

"During that entire time, only Mr. Parr, his roommate—or maybe I should say his live-in landlord—only Mr. Parr was home that day, correct?"

"I can't speak to who was where that entire day."

"I'm speaking of the time period your team was at the apartment. During that time, the only resident of that unit that you encountered or saw was Mr. Parr, correct?"

"That's correct."

"Thank you. Now, let's go back to when your team knocked on the door. Did Mr. Parr open the door immediately, say, within two or three seconds?"

"No, but in my experience nobody answers a door that quickly."

"Did he answer within five seconds?"

"No."

"Ten? Twenty?"

"Sir, when my officers are executing a search warrant, I don't task anybody with staring at his watch to count the seconds. There may be weapons in there. We've got lives on the line."

"Of course. Let me explain where I'm coming from. I've got witness interviews from residents of the building stating that you were at the door for well over a minute, and in fact it reached the point where officers were threatening to break the door down, before Mr. Parr finally came to let you in. Would you agree with the witnesses on that?"

"I haven't heard any witnesses here today, sir."

Like most seasoned police officers, Milton had plenty of experience testifying in court. He knew how to obfuscate and how to stand his ground.

I said, "That's correct. But what I'm asking is whether your recollection about how long Mr. Parr took to answer the door is consistent with the statement that it took well over a minute. In other words, do you remember it being much longer than that, or much shorter? Or about the same?"

He glanced at Varner, perhaps hoping for an objection, but there was nothing in my question to object to. After a second he said, "It could've been about that long."

I nodded, confirming what he'd said. "It could've been well over a minute. Okay, thank you. And you didn't just stand there that whole time, correct? You would've knocked a few more times?"

"Yes."

"And you would've announced that you were the police, that you had a warrant, and so forth?"

"That's our procedure, yes."

"And you followed procedure that day?"

"Of course we did. I run a tight ship."

"You run a tight ship. Okay, so you or your officers announced all that pretty loudly, I assume, to ensure anyone who was inside understood the situation?"

"Reasonably loudly, yes."

"Okay. Now, we've seen some photos your team took in the apartment. Would I be wrong in saying that, as two-bedroom apartments go, it looks to be about average in size?"

"I'm not sure what you mean by average."

"Well, did it strike you as unusually large?"

"No."

"It wouldn't take a man a full minute to walk from one end of it to the other, would it?"

"Uh, not normally, no."

"Okay. I know I can cross my own living room in three or four strides. Does that sound pretty similar in size to the living room in the apartment?"

I saw him hesitate—should he keep fighting my questions, or would that make him look bad to the judge? Eventually he made the right choice: "Yeah, that sounds pretty similar."

I took four strides across the courtroom, saying, as I walked, "So this is taking me all of about two seconds, right? And would you say I'm walking at a pretty normal speed?"

"Normal enough."

"Okay. So is it fair to say that Mr. Parr could've walked back and forth all over the apartment, several times if he so chose, in the time that elapsed between your team's arrival and him finally coming to the door?"

"I don't want to speculate about what he might have been doing. I've got no basis—"

"I'm not asking you to speculate. You don't have X-ray vision; you couldn't see through the door, correct?"

"Of course not."

"So what I'm asking is not whether you know what he did while you were waiting outside. You don't know that, do you?"

He took a second to answer. I could tell he was not happy to find himself outmaneuvered. "No," he said.

"Of course not. You couldn't possibly know what he did in there while you were waiting outside. He could've been doing cartwheels, or fixing himself a snack, or flushing drugs down the toilet for that matter. What I'm asking is whether, having spent three-plus hours in that apartment yourself, you think Mr. Parr could walk from one end of it to the other in less than a minute?"

"Of course he could."

"Several times, if he wanted, correct?"

"In the abstract, sure. But I don't recall, nor did I see it written in the report, any sound of footsteps or anything of that nature."

"Well, didn't the photos we've been looking at show that the apartment was carpeted?"

"Yes."

"And didn't you just testify that your team was out there knocking and loudly announcing yourselves?"

"We announced ourselves at least once, yes."

"So you can't tell me that you would've heard all of his movements, can you?"

"Not all of them, necessarily, no."

I could tell Warrington had gotten my point, so I moved on.

"Okay. So you've testified that when Mr. Parr did finally let you in, two of your officers took him aside and the rest of the team did the usual sweep through the apartment, correct?"

"Yes."

"And Mr. Drayton was not present at any point."

"No."

"So it was Mr. Parr who would've informed you as to whose bedroom was whose?"

"Yes, it was."

"And when you observed that Mr. Drayton's bedroom was locked, what did you or your officers do about that?"

"Officer Montgomery asked Mr. Parr if he had a key."

"And he claimed not to have a key, correct?"

"That's what he said, yes."

"So you took that at face value and broke the door down, correct?"

"After establishing it was locked, and knocking on it, yes, I ordered my officers to break it down."

"Did it occur to you that Mr. Parr might've been lying about not having a key?"

"I was there to execute a search warrant, not to have a conversation with Mr. Parr. I followed department policy. If the resident won't cooperate, then we do what's necessary."

"So you knew he might be lying, but that didn't matter to you?"

"Objection!" Varner said.

"I'll withdraw that question. Is it fair to say you've testified that only Mr. Parr was in the apartment when you arrived, not Mr. Drayton?"

"Yes."

"And three to four minutes elapsed between the arrival of your police cruisers and the moment you first knocked on the door?"

"Yes."

"And another full minute or so before Mr. Parr opened the door?"

"Yes."

"During which time he could've walked back and forth across the apartment several times?"

"I don't know that he did—"

"But he could have?"

"Yes."

"You certainly can't say that he didn't?"

"I... No."

"As you sit here today, you can't testify that he didn't spend that time moving drugs from some other part of the apartment into Mr. Drayton's room?"

"Objection. Assumes facts not in evidence."

"Your Honor," I said, "this is just a preliminary hearing. The rules of evidence that would apply at trial don't operate as strictly here."

Warrington nodded. "I'll overrule that, but I will ask you to tone it down."

"I apologize, Your Honor. Detective Milton, based on your knowledge of the apartment, in the minute or so that your team was outside the door, would it have been physically possible for the average person to carry a cardboard box from one room of the apartment to another?"

"In theory, if that other room was not locked, yes."

"And as you've testified, you didn't verify Mr. Parr's claim that he didn't have the key, did you?"

"We didn't strip-search him, no."

Behind me, somebody laughed.

"You simply had your officers break the door down?"

"Per our usual policy, yes."

"And as we saw in the pictures, what you found in there was a brown cardboard box with no identifying marks?"

"That's correct."

"No fingerprints were recovered from it?"

"No. Not Mr. Drayton's or Mr. Parr's."

"And you found nothing else in there, no drugs or drug paraphernalia elsewhere in Mr. Drayton's room?"

"We did not."

"So, none of the usual indicators that this was the bedroom of some-body who used drugs?"

"What we found in his room was ten and a quarter pounds of marijuana."

"And as you sit here today, are you aware that Mr. Drayton has no drug crimes in his past, no criminal record or history of illicit drug use at all?"

"I'm not aware of what his criminal history is."

"I'll represent that he has none. Was there any other place in the apartment where your officers found drugs?"

"Yes, a so-called hash pipe was found in the kitchen, and a marijuana cigarette was recovered from Mr. Parr's nightstand."

"And was Mr. Parr arrested for that?"

"He was."

The time to play my card had come. "And were you aware at the time that, unlike Mr. Drayton, Mr. Parr had two previous convictions for marijuana possession?"

He looked at Varner but got no sign from him.

He said, "I was not."

"So, you searched the apartment of a convicted marijuana user, Mr. Parr. You found a marijuana cigarette in his nightstand. You found ten pounds of marijuana in his spare bedroom. Correct?"

"I don't know that I'd characterize that as his spare bedroom—"

"Well, was it a bedroom?"

"Yes."

"And wasn't there another bedroom, which Mr. Parr occupied?"

"Uh, yes."

"And as the State has stipulated, Mr. Parr was subletting the bedroom we're talking about to Mr. Drayton, correct?"

He glanced at the prosecution table. The look on Varner's face must've told him the answer. He gave a grudging nod and said, "If I understand correctly, yes."

"So, back to my original question. You found ten pounds of marijuana in Mr. Parr's spare bedroom, correct?"

He studied me, looking for a way out. "If that's a correct characterization of the room, then yes."

"So does it make sense to you that the defendant here today is Mr. Parr's *subletter*? Rather than Mr. Parr?"

"The drugs were found in his—in Mr. Drayton's bedroom."

"But you've testified that Mr. Parr was there alone when you arrived?"

"Yes."

"And you've testified that in the minute-plus that you and your officers were outside banging on the door, loudly announcing that you were the police, Mr. Parr could've carried that box across the apartment and put it in his spare bedroom before answering the door?"

He glared at me.

After giving him a second to respond, I said, "Your Honor—"

"The witness will please answer the question."

"Yes," Milton said.

"Yes, Mr. Parr could have carried the narcotics to his spare bedroom before answering the door?"

"Yes."

"Thank you. I have no further questions."

When I turned and walked back to the defense table, Jacob was looking at me with the kind of perfect trust that you only ever see in people who are still young. He thought I'd won his case then and there.

He'd never been to a preliminary hearing before. I'd probably been to a thousand of them. So, unlike him, I wasn't surprised when we lost.

4

MARCH 16, 2022

After working all day in the office, I drove over to the Carters' house to meet them in person. On the causeway, the palm trees flashed past until I turned inland to take the road north. I was coming up in the world: instead of the base-model Chevy Malibu I'd been driving for a couple of years, I now had a dark blue Subaru Outback.

My boss, Roy, had argued hard for a BMW, one of the few cars that, in his view, were appropriate for a lawyer to drive. While I duly admired his new black 8 Series, which he gave me a ride in so I could appreciate its excellence, it wasn't for me. I didn't have ninety grand to drop on a car, and even if I did, I would not mentally have been capable of giving up that much money in exchange for a vehicle.

The Carters lived in the part of town where my realtor thought I ought to live. I didn't remember Bobby from high school—he was a few years younger—but what I'd learned about him from Laura and the internet told me he probably didn't feel any more at home there than I did. He'd grown up in Basking Rock's biggest trailer park and joined the military at eighteen to have a shot in life. The North Side kids never did that. They had names like Emma and Sebastian; they came from generations of doctors, lawyers, and politicians, and after high school they headed to Vanderbilt or USC.

The GPS on my car, which I'd resigned myself to using since I couldn't figure out how to turn it off, took me up a hill, around a few bends, and onto Fox Chase Lane, a cul-de-sac with the Carters' large brick home at the end. I parked on the street and saw Marianne wave through a window on her way to open the front door. It was an hour or so before sunset, and the last rays made the top half of the house glow deep red. The rest was already in shadow.

The door swung open, and there was Marianne, with Bobby looming behind her. He looked about the height and width of a commercial fridge. He held out a baseball mitt of a hand, and we shook.

Once I'd stepped inside, Marianne said, "Can I get you something? These days Bobby likes a sparkling water mixed with cranberry juice, but we've got everything—beer, wine, Coke, tea. Just say the word."

"I'd actually like one of what he's having, if you don't mind. Sounds very refreshing." It was nice not to have to make an excuse for declining alcohol.

"It's good stuff," Bobby said, leading me to the living room. "I've been sober for eleven years, and Marianne knows how to keep things interesting."

"Is that so. Well, that's great." I wondered how that worked, keeping beer and wine in the house when he presumably had to make a daily effort to maintain sobriety, but I didn't ask. Unless he steered the conversation that way, I was not going down that rabbit hole at our first meeting.

After we sat down, Marianne came in carrying a tray laden with glasses, a pitcher of cranberry juice, a bottle of soda water, a crystal bowl of lime wedges, and even a miniature ice bucket with tongs. I felt ungentlemanly for letting her carry it all, but before I could even stand up from the plush chair, she set the tray on the coffee table and began putting our drinks together. As she squeezed lime juice into each glass, she said, "Leland, we really do appreciate you coming over. I know this is a little out of your way, so thank you. It's just easier to talk about things in, you know"—she gestured to the room— "the comfort of your own home."

"I completely understand."

"I've pretty much been camping out here these past couple of weeks," Bobby said. "Last time I went to work, it was pretty rough."

"To work? Oh, your other location?"

"Yeah, the one by the beach. Last Thursday, I think it was."

"He had a manager call off," Marianne said. "When that happens, he goes in."

Bobby nodded. "In the middle of the dinner rush, this reporter shows up from the *Patriot*, getting right in my face with her camera. She was only a little thing—would've fallen down if I sneezed. Still, I don't like it."

"Yeah, and that's got to be a little weird for the customers."

"And the staff! The two locations shared staff, so…"

"Uh-huh, so their workplace just burned down. Yeah, sounds uncomfortable. Did she identify herself? Show a press card?"

"Yeah, she said pretty loud what paper she was from. Or website, I guess. And it was just… I mean, come on. We got forty people in there waiting for pizza, you know?"

Marianne looked at me and said, "So, for me, it raises some questions." She paused, looking thoughtful. She didn't speak slowly—I had yet to meet a New Englander whose speech sounded slow to my

Southern ears—but the way she talked seemed to somehow slow time down.

"The biggest question for me," she said, "is, what's her goal? What's she trying to accomplish, pulling that ace-reporter shtick in the middle of the dinner rush?"

I said, "I think you hit the nail on the head, there. Because as of now there's no news to report at all, is there."

She gestured in my direction, palm up, slow nod, as if to say, *Exactly.*

I said, "I mean, what caption is she going to put on the photos she takes? It's not even a homicide at this point. It's an accidental fire. What's making the *Patriot* treat it like something else?"

She seemed to freeze up a little. I could practically see stop signs in her eyes. I remembered how she'd asked me to talk to Bobby in a way that didn't make this sound like a big problem. The interest our local news was showing in what so far was a nonstory was strange, and it worried me, but maybe I'd just stepped too close to one of his sinkholes.

She was the one who'd asked the question, though.

I decided she'd given me that idea the way you give a hound dog a scent. A trail for me to follow—but not now, not here.

In a moving-on tone of voice, I said, "Anyway, yeah, I'm not a fan of the local rag. They'd turn a garage sale into clickbait if they could."

She chuckled, picked up the cranberry juice and said, as she sloshed it into our glasses, "There's not much in the way of, let's say, thoughtful news down here, is there." She set the bottle down and swirled a drink with a long silver spoon. "Not much thoughtfulness or insight in general." She handed me the glass and said, "That's not a comment on the South, of course. I wouldn't say there's a surfeit of insight anywhere I've ever been."

43

"I'm with you on *that*." As I took a sip of my drink, I caught sight of the little tree I'd noticed during our Zoom call. It looked like a gnarled, ancient oak, but it was only about fifteen inches tall.

She said, "You like that bonsai? Bobby actually grew it. What'd it take you to get it like that, honey? Four years?"

"Well, counting the whole thing," he said, "almost five."

"You *grew* that? What, from seed?" I got up and went over for a closer look. It was covered with jagged leaves no bigger than my pinky fingernail.

"Yeah. It's a Lebanon oak. Buddy of mine brought a pocket full of acorns back from Iraq."

"My goodness. I never picture Iraq having trees, besides palm trees, but I guess I was wrong."

"Those grow at altitude," he said. "Up in the Kurdish territories."

I kept looking at the tree, giving him a minute to go on, but he didn't. Eventually I said, "And what'd you do, trim it all the time to keep it small? Is that how these things work?"

"More or less. You pretty much train it to grow how you want, every day."

"Man, the amount of *time* that must've taken!"

"Well, I'm the kind of guy likes to work with my hands."

"That why you got into the pizza-making business?"

"Yup. And not just the cooking part. I built both my locations out from a shell. From nothing. Those buildings were worthless when I started."

Marianne nodded sagely and said, in her low, soothing voice, "Talk therapy only goes so far. Trauma lives in the body. And the body's the only thing that can work it out."

I wasn't sure how to respond to that, or if I should. I was getting the sense that sometimes what she said wasn't for conversation. It was there either to signal something, or just to hang in the air like incense, creating a mood.

I went back to my chair, saying, "Well, it's real interesting that you got that all the way from Iraq."

Bobby gave a grim, hard-won smile. "Yeah, I kind of needed to. We got oaks, they got oaks. That's one way we're the same. So I got one of theirs, and I'm taking care of it."

And constraining it, I thought. Keeping it small. I had a mental image of that tree filling one of the sinkholes in his yard, its little roots knitting the ground together.

I took another sip of my drink. I needed to get to the point—I'd come over mainly to hear Bobby's story about the fire and get any background he could provide—but I wasn't sure how to get there without hitting some kind of hidden conversational trip wire.

I looked at Marianne and said, "So, uh…"

She nodded and rose from her chair. "I'm actually a little hot," she said, heading to the other side of the room. "I know it's only March, but where I come from, we'd still be wearing snowsuits at this point." She pressed a button on the thermostat, and I heard the AC come on with a low hum.

As she came back, she gave us a smile and said, "You should see me in the summertime. I pretty much melt."

"Aw, baby," Bobby said, "I shouldn't keep you down here. It's just cruel."

His smile was blissful, and he seemed to have sunk an inch or two lower in his armchair. I noticed the air conditioner's hum again and wondered if that's what had relaxed him.

Marianne sat down, leaned forward to rest her elbows on her knees, and said, in a tone even more soothing than usual, "So… I guess it's time."

She took a deep breath. So did Bobby.

She looked at me and said, "Why don't you start by telling us how fire investigations normally go? This is all new to us, so I've thought, you know, it's possible we're getting stressed about things that are completely normal."

It was not normal for the press to be hounding a man at work when it wasn't even determined whether there'd been a crime, much less any charges laid on him for it. And it was not normal for the whole town to be whispering that he'd set the fire for the insurance money. But she'd given me the topic sentence of the talk she wanted us to have, so I started there.

"Well, yes. Any time there's a fire that kills somebody, there's—if it's not immediately apparent what all happened, there's going to be an investigation. They've got to do it. And that's going to involve talking to everybody connected with the fire. So, the— I understand y'all don't own this building, right?"

Bobby shook his head. "It's a long-term lease."

"So they're going to talk to the landlord, they're going to talk to the tenant, which is you, they're going to talk to anybody that has any connection, probably including neighbors, employees, and what have you. That's all par for the course."

"So why would we need a lawyer?"

"Well, to answer any questions you have, but also…"

I tried to think how to explain why a lawyer was useful without making the situation sound dangerous.

Marianne saw my conundrum and stepped in. "Leland," she said, "I don't think I mentioned this to you, but way back when I was young, I was an insurance paralegal."

"Oh, really?"

"Yeah. Not the most fascinating chapter of my life, so it doesn't come up a lot. But the attorney I worked for represented the insureds, right? The people who'd filed a claim and were having to drag their insurers over the coals to get money out of them."

I recalled my own travails with car insurance and Noah's health insurance after my wife's fatal accident. "Those folks never do seem to want to pay out, do they."

"Right?" She was looking at me, wide-eyed, and I realized we had hit upon a pet peeve of hers. "Isn't the whole point of insurance to compensate you when you suffer a loss? But that's the one thing they never want to do."

"Mm-hmm. Sadly, that is the truth. Speaking of that, what kind of insurance did you have there?"

She counted off on her fingers: "Let's see. Liability, renter's insurance for the contents, business interruption—although that was a real basic policy—and workers' comp, of course. The building itself, that wasn't ours to insure."

"And you put in a claim on the contents and so forth?"

"Well, we *want* to, because that was a big loss. I did give them notice. But I was thinking we might want to wait to file the actual claim until things… settle down a little."

"I think that makes sense. So all you need at this point is some guidance. Having an investigation like this going on, it's stressful, but it really is routine."

Marianne said, "Are things on the up-and-up in this town? I had the sense it could be a little…" She winced, as if she didn't like the words that came to mind. "I don't want to say *corrupt*, but very… Like, the folks in power tend to help their friends, hurt their foes, that kind of thing. And again, I'm not saying that because it's the South. It's just, I heard some things."

"Well, in all honesty, I think it can be that way a lot of places. That's just human nature. And… yeah, it was maybe more than a little bit like that around here until recently. But we've had a changing of the guard, in terms of local politics, so I don't see that being as much of a concern anymore."

She turned to Bobby and said, "See, this is what I mean. Working with that insurance lawyer, I learned there are situations where you've done nothing wrong, so you shouldn't need a lawyer, but you do. Because they know the terrain. They know who's in charge, what to expect and how things work."

"I hear you. That does make some sense." Bobby was looking off somewhere, out a window maybe. He mused, "They know how the game is played."

"Yep, yep." I was nodding, but the way he'd put that hit me wrong. How the game was played? We were talking about a fire that had killed a young woman.

I needed to get his story and figure out if he was someone I wanted to work for. I sat forward to get this show on the road and said, "Okay, so, Mr. Carter, can you tell me what happened here? I hope you don't mind, but I like to take notes, if that's okay."

He nodded, so I got my legal pad out of my bag. "First off, I need some context. How long had you been renting that space from Mr. Boseman?"

"Oh, jeez," he said. "What's it been, six or seven years?"

"Mm, it must be seven," Marianne said. "It was a five-year lease, and you just re-upped it like two weeks before the pandemic hit, right?"

"Oh, yeah. My five-year sweetheart deal."

I looked up from my notebook. "Sweetheart deal? How so?"

"For the build-out. Like I said, it was a shell. I put in the restaurant and the apartment. So initially he gave me a deal on rent, basically for helping him see if we could make that space work."

"You remodeled the apartment?"

"I didn't remodel nothing. I built it from scratch."

There was only one apartment in the building. That was where Dixie Ward had died.

"So you must've been real familiar with it, huh?"

"Yeah, until he redid it this past year. I don't know if he kept my floor plan or not."

"Oh, I read something about that. It was still being redone, so Miss Ward was supposed to be staying someplace else?"

The news had said investigators still didn't know why she'd gone there on the night of the fire.

"No, that remodel was last summer. There was some repair being done right before the fire. God, that poor girl," he said, looking at the rug in front of him.

"Did you know her at all?"

49

"Just, like, to say hello to. I'm only there—or I mean, I *was* only there—two or three times a week. And about the same at the other location."

"And not for a whole shift," she said.

"Unless a manager calls off. But yeah, she came down for pizza sometimes. Real pretty girl." He flashed a smile at Marianne and apologized.

She laughed, a warm, full-throated sound. "Oh, honey," she said, "you're married, not *dead*. That's allowed. Anyone with eyes could see how pretty she was."

"You know what," I said, "we're going to want to make sure they consider the contractors. I've certainly heard of fires caused by workers leaving stuff plugged in, and so forth." I made a note of that.

Marianne lit up. "Oh, I can't believe I didn't think of that! You're absolutely right." She paused, shaking her head slowly. "Isn't that—I'm pretty sure something like that is what made Notre Dame catch fire, in Paris, isn't it? Contractors making a mistake?"

I was not up on happenings in Paris. I vaguely recalled news reports of a cathedral in flames. I said, "Well, it sure does happen," and scribbled a note to myself to follow up.

"Not when *I* do the work," Bobby said. "I know the damn electrical code."

"You do," Marianne said gently. "You take care."

The whole room seemed to fall into a hush. I heard him take a breath.

"So, anyway," I said, "I take it you weren't the one working on the apartment this time?"

"No, I think it was the same outfit from Charleston he used last year for the upgrade." He looked at Marianne. "What was that granite you saw?"

"Oh, the blue Bahia? Yeah, it was gorgeous. We were over there one day during the remodel and saw his contractors lugging this huge slab up the back stairs."

"There went your baby," he said.

She laughed and explained, "I recognized it, because that's what I'd wanted for our kitchen at first. Blue is such a soothing color, isn't it? But I was surprised to see it at the building. Who puts that in a rental? It's over a hundred dollars a square foot. We ended up going with Carrara marble and blue cabinets."

She gestured to a doorway, and I leaned back to take a look. Through it I saw white counters and cabinets the color I'd always pictured water being in the Caribbean.

"Bobby did that," she said. "Everything. From start to finish."

"Did he? That looks like real nice work."

"It is. He's very… attuned, I would say, to the physical world. To the things he works with. They're not just objects to him. They respond to his touch."

"Huh. Well, uh…" It took me a second to remember what I'd been asking about. "Okay, so… Bobby, you mentioned the pandemic. If I can ask, how'd your business fare while that was going on?"

"Oh, we did great, actually. Most of our business was takeout anyway, or delivery, and the demand just went up and up. I even cut a hole in the side wall so we could put in a takeout window, so the lines inside wouldn't be as long." He shook his head and said, "It kind of feels wrong, you know, to profit from a thing like that pandemic. Something that did so much damage to so many people."

I was liking him better now that he'd started sounding like he had a soul.

"Yeah, that must have been hard," I sympathized. "But, putting my lawyer hat on, I'm glad to hear it. That's something worth mentioning to the fire inspector. Anybody would understand that if your business is doing well, you probably wouldn't want to destroy it."

"Bobby's a builder," Marianne said. "Not a destroyer."

"Well, good." I let that sit a second and then got to the point: "Bobby, can you tell me what the fire inspector wanted to talk about when you met up?"

"Oh, where I was on the night, whether any of our kitchen equipment or electrical was malfunctioning, how business was going." He shrugged.

"Yeah, those are the standard questions. And what'd you say?"

"Well, on the night, you can ask her." He gestured to Marianne. "I was home in bed. I mean, they say it started around 3 a.m. So I don't know how I'm supposed to have a better alibi than that."

"Rest assured they're probably asking a lot of folks questions. And given it was 3 a.m., that's probably most everybody's alibi."

In her late-night, smooth-jazz voice, Marianne said, "Isn't that what I told you, Bobby?"

"Yep. Yes, it is."

They smiled at each other.

"You know what," I said, "speaking of that, my PI can run a request to your phone company for records of your whereabouts on the night. Or your phone's whereabouts, at least. That might be a good thing to have in our back pocket, so we can deploy it if we need to."

"I like that idea," Marianne said.

"Okay," Bobby said. "What all do you need from me for that?"

I told him. It was a simple process.

I decided not to ask him anything else at this point. I'd found that revelations, if they came at all, came later. Folks had to develop trust in me first.

And I was going to give him a chance to. He needed guidance, he had the means to pay for it, and there was a good chance he had nothing to do with the fire. I couldn't see much motive for destroying a business that was doing well, and the immediate enthusiasm for the cell phone location check was a good sign.

After we wrapped things up, Bobby walked me out to my car. I told him I'd send an engagement letter over for him to sign in the morning, beeped my key to unlock the doors, and tossed my bag over onto the passenger seat.

Bobby had stopped on the edge of his lawn, on the other side of the car. My Subaru didn't come up much higher than his waist. In a voice that seemed quiet, considering we were outside, he said, "Man, that lead investigator. He's a piece of work. You know him?"

"Little bit." Flanders was a humorless, sharp-faced man. Not the kind of guy I'd ever want to hang out with, but he was good at his job.

Bobby seemed a little rattled. "Way he looks at you," he said, "makes you feel like he knows something you don't. Kind of guy who could convince you that he saw you commit a crime right in front of him, and the only reason you don't remember committing it is because you plumb forgot."

"Uh-huh." When he didn't go on, I said, on a hunch, "What else did he ask you about?"

He glanced back at the house. The front door was shut.

He looked at me and said, even more quietly, "Stuff about Dixie Ward. Like, did I *know* her. How well did I know her. Had we… you know."

I nodded.

"We *didn't*," he said. "I talked to her. That's all."

I nodded some more.

I asked, "You ever talk to her on the phone? Or text? Anything electronic?"

"Maybe once? But that was I don't know how many months ago."

"Okay."

Marianne opened the front door and called his name.

He replied, "I'm coming, baby!"

"Anyway," I told him, "we'll talk."

"Yep. Good night, now."

I waved to his wife, calling out thanks and goodbye, and then got in my car and left. The streetlights had come on, and in my rearview mirror, they lit up the daffodils in the Carters' yard so it looked like the lawn was filled with sparks.

5

MARCH 21, 2022

I parked beside the tallest palm tree outside Roy's office, grabbed the box of a half-dozen donuts I'd just bought, and went in. It was going on eleven in the morning, so I wasn't surprised to see Roy heading out of his office with a client, carrying his golf bag.

"Hey, Leland," Roy said, stopping and leaning his clubs against the wall. "You know Hank Manigault?" On the very short list of things that could make Roy willingly delay a round of golf, schmoozing was near the top. "We're heading up to Kiawah Island."

"Yeah, great to finally meet you." I set the donuts on Laura's desk and shook Hank's hand. I knew he was one of the more successful entrepreneurs in town. Lately Roy had been advising him on something to do with his insurance franchise, but he ran some grocery stores too.

"You the guy who's defending the Drayton kid up in Charleston?" Hank asked.

"The very same."

"Good!" Hank said. "That boy needs a strong hand to get him out of that mess."

"Oh," I said, "you're familiar with the case?"

It hadn't been in the news. Jacob's reputation was still unblemished. I assumed that was because our local media magnate, Fourth, ran in the same circles as Jacob's dad.

"Yeah, his dad and I go way back. I tell you what, you get him off, and I might just about forgive you for what you pulled on Ludlow last year."

He gave me a friendly punch on the arm, laughing. Apparently, he was a fan of our corrupt former solicitor, whose recent downfall was partly my doing.

"Naw," he added, "I know it wasn't your fault. That Tucker guy set you right up, didn't he."

"Well, he sure did say his piece. And I can't change what a witness says on the stand."

"No, I guess you can't."

Roy slung his bag over his shoulder again and said, "Anyway, we're going golfing to celebrate the fact that Hank's agency didn't have any policies on that building that burned down."

"Oh, it's not just that! He's being modest." Hank clapped a hand on Roy's other shoulder and told me, "This guy here got me out from under Boseman's properties last year. Just in time!"

"Yeah? How so?"

"Hoo, boy. Long story. Suffice to say, I've sold a lot of policies to Clyde Boseman over the years, on a few different properties, and he's... uh, well, he's interesting. There's pros and there's cons."

The two of them laughed.

"Let's leave it at that," Hank said. "He's one of those clients that's hard to handle when you got him, and hard to get away from too."

"You have to make *him* want to get away," Roy said. "It has to be his idea."

"Yeah, I don't know how you did it."

"You gotta know how people work. Anyway," Roy told me, "hold the fort. Keep the wheels turning. I'll see you tomorrow."

When they'd cleared out, Laura pointed at the donut box and said, "Is one of those for me?"

"You know it."

I'd gotten into the habit of bringing in some of her favorite Bavarian cream donuts once a week. I'd yet to convince Roy to give her more than a token raise—she'd never asked for any raise at all, but she deserved plenty—so I tried to make up for it in small ways here and there.

I went to the coffee maker, and Laura got two paper plates out of a cabinet. We had a ritual. Back at her desk, she stuck her bifocals up in her hair, and we chatted over donuts and coffee.

"I put a message on your desk," she said. "Marianne Carter called. She was upset about what's in the paper this morning." Laura was old enough that she referred to the *Southeast Patriot* website as "the paper."

"Oh, something bad?"

"Leland, are you *ever* going to get in the habit of reading the news? I don't know how you expect to find out what's going on around here."

I smiled. "I find out from you! Over donuts! I've tried to read what old Fourth and his minions put out, but more than a paragraph and my blood pressure starts to rise."

"Well, I expect Mrs. Carter felt the same way when she read what he printed this morning. I'll send you a link. It's just another one of his… not hit pieces, exactly, but you know how bad he makes things sound sometimes."

"Oh, yeah."

"Today it was along the lines of 'Bobby Carter's lying low. What could that mean? What's he got to hide?'" She shook her head, incensed at the unfairness of it.

"It means there's no case," I said, "and Bobby doesn't want to hear the gossip. Man, at this point the *Patriot*'s just making news up so they can sell more papers. Or ads, I guess. Clicks, or however they make money now."

"I don't know how he lives with himself. His daddy built up an empire—he could sell it and never work a day in his life. Why's he want to spend his time on this earth spreading rumors?"

"I know. What would you do if you had his money?"

"Oh, my." She thought about it for a second. "Well, you know what, I'd get a bigger house so my grandkids could all stay the night, and then I hope I'd do what Dolly Parton does. Give free books to every poor kid in South Carolina, something like that."

"Oh, yeah. I've always liked her. Well, I hope you get those millions."

I raised my cup of coffee to that idea, and she raised hers.

We finished our donut break, and I went to my office to give Marianne a call. After quick hellos and my expression of sympathy about the article, she said, "I know this is probably a long shot, but is there anything we can do about this coverage? Why are they allowed to publish all those insinuations that make it sound like he's the bad guy?"

"Yeah, it's annoying as hell. But, first off, Marianne, before I start answering any questions, I want to ask you to please not share anything with me that Bobby told you in confidence, and please understand that I can't give you advice to relay to him. The way the law works, with attorney-client privilege, it's got to be between him and me."

"Okay. Huh. I thought… Obviously I'm not a lawyer, so stop me before I embarrass myself, but isn't there something like attorney-client privilege between spouses?"

"Well, kind of, but not exactly. The main difference is, if he tells *me* something in confidence, I'm not allowed to reveal it. Not in court, not to a friend of mine, nothing. But if he tells *you* something, you could tell anybody you like, if you wanted to. You could even get up on the witness stand and testify about it if you so chose—"

"*Really?* Wait, where did I…" She laughed. "Did I misunderstand what they said on *CSI* or something?"

I laughed. "I don't know what they said on TV, but the way it works between spouses is that the State can't *force* you to testify. Anybody else he talked to—apart from me, his lawyer—they could subpoena them and make them testify, and if they refused, they'd get hit with contempt of court. But you can refuse, and the State can't punish you for it. Or you can decide not to refuse. It's up to you."

"Oh. Okay, I think I get it."

She sighed and was quiet for a moment.

I looked out the window. It was windy. The palm fronds were blowing around. I wondered if that would get in the way of Roy's golf game.

"Okay, then," she said. "Thanks. I needed to, uh… rearrange my mental files a little. I don't want to put anything at risk by getting in the middle, here. I just—we're both pretty upset about this article, and the whole process."

"I hear you. It's a hard thing to go through, and there's a lot about it that's unfair. And you know what, like we talked about at your place, if this had happened last year, I'd be a lot more worried than I am. The solicitor we had then was not a good guy, and cases weren't handled right."

After a second, she said, "Wait. You're talking about the prosecutor?"

"Yeah. The guy we've got now, Ruiz, he's a straight arrow. I know him, and I trust him. So I'm a lot less worried than I used to be about things being handled wrong."

"Okay, so… it's a little unnerving to be talking about the prosecutor at this point."

I realized my error. In her head, this whole situation was a printout on the fire inspector's desk, and now that I'd given them the guidance they needed, we were simply waiting for the inspector to check the "Accident" box and move on. It hadn't occurred to her that in a small town, everybody in local government knew everybody else, and they talked. I hadn't spoken to Ruiz about the situation myself, but there was no way he wasn't keeping an eye on it.

I took an upbeat tone. "Oh, I don't mean he's involved in the investigation. I just meant it's a small town, and folks talk. With the solicitor we had before, I might've had a concern that he'd be looking at this from a political angle, to see if he could meddle with the investigation, maybe make something out of it to get himself reelected. But with the new guy, that's not going to happen."

"Oh. I see. Okay." After a thoughtful pause, she added, "This isn't a particularly original idea, but I've always thought the good thing about a small town is that everyone knows everyone else, and the bad thing about a small town is… that everyone knows everyone else."

I laughed and said, "Yes, indeed."

An hour or so later, I drove toward the beach to meet Terri for lunch. She'd called to let me know the cell phone check had come back saying Bobby's phone hadn't pinged anywhere but his own house between midnight and 7 a.m. on the night of the fire. That made me think it was pretty unlikely that his current troubles would turn into a case. Still, on the off chance they did, we'd decided to visit his remaining location—both to try his pizza, which had a good reputation, and to get a sense of who the employees were and how they got along.

In the parking lot beside the little sand dune that marked one end of the beach, I saw Terri's green Forester and parked near it. She saw me from the other side of the dune and walked back around. It was a bright, sunny day, but she was hugging herself to keep warm—the breeze off the ocean was chilly.

"Where's Squatter?" she asked. "Doesn't he like pizza?"

"He does, but the health inspector doesn't like dogs in restaurants."

"Yeah. I left Buster at home too. I didn't think the waiter would want a rottweiler on the terrace."

"You going to be okay sitting outside?" We'd agreed to go inside first, to look around, and then sit outside to talk, away from eavesdroppers. "I got a fleece, if you want."

We went to my car to get it. She said, smiling, "I still can't get used to you in that Subaru. I get this cognitive dissonance thing. Like you're *supposed* to be in a low-end car."

"Oh, come on, now."

"No, it's like that old detective show, that little guy with—*Columbo*, that's it. Him and his rumpled trench coat. If you saw him in a nice wool overcoat, or a tux, it wouldn't seem right."

I got my fleece out of the back seat and was dismayed to see how it looked in the sunlight. "I'm sorry about the dog hair. Listen, we can eat indoors if—"

"Oh, I live and breathe dog hair." She took the fleece.

We headed for Bobbino's Pizza Pie, which was in a brick building about halfway down the beach, across the street, facing the water.

She said, "So, you met the two of them last week? What's your sense of them?"

She wasn't about to say any names when we were out walking around in public.

"You mean, personally?" I shrugged. "I liked them well enough. Although there were some weird moments."

"How so?"

"Well, just on first impressions, for instance, it'd be an uphill battle if this ever got to the point of being in front of a jury." I glanced around to make sure nobody was near enough to overhear. Nobody was, but I lowered my voice anyway. "I mean, a gigantic ex-con married to a hypnotist doesn't make for the most relatable couple."

She laughed. "You mean a decorated veteran married to an alternative healthcare practitioner."

"Yeah, that does sound better. Although, does that really count as healthcare?"

She shook her head in dismay as we waited to cross the street. "You're going to need to learn more about hypnotherapy if this does turn into a case. I've seen some pretty great outcomes with it for addiction. In some people it works real well."

"Seriously? Huh."

I had yet to go wrong by respecting Terri's opinions, and she had the background to know what she was talking about. On top of being a private investigator, she'd gotten her master's in social work, and she was one of several women helping run a program in town for women recovering from addiction.

As we crossed the street, I said, "There's something strange about the way the wife talks, though. It almost felt like she was trying to hypnotize *me*."

She chuckled. "Did it work?"

"I hope not."

Ahead, we could see the pizza place's terrace had four tables, only one of which was in use. I wondered if business was down as a result of the news coverage.

"Is there any reason you can think of that old Fourth would have a grudge against them?" I asked. "Or either of them specifically?"

"Oh, to explain the coverage?"

"Yeah."

"Nothing I've found yet. She moved here about twelve years ago—"

"How'd they meet? Did she already know him at that point?"

"You didn't ask them that?"

I tried to remember why I hadn't. "I guess it didn't come up."

She laughed. "Maybe she really did hypnotize you."

"Maybe so."

"Well, she was in Charleston at first, for a year and a half or so. Practicing as—what she does."

She didn't name Mrs. Carter's profession, because somebody coming toward us on the sidewalk was getting a little too close.

"And that's how they met," she said. "After that, she moved here."

We were silent for a moment, waiting for the other person to pass us by. When they'd gotten far enough away, I said, "Wait, what's how they met?"

"He was her patient."

"She dated her own patient? And married him? Hoo, boy. That's some very *alternative* healthcare."

"I mean, I don't know the timeline. It's not like I hacked into their email. So I couldn't tell you if they started dating while she was still treating him."

"Maybe they didn't. If it gets to where I'm going to have to explain this to a jury, I'll ask."

"You think it'll get that far?" She sounded skeptical.

"I don't know." As we approached Bobby's restaurant, I got a whiff of pizza and said, "Man, you smell that?"

"Mm. Melted cheese is my happy place."

"Mine too. Yeah, so, what caused the, uh, incident, we'll find out soon, I guess. We're still waiting on the inspector's report."

"So we don't even know if it was… not accidental yet?"

I could tell from the pause that she would've said arson if we'd been speaking in private.

"Nope. We don't."

The waiter on the terrace, a high school kid, nodded and said hello. He was wearing a bright orange T-shirt that said *BOBBINO'S*. This was the kind of place that would be called a pizza joint, not a restaurant: porch furniture with shabby umbrellas out front, rough wood floor inside, a display case and takeout register near the door.

To the kid, I said, "We're just going to walk around a little. Haven't decided if we want to eat inside or out."

"Sure, cool."

Inside, it took a second for my eyes to adjust, so at first all I saw were the freshly baked pizzas lit up in the display case. Every one of them was missing several pieces. Only about half the tables inside were occupied, which seemed light for lunch, but it looked like the place did a brisk business in takeout slices.

Terri was asking the kid at the register about the pizza. When I walked over, she gestured toward me and told him, "Oh, my friend's nephew is looking for a job. Is this a good place to work?"

The kid shrugged. "I mean, yeah? It's pretty chill. They're not hiring, though. But we get free pizza on our breaks, so, no complaints."

I didn't have a nephew, but I went along with it. "Cool. Must be nice to work near the beach."

He looked out the window and shrugged. Those of us who grew up in a beach town didn't tend to be that impressed by it.

I said, "They keep you busy? Lotta hours?"

"I mean, they did. Little less now, since there was, uh, like a couple weeks ago, that fire? That was our other location."

"Oh, man."

"Yeah. So I guess now the owner's got double staff and no place to put them."

"Oh, he's keeping them on?"

"He's trying to. We all got, like, an offer to quit if we wanted, with a week's pay and a recommendation letter, he said. Couple guys took it. So he's not hiring now. But I don't know, I worked here last summer, and it was real busy then. Maybe things'll pick up."

"Okay. Well, thank you."

We ordered a couple slices each, plus soda pop, and went outside with our trays.

The pizza was good, and the sun was hot on my back. "Well, it sounds like he's treating his workers decent," I said, wiping my mouth.

"Mm-hmm. That's a point in his favor."

"Yeah. He seemed like a good guy. Or not a bad one, anyway. But a little... I don't know, traumatized. Like the kind of person you've got to speak a little carefully to."

"How come?"

"Oh, his wife made it sound like he might flip his lid if I got too candid about how big this problem of theirs could get."

She winced like that was not a good sign.

"Yeah," I said. "Assuming he had nothing to do with it, I sure hope it blows over. A guy like that isn't going to handle cross-examination very well."

"Oof. No." She shook her head. "And then imagine how Fourth would cover that." She gestured to indicate a banner headline. "'Emotional Breakdown during a Devastating Cross—Sign of a Guilty Conscience?'"

"God, I hate that guy. I wish he'd cover all my cases the way he's covering Drayton's." Which was to say, not at all.

She laughed. "No, you don't," she said. "Because the only way that would happen is if you specialized in defending all the rich boys in town. All the ones whose dads are friends with him." She picked up a couple of basil leaves that had fallen onto her plate, put them back on her slice, and took a bite.

"Yeah, but even then," I said, "He'd probably run some campaign that would end up convincing my clients to fire me. He has it in for me."

"He has it in for both of us."

"Yep."

He'd all but slandered us on his website the previous summer, telling a story so appalling it got Terri briefly arrested. We'd talked about filing a lawsuit against him for it, but the defamation lawyer we met with had made it clear that it'd be a long and expensive fight.

Life was short. We were not inclined to waste it shoveling dollar bills into a bonfire to try to punish Fourth.

I looked at the beach. A couple of young guys were playing Frisbee, and a seagull was floating on the wind.

"If this thing does turn into a case," I said, "maybe I ought to refer them to somebody who specializes in, uh…" I looked around. Nobody was nearby. "…in arson defense. I've never defended one of those, and it must be fifteen years since I prosecuted one. I'm not up on the science of fire investigation at all anymore."

She shrugged. "So you hire an expert."

"I could." I took a sip of my Coke. "Or I could do them one better than that, by pointing them to a lawyer who actually knows what he's doing. And who Fourth doesn't hate."

6

MARCH 31, 2022

I followed Jacob's car over a bridge, around a corner, and into the parking lot of the Palmetto Shooting Range. We were a little ways south of the Charleston city limits. I was off the clock, about to hang out with my client in his natural element.

Like most gun ranges, the place was a low, sturdy building with hardly any windows. It sat on the green lawn like a giant cinder block, with no decoration other than American flags: one up on a pole, flapping in the wind, and another painted over the front door.

We parked our cars. As I walked over, Jacob opened his trunk, slung a duffel bag over his shoulder, and pulled out his black plastic gun case.

"Hey there," he said. Gesturing to the black case, he added, "By the way, thanks for getting this back for me."

"Course. That's my job."

The police had seized all the weapons they'd found in his room, calling them "fruits of the crime" of drug dealing, but Jacob had told me this particular pistol was a gift from his dad. That meant the cops' reason for holding on to it didn't apply, so I'd reached out to his dad to get a receipt to help me prove it. Getting that pistol back in Jacob's hands had still taken nearly three weeks and the threat of a hearing.

That wasn't the only time I'd been deputized to talk to his dad. Where possible, Jacob preferred to pay me to do it rather than talk to the man himself. Their conversations tended to get contentious.

We went inside. It wasn't crowded; weekdays right after lunch weren't prime time for gun ranges. The man selling tickets—they rented firing lanes by the hour—greeted Jacob with a loud hello and a handshake that would've knocked some men over. Jacob was a skinny kid, but he took it fine; he made up for what he lacked in size with a good stance. The ticket seller's colleague stepped out from behind a display case full of guns to whack Jacob's palm with a handshake of his own. Jacob introduced me, and I got the same treatment.

"I swear," the display-case guy told me, hitching up his jeans, "there ain't enough folks these days willing to stand up for a man's rights. Good to see you doing it."

"Well, I'm happy to."

The ticket seller said, "He's been coming here since he was, what, ten years old?"

"Yes, sir," Jacob said.

"Yep. Since he was ten! I know this kid. And when all that bullshit started, I knew right off that them cops made a mistake. I don't know what they was thinking. I mean, look at him! He look like a drug dealer to you?"

The other guy shook his head and laughed.

I wasn't about to tell him that Jacob looked a lot like five or six of the dealers I'd successfully prosecuted back in the day, and so did his fresh-faced young roommate with the gang connections. We called them dorm room dealers, the college boys who sold to their friends.

I also wasn't going to tell him that Jacob had known perfectly well that his roommate was a dealer. He'd worried about it when he first found out, but then he'd taken the easy way out: he told himself he'd move out in a few months, when the lease was up. I couldn't imagine doing that in his shoes, but then, I was not of the generation that grew up after half the states in the country had legalized weed. At his age, my friends and I were well aware that a single joint could get you a record and thirty days in jail.

I didn't say any of that. I just said, "Well, I'm real glad he's got your support."

"Aw, hell yeah!" said display-case guy. "Listen, when's your trial? We'll be there, both of us. We got you."

"Thanks, man. I mean, if it happens, it's supposed to be…" He turned to me. "When is it, again?"

"It's scheduled to start on June 6."

Display-case guy said, "And how long you think it'll last? Will it be done by July 4?"

"Oh, yeah. Easily."

He slapped his leg and crowed, "I tell you what, Jacob, we're going to celebrate with you on Independence Day!"

The ticket taker said, "Yeah, man. Count me in. For the trial and the holiday."

"Yeah, I'll be there in court with you wearing full-on red, white, and blue."

Jacob chuckled, but I could tell he was moved. He thanked them both and paid for our lane, over the ticket seller's objections—the guy wanted to let us shoot for free—and then we stepped over to the display case. The other guy went back behind it to wait on us.

Jacob told him, "Mr. Munroe here's not a regular shooter."

"Oh, uh-huh," the man said. "Well, what you feeling like today? Revolver or semi-auto?"

I said, "I'll go with a revolver. More of a classic feel."

"Yes indeed. You got one you like? Or you want me to pick one for you?"

"How about that?" I pointed to a long-nosed silver one that looked straight out of the old cowboy movies I'd liked when I was a kid.

"Ruger Super Redhawk," he said, nodding approval. "Real powerful, real accurate. This one's a .480 Ruger, but I got it in a .44 Magnum too."

The Magnum sounded a little too Clint Eastwood for me. Challenging somebody to go ahead and make my day was not my style. I said, "I'll go with the Ruger."

He got it out, and we headed for the other register. He grabbed a box of ammo for me on the way, and a set of earmuffs from the next shelf —like the guns, they rented ear protection to folks who hadn't brought their own.

I saw Jacob opening his wallet. "Put that away," I said. "Thanks, but I can pay for my own gun."

I did so. As we waited for my credit card to be authorized, I told him, "I ought to warn you, not only has it been a while since I went shooting, but I never did have great marksmanship in the first place."

"Well, you're a southpaw, aren't you?"

"Yep. Why?"

"My coach says y'all are wired different. He's seen more than a few lefties who are right-eyed."

"Right-eyed? How d'you mean?"

His friend ripped my credit card receipt off the machine and said, "You ain't heard of that? Oh, man. Show him the thumb thing."

Jacob said, "I was going to. Stick out your thumb."

He did an arm's-length thumbs-up to show me what he meant. I did the same.

"Now look at your thumb," he said, "and tell me what's behind it."

"That flag," I said. Another Stars and Stripes was hanging on the wall behind the cash register.

"Okay, shut your left eye. Is the flag still behind it?"

"Uh-huh."

"Okay, switch eyes."

I shut my right eye, and the backdrop changed: my thumb was suddenly superimposed on the rack of ammunition to the right of the flag.

"Whoa!"

"It moved, huh?" Jacob said. When I confirmed it had, he and his friend laughed and congratulated each other. "You've been aiming with the wrong eye," he told me. "Come on, I'll show you."

I took my stuff, and we headed for our lane. The place had six firing lanes divided between three bays, and his ticket-seller friend had given us a bay all to ourselves. As Jacob unlocked the door, I asked, "So you've been coming here since you were ten? Why'd y'all drive all the way up here instead of going to one of the ranges in Basking Rock?"

"My dad didn't think too highly of the ones down there." He swung the door open. "Lot of riffraff went shooting there, he used to say."

"Huh."

We walked into a dark gray cement room with a bench on the wall beside the door and two shooting booths facing down the white cement lanes. Through the wall to our left, I could hear muffled gunshots from the next bay.

"Far as I can tell," he said, shutting the door and setting his things on the bench, "my dad thinks about ninety-eight percent of the world is riffraff."

I laughed and said, "I guess I probably fall into that category."

"He didn't use those words, but yeah."

Jacob's dad had adamantly opposed hiring me to represent him. He had an old friend in Charleston who did criminal defense, and that's who he'd wanted. Jacob, however, had a trust fund from his grandma and a strong desire to make his own decisions.

I set my things down on the other bench, except for the ammo box. As I used my thumbnail to slice through the tape holding it shut, I said, "You know what, I've been meaning to ask you since the hearing. Just to get a sense of what kind of ammo I've got available for your case, so to speak. Have you thought about sharing what you know about your ex-roommate and his pals in exchange for pleading down to a misdemeanor?"

Jacob winced. "I don't want to spend the rest of my life looking over my shoulder."

"I can understand that. It just sounded like you knew enough to put them away for a good long time."

I shook six bullets into my palm, set the box down, and popped out the cylinder of my gun to load it.

"But they got friends," Jacob said. "Like, cut off one head, and another grows."

"Well, that's fair enough."

I hadn't sounded Varner out on what he'd offer in exchange for good information. There wasn't much point unless Jacob was at least willing to consider the idea.

He opened his duffel bag, took out his earmuffs, and put them on.

"Okay, anyway, when you shoot," he said, "try this." He aimed a left-handed finger gun at me, twisted his head to the left, and looked down his arm with his right eye open and his left one squinted shut. "It's a little awkward, but you got to do it, since your eyes and your hand don't match."

"Huh. Okay."

I put my own earmuffs on, and we got into our shooting booths. "Booths" was an exaggeration; they were more like doorways two feet deep. Their purpose was to stop spent shells, which semi-auto pistols ejected with each shot, from flying over and hitting the other guy.

We each faced a paper target printed with the blue silhouette of a man's torso and head. Mine was seven yards down the lane. Jacob's was twice that, down at the far end, just before the bullet trap.

I heard him start firing and lost count at five shots.

I took the stance he'd told me to, aimed, and fired. A hole appeared in my target's shoulder. For my skill level, that was pretty damn good. I emptied the chambers. All six shots hit the torso.

"Damn," I said, in disbelief that Jacob had made my aim so much better with something that simple. I pointed the gun again and did the trick he'd taught me, shutting my right eye, watching the target seem to jump to the left.

He was still shooting, so I couldn't thank him yet for the tip. As I went back to the bench to get more ammo, I saw two empty clips on the floor. That meant he'd fired more than twenty rounds. I got behind him to look down his lane. He'd shot a straight line of perfectly spaced holes down the center of his target, from head to crotch.

He finished up another line, this one from shoulder to shoulder. Then he popped the old clip out and a new one in and fired ten more shots across the shoulders to eliminate most of the paper left between the holes. A second or two after he finished, the target, still shuddering from the impact, tore itself apart in slow motion, and everything below the shoulders fell to the floor.

I was nearly home, cruising down the Basking Rock exit ramp with "Jolene" turned up on the radio, when my phone rang. At the Subaru dealership, the salesman had told me my phone could interface with the car for hands-free use via voice commands, but he'd stopped talking when I showed him my battered black flip phone. That thing couldn't interface with anything but my ear.

It was Marianne Carter's number. I merged onto the main road, turned the radio off, and picked up.

"Leland," she said, "the police are here. I don't know what to do."

"Dammit." I heard banging and a muffled shout. "What do they want?"

"They want Bobby. They say they've got an arrest warrant."

"What the hell?" I realized they must be banging on the door. "Are they on the porch?"

"Yeah. I haven't let them in yet."

"Okay, ask to see the warrant. I can't remember if you've got a mail slot, but—"

"Yeah, we do."

"Okay. Tell them to put it through the slot. If you can, if things stay calm, take a photo of it and send it to me. Then set your phone so it's recording, if you can. At least the sound."

"What if they don't stay calm?"

"Keep your hands visible. Make sure Bobby does too. Tell him I'll be right there."

7

MARCH 31, 2022

As I sped toward the Carters' house, I called Ruiz on his cell. It rang several times. I knew he might be in court, and I was preparing to leave a voicemail when he finally picked up.

"Hey, Leland. What's up?"

"Hey, Ruiz. Well, I got retained recently by Bobby Carter—"

"Oh, my."

"Yeah. And I just got a call from his wife saying there's police on their porch with, apparently, an arrest warrant."

"With— Are you kidding me?"

"Does that mean your office isn't involved? Yet, anyway?"

"No, and frankly I'm a little pissed off that I didn't get a heads-up."

"You and me both. Listen, is there any way you can call them off for now, so we can do this the right way? He'll present himself for arrest, I can represent that to you right now. I just don't want a decorated veteran with a history of PTSD being dragged out of his home—"

"Yeah, I get your drift." He sighed. "I wish I could. But that's got to be SLED in there. It's not us. If it was, I would've heard about it beforehand."

SLED was the statewide police force, as opposed to city or county law enforcement. SLED had jurisdiction over certain crimes. Now that Ruiz mentioned it, I recalled that one of those crimes was arson.

"Oh, yeah," I said. I kicked myself for having assumed our local police would be handling the case. It was another point in favor of referring the Carters to an attorney who knew how to run an arson defense.

I wasn't about to tell Ruiz that. I just said, "Dammit."

"Yeah. I don't know anyone in SLED. Maybe Ludlow had some connections there, but he didn't do introductions for me before he left."

From what little Ruiz had told me of Ludlow's sudden departure, I had the impression that the man had not gone gracefully.

"Okay," I said. "Well, just so you know, that's what's going on. I'm heading over there right now and, frankly, I don't know what I'm going to find."

"I don't suppose you need reminding," Ruiz said, "of your rights in regard to taking video of the police."

I was surprised to hear him suggest that. He was a by-the-book, conservative guy. More than once, I'd told him he must've come out of his mother's womb in a suit and tie.

I said, "Yeah, I appreciate that."

We hung up. As I closed my flip phone, I realized I couldn't take video with it.

Unless someone else had the presence of mind to do it, whatever was about to go down wasn't going to be recorded.

I turned onto the Carters' street and saw four SLED cars in front of their house: two in the road, one in the driveway, and one sideways across the front lawn. Nobody was on the porch. Behind two of the police cars, officers stood with their guns drawn and pointed at the front door. They weren't in shooting stance, but they were ready to be.

I parked a couple doors down—driving right up to them seemed like a bad idea—and got my bar card out of my wallet in case they wanted to see it. I tucked it into my shirt pocket, got out, and walked toward them with my hands visible. As I got closer, I called out, "Officers? Afternoon, officers. I'm Mr. Carter's attorney. I appreciate your caution, but he's willing to go peacefully."

They took turns looking at me. None of them answered.

When I got up to them, I said, "Can I ask, who's the commanding officer here?"

The cop behind the car in the driveway said, "Officer Rappaport. He's inside."

"Thank you. Now, I'm just going to head on in there, if y'all don't mind."

He squinted at me warily. "You say you're the suspect's attorney?"

"Yes, I am. I got my bar card in my pocket here if you'd like to see it."

He gave me a hard, appraising look, and finally said, "Naw. You can approach and announce yourself."

"Thank you."

I headed up the walkway. Crushed daffodils stuck out from under one of the wheels of the squad car on the lawn. Parking there was an unnecessarily aggressive move, and it didn't make me optimistic about Officer Rappaport.

When I knocked on the front door, it swung open.

I leaned in, looking toward the living room.

Two police officers were sitting on the couch, facing me, nodding as they listened to Marianne. She was perched on an ottoman with her back to me. I couldn't hear what she was saying, but I recognized her low, soothing tone. Two other officers sat on the love seat that was positioned at a right angle to the sofa. None of them appeared to be on high alert.

I took a deep breath and recalibrated. So far, things were calm, and I needed to downshift out of high alert to avoid aggravating the situation.

I put my left hand on the inside of the door frame to make sure it was visible. With my right hand, I reached out to knock on the open door, calling out in a friendly tone, "Afternoon, folks."

The commanding officer's eyes shot up to mine.

I gave him a nod and a wave. "Leland Munroe here. I'm Mr. Carter's attorney."

Marianne said something reassuring to him and then twisted around to smile at me. She moved in a slow, relaxed way that brought to mind the way my late wife used to move after getting a spa treatment. "Leland," she said, as if my arrival were a pleasant, neighborly surprise. "Come on in. Officer Rappaport is here with a few of his men."

She was speaking like a Southerner—that is, at about half of her usual speed.

I went in, walked over to the commanding officer, and held out my hand. "Afternoon," I said. "Nice to meet you."

"Afternoon," he said, and we shook.

I smiled hello at the three other cops, and I gave Bobby a nod. He was lying in his recliner with his feet sticking out in front of him on the foot support. His eyes were half closed, but he nodded back.

This was, bar none, the strangest arrest I had ever seen.

Marianne said, in a tone of mild regret, "So, Officer Rappaport here was just explaining that it looks like Bobby's got to go downtown."

Officer Rappaport said, "Yes, ma'am. I'm afraid he does."

I adopted the same relaxed tone and said, "Oh, my. Well, would you mind, Officer, letting me see what you've got there, in terms of a warrant?"

Marianne said, "That's it on the end table there."

"Oh, thank you."

She went back to her conversation with Rappaport.

I picked up the warrant. The stated charges were first-degree arson and involuntary manslaughter. I looked at the next page for the facts supporting probable cause. It said that fire investigation canines had alerted at certain points on the restaurant floor, and tests done at those points had found accelerant.

I looked at Marianne. She was laughing at something Rappaport had said.

I kept reading. The warrant said that Clyde Boseman, the owner of the building, had been out of town on the night of the fire. Investigators had looked into his finances and found no sign of trouble. That, of course, indicated he had neither opportunity nor motive to start the blaze.

The other cop on the couch had taken his hat off to scratch his head. One of the two on the love seat was flipping through a magazine.

I hadn't noticed it before, but something was playing on the Carters' sound system. The volume was so low I had to concentrate to identify what I was hearing. It sounded like a combination of ocean waves and violins.

The conversation paused, and Officer Rappaport said, "Well, ma'am, I'm sorry, but I think we've got to get moving now."

"Okay," she said, nodding slowly. "All right. Um…"

She turned to look up at me from the ottoman. The glint of panic in her eyes surprised me. It was so different from her tone of voice and her body language that it was like looking at a different person.

She'd done everything she could, I realized. She'd drawn on every skill she had to get these folks calmed down and keep this situation from spinning out of control. But now she needed help.

I said, "Officer Rappaport, I'm just going to take a moment to explain to Mrs. Carter what will be happening next." I gestured to the fine home we were in and said, "I'm sure you can appreciate she's got no experience of the criminal justice system. This is all new to her."

He gave a shrug that said *Get on with it.*

"Okay. Mrs. Carter, what's got to happen now, the first step we've got to go through before we can get things cleared up, is Bobby's got to go downtown and wait there overnight for his bail hearing. Those happen twice a day, and the next one's at eight thirty tomorrow morning. I'll be there for it, of course."

In a whisper, she said, "Overnight in— You mean… he has to sleep in *jail?*"

Her calm tone had given way to the anxiety that I nearly always heard in people whose family members were about to be put behind bars. I didn't know if emotion had finally gotten the better of her or if she'd simply realized that sounding like a human tranquilizer wasn't going to help at this point.

I nodded gravely. Her face fell.

Over on the recliner, Bobby had shut his eyes. He was awfully still.

"Officer," I said, "I need to just speak with my client a moment. Mrs. Carter, if you want, why don't you get ready to go. I'll drive you, and maybe you'll be able to see Bobby for a little while before visiting hours end. We can follow the car he's in."

She looked at me wordlessly—processing it, I figured. After a second, she said, "Should I… pack a bag for him, or…?"

"No, that won't be necessary." Or allowed. "Except, if there are any medications he'll need—"

She shook her head to say he wasn't on any, then stood up and went to the next room.

"Okay, Officer," I said, "this won't be long. My client knows he's got to go with you, and it's going to be just as peaceable as it is right now. But I do need a moment to talk with him first."

Rappaport stood up and said, "You'll be able to speak to him in confidence after he's booked. There's rooms for that at the jail." He nodded to his men, and they stood up, too, one of them putting his hat back on as he did.

Marianne came back with her purse, made a beeline for Bobby, and leaned down to whisper in his ear. Whatever she said took a while; I could see that Rappaport was getting impatient.

When she finished, Bobby righted the recliner and stood. She took his hand, held it tight, and they walked right past the cops by the love seat.

Rappaport barked, "Mr. Carter!" as his hand moved toward his belt.

I stepped between him and them, saying, "Hold on, now," in my own version of Marianne's mesmerizing drawl. "This is a peaceful situation. They're cooperating. You just tell us which car he ought to go to, and that's where he'll go."

He backed off, and all was well again until we passed the window in the hall.

"Mr. and Mrs. Carter," I said, "hang on just one second."

I'd spotted a white van out the window and wanted to get a better look.

"Uh, Officer Rappaport," I said, "would you be able to order your officers in the driveway there to come around the back? We got a TV van out front, and knowing those reporters, I think there might be a real unpleasant disturbance if we come out the front door."

My true concern was avoiding embarrassment for the Carters—I didn't think Dabney's reporters would cause a scene—but I was betting on Rappaport not being as familiar with the local media as I was.

He took a look out the window, and he decided to err on the side of caution. He tapped his walkie-talkie and told his boys in the driveway to pull around the back of the house, and then he told the ones out front to keep the roadway clear for us to leave.

The Carters led us back through the living room, across the huge kitchen and into the mudroom. The squad car parked as close as it could, and after leaning down to kiss his wife, Bobby walked outside, folded himself into the back seat, and had the car door slammed behind him by Rappaport, who then took an officer down the driveway on foot to help keep the way clear.

As the squad car turned around, Bobby kept his eyes on Marianne. When it rounded the corner of the house, he ducked down.

Beside me, she nodded in a satisfied way and said, "I told him not to let those bastards get a picture."

She went back inside. I followed her. In the kitchen, she sat at the island, set her elbows on the marble countertop, closed her eyes, and rested her chin on her balled-up fists. She sat that way for a solid minute, taking slow, even breaths, and then she sat back and asked, "Will they really let me see him tonight?"

I looked at my watch. It was later than I'd thought. "If they book him real quick," I said, "you could make it in before visiting hours are up."

"Do they usually book people quickly?"

In the average case, I knew, there was at least a fifty-fifty chance they would. But Bobby wasn't an average case. The police, like most folks in Basking Rock, wouldn't forget a person's past.

I shook my head. "I wouldn't bet on it."

She looked down. I could see she was upset. She got a hold of herself and said, "They have to let you in, right?"

"As his lawyer? Yeah."

"Okay. Good. Tell him I stayed here because if I can't see him anyway, I'm sure as hell not going to walk out there and end up on the front page. And tell him— This is going to sound weird."

85

She didn't go on, so after a second, I said, "In this job, I hear things you wouldn't believe. You tell me whatever you want."

She gave a little chuckle, but she wouldn't look at me. Talking to her countertop, she said, "He's going to be okay physically, right? I mean, how many prisoners are bigger than him?"

"Not many. And so we're clear, Marianne, whatever you may have heard about violence in prisons, that's not a prison he's going to." Not tonight, at any rate. "It's a jail. They'll be holding him with whoever else got arrested recently—some good old boy with a DUI, that kind of thing. Not hardened criminals."

Her shoulders relaxed, and she said, "Oh, good."

"So what was it you'd like me to tell him?"

She looked up at me and asked, "Are there clocks in the jail?"

"Clocks?" That was not a question I'd expected.

She nodded. I pictured various parts of the county jail. "Uh, yeah," I told her. "There's wall clocks in a lot of different rooms. Ugly old things from the eighties or whenever."

"Good. Tell him to keep looking at the clocks."

"Keep looking at the clocks? Really?" Personally, I thought clocks must be a minor torture device for a man behind bars: they mocked you with the fact that life was passing you by and the only thing you could do was wait.

But I wasn't about to depress her with that.

She was looking at me with a slightly unnerving expression. It made me feel like I was being x-rayed. Then she said, "You've never been in combat, have you?"

86

"Nope. Matter of fact, apart from a trip up to Niagara Falls, I've never left the US of A."

She nodded, like that confirmed something for her. "I've worked with a lot of people who have," she said. "And what they tell me is that when you've been in combat... what you've done, honestly, is left this world. You've left the world that you and I are in right now and walked into hell. The guy right beside you gets hit by a sniper in mid-sentence, and you're untouched. Next time it might be the other way around. It's chaos, and the chaos could start at any moment or end at any moment—there's no rhythm to it, nothing predictable, nothing you can count on at all."

I shook my head. What was there to say?

"But clocks," she said, "they're predictable. They only go one way. They only go at one speed. They have a rhythm."

"Oh," I said. "I get it."

"They're boring," she said. "Regular. Ordinary. And it helps him, somehow, to look at them."

"Okay. I'll tell him."

She nodded. Then she said, "You've got to do more than that." No sign of the hypnotist voice now. Even the South was gone from her tone. "You've got to stop this thing. You've got to get him home."

8

APRIL 1, 2022

I'd been right about how the local cops would handle things. It was pretty clear they remembered what Bobby had done when he first got back from Iraq. He got none of the favors or greased wheels that an inmate with no history might've gotten. They slowed his paperwork down so he missed the morning bail hearing, and I was pretty sure they would've made him miss the afternoon one, too, if I hadn't intervened. Bond hearings were supposed to be held within twenty-four hours of arrest, but if you missed the last hearing on Friday, you'd be stuck in jail all weekend.

Since the charges against Bobby didn't carry a potential life sentence or death penalty, the bond hearing wasn't up at the courthouse. It was held right at the jail, in one of the magistrate's courtrooms on the ground floor. I waited outside, in the shade of an oak tree, for Marianne. She was bringing the manager of the beachfront pizza restaurant. The one benefit of the cops' efforts to keep Bobby locked up longer was that it had given me time to prepare the two of them in case the magistrate wanted to ask them about Bobby's ties to the community.

I saw them walking over from the parking lot and raised a hand to say hello. We'd talked about what to wear, and Marianne was dressed perfectly for the occasion in a gray skirt suit with a pink blouse. As they got closer, I saw she'd even switched out her yin-yang pendant for a strand of pearls. I wanted the magistrate to see my client's wife as a conservative, well-to-do, feminine woman, and she'd hit a home run on that front.

The manager, who was in his late twenties and wore his blond hair tied back in a skinny ponytail, looked like he'd borrowed his big brother's funeral suit. That was fine. The main thing at a hearing was to look the part, whatever your part was, and dress respectfully.

"Good to meet you, Kevin," I said, reaching out and shaking his hand. "Thanks for your support. I know Mr. and Mrs. Carter really appreciate it."

"Yeah, of course. I just can't believe it got to this point. I mean…" He looked up at the jail, wide-eyed, shaking his head.

"You ever been here before?"

"No, sir. I only ever been to traffic court once, to fight a speeding ticket. Man, *this*…"

"Yeah, it's something else. Come on, let's get through the metal detector. That can take a little while."

Inside, we waited in the hallway by the courtroom with half a dozen other lawyers. I recognized a couple, and we exchanged collegial hellos. I figured the prosecutor must be one of the ones I didn't recognize. There were some new faces at the solicitor's office, and the previous year, not long after he'd taken over from Ludlow as district solicitor, Ruiz had started assigning his underlings to my cases instead of showing up himself. I understood why. Since folks knew us to be friends, and on top of that, our kids were dating, it might create an appearance of impropriety if he appointed himself to go up against me in court.

Through the window in the courtroom door, I saw the bailiff heading over to let us in. These bond hearings were cattle calls, with everyone showing up at the same time and waiting their turn. We walked in, and I led Marianne and Kevin over to the defense side. In the courthouse they would've been seated in wooden pews, but here it was just several rows of black metal chairs.

The court reporter was getting set up, but the bench was empty, so folks were still talking. Kevin asked me, almost whispering, "When do they bring Mr. Carter down? I'd like to shake his hand."

"Oh, I'm sorry. I explained to Mrs. Carter, but not to you. They do these things remotely, as far as the folks being held in jail are concerned. You see those screens up by the bench? That's where he'll appear."

"Aw, man. Okay."

They'd made hearings remote during COVID, setting up a room elsewhere in the building with a desk and a laptop for prisoners to use, and it turned out the staff preferred it that way. The bailiff got a lot less unexpected exercise, because unruly prisoners—there were always a few—couldn't pull their theatrics in the courtroom anymore.

The bailiff announced Magistrate Porcher, and we all stood up. I'd been before him a couple of times. His family was an old one around here, so everyone knew to pronounce his name with a French flourish: por-*shay*. He made his way to the bench. His back was bent, his hair was white, and although Roy told me Porcher's judicial mind had been highly regarded when he was younger, we were not the only lawyers who thought he ought to have retired long ago.

The bailiff called the first case, and the woman at the solicitor's table rose to speak. She was maybe forty, with perfectly coiffed blonde hair.

"Your Honor, may it please the court," she said, "Ginevra Barnes for the district solicitor."

That caught my attention, but I reminded myself that Barnes was a common name. Fourth was about twenty years older than she was, and dark-haired. And to my knowledge, nobody in his family had gone into the practice of law.

Still, I was concerned. I slipped my phone out of my pocket and discreetly texted Terri, hoping she'd be available to look this woman up.

The case was a DUI, the driver was on his fourth offense, and this time he'd sent somebody to the hospital. He did not get bond. On the screen, he protested that staying in jail would cost him his job.

"Your Honor," Ms. Barnes said, "the State submits that letting him out on bond could cost some innocent person their life."

The magistrate agreed. On-screen, the DUI guy blew up, shouting curses. A prison guard came in, and after a brief scuffle he was subdued and dragged out of the room.

My phone buzzed. Terri's text said *It's 2022. You need to get a smartphone & look stuff up yourself.*

I chuckled. She was right.

Her next one said *Anyway she's Fourth's SIL.*

I sent her a question mark.

She wrote back *Sister in law.*

Well, dammit.

I wrote *Thx*. Then I flipped my phone shut and stuck it back in my pocket.

Ruiz knew that Fourth would gladly ruin me. He also knew I'd gladly drop Fourth off a very high bridge. I wondered if I could convince Ruiz that putting any member of the Barnes family on a case of mine would create an appearance of impropriety.

But I knew what his answer would be. *It's a small town and an even smaller legal community. You can't avoid that kind of thing.*

And although I didn't like it, that was true. He had to pick the right prosecutor for each case. If awkward connections came up between counsel, it was on us to act like professionals.

Which, right now, meant me giving Ms. Barnes a chance. For all I knew, maybe she didn't like Fourth either. I imagined that being his sister-in-law might be a special kind of hell.

After a few more cases were heard and disposed of, it was our turn.

I stepped up to the defense table and nodded hello to Ms. Barnes. She looked away and busied herself with one of the binders on her table. When I'd been a prosecutor, showing up in court to argue ten bail hearings in a row, my table had never looked half as organized as hers did.

I turned to the bench. "Your Honor, Leland Munroe, counsel for Bobby Carter."

"Oh, okay, then," Porcher drawled. "I was wondering who'd take the arson case. Should've figured it'd be you."

I gave him the obligatory chuckle. Porcher sometimes talked like he was sitting on the couch in his living room, instead of up on the bench. I'd heard he was more formal in his youth, so I figured he'd reached an age where he just did not care anymore.

He said, "That your boy up on the TV now?"

I looked at the monitor beside the bench. Bobby was there. I realized that, since he wasn't in the courtroom, the magistrate couldn't tell how big he was. I hoped that would play in our favor; it made him less physically intimidating.

"Yes, Your Honor, that's Mr. Carter there."

Ms. Barnes said, "Your Honor, if I might recap for the court reporter, Mr. Carter's been arrested for first-degree arson under section 16-11-110 and involuntary manslaughter under section 16-3-60."

She wasn't recapping anything. Porcher should've announced those details himself, for the record, right off the bat. They needed to get into the hearing transcript, and the court reporter couldn't put them there unless somebody said them out loud.

Porcher asked, "And I take it your office plans to charge him with those offenses?"

"Your Honor, yes, we do plan to bring this before the grand jury. As Your Honor I'm sure is aware, this case arises from a fire on February 24, 2022, in the restaurant Mr. Carter operated in downtown Basking Rock. That fire killed a promising and much-loved young woman, Dixie Ward, who had recently graduated with her degree in hotel management and started her career at the Sea Island Inn." That was one of the better hotels in town.

"And it's been determined to be arson?" Porcher asked.

"It has, Your Honor. That's the conclusion of Dr. Willard, the South Carolina Law Enforcement Division expert, or SLED expert as I'll refer to him, who was assigned to the investigation. The fire that killed Miss Ward was intentionally set. And as I'm sure Your Honor is also aware, both of the crimes Mr. Carter was arrested for are felonies, and on the arson charge alone he's facing a minimum sentence of thirty years."

"Okay, then. What's the State's position on bond?"

"Your Honor, the State submits that Mr. Carter should not be released on bond. If I may just state for the record, first-degree arson is one of the violent crimes set forth at section 16-1-60 as being suitable for a denial of bail. And I want to underline that, even if the arson that Mr. Carter was arrested for hadn't killed anybody, denial would still be appropriate. The vast majority of violent crimes for which Your Honor has the discretion to deny bail are not crimes that result in death. But here, of course, the arson in question killed a vibrant young woman with her whole future ahead of her, and it has shattered her poor family."

Porcher nodded gravely and looked down. I sensed that he was about to turn the floor over to me. Ms. Barnes must've sensed it, too, because she added, "And Your Honor, I would also note that section 17-15-30(B) requires that the court consider the record of the accused. What I can tell you right now is that Mr. Carter previously served four years in the state penitentiary for bank fraud and passing bad checks."

Porcher frowned and looked at Bobby on the screen. After a second, he said, "Carter. Yeah. You know what, I believe I do recall hearing about that case, now that you mention it." Looking back at Ms. Barnes, he added, "Can't recall the details, though. It's been a while."

"Well, Your Honor," she said, "I'm afraid at this moment I'm not able to give you the full picture of his previous crimes, because this case has progressed very quickly. The arrest warrant only issued yesterday afternoon, and I wasn't informed until the paperwork for this hearing came across my desk about two hours ago. I did call SLED as soon as I got that, but they weren't able to get me a copy of his criminal history before I had to leave for today's hearings."

"Okay," Porcher said. "So do we know if the fraud and so forth are the extent of his history? Does the State need some time to look into that?"

For Bobby's sake, I had to take the wheel of this conversation.

"Your Honor," I said, "I believe I can shed some light on that. As part of my due diligence in this case, I looked at Mr. Carter's record myself. I had my private investigator pull it. The conviction Ms. Barnes mentioned is his only one, and that was fifteen years ago, shortly after Mr. Carter returned from his second tour in Iraq with combat injuries and, unfortunately, some related mental trauma."

As I spoke about Iraq, Porcher nodded in a way that made me think he had more than a merely theoretical understanding of what I was saying. It occurred to me that he was of the generation that had served in Vietnam. I decided to keep going in that vein.

"Bobby Carter is a decorated veteran," I said. "Prior to his service in Iraq, he had no criminal record at all. His worst offense was two speeding tickets. The acts he committed after returning from combat, which led to his incarceration, were completely out of character. But I would note that, even so, those acts were not violent. Mr. Carter deeply regrets what he did fifteen years ago, but in a bond hearing I believe it's important to let the court know that those acts did not cause anybody any physical harm. After his release from prison in 2011, Mr. Carter finally received the treatment he needed for the trauma he'd sustained in Iraq, and since that time he has not reoffended. To the contrary, Your Honor, he met and married his wife, Marianne Carter, who's here to support him right now."

I gestured to her where she sat, in the front row.

"And, Your Honor, with the love and support of his wife, Mr. Carter has spent the last decade building a successful restaurant business that provides jobs to a number of folks here in town. Next to Mr. Carter's wife is Kevin Moreland, the manager of his beachfront restaurant, who also came here today to show his support. They're both prepared to speak to his ties to the community and other issues."

"Uh-huh," Porcher said. "Well, I don't know that we'll need that, especially since we've got, uh…" He gestured toward the gallery behind me. "There's a number of other folks here waiting their turn to request bond, just like your client's doing."

"I understand, Your Honor. Well, then, let me just summarize some pertinent facts real quick. Mr. Carter was born and raised right here in Basking Rock, and in addition to his restaurant business, he and his wife own a home on the North Side. So his ties to the community are strong. And as Mr. Moreland would've testified, Mr. Carter frequently works at the restaurant himself, which I think speaks to the fact that his financial wherewithal depends on him being here in town. It's a good old-fashioned pizza shop, not a business you could run remotely. Mr. Carter has no record of flight or failure to appear at court proceedings, and when he was arrested the other day, he went peacefully, without so much as raising his voice, much less trying to flee. So in addition to the fact that he's got no history of violence at all, the evidence points to him not being a flight risk."

I glanced at the screen. Bobby looked nervous as hell. Anybody would be, in his shoes.

Porcher said, "Mrs. Barnes, does the State disagree?"

"We do, Your Honor. We understand that Mr. Carter has significant ties out of state, in New England, through his wife's family. His restaurant skills are portable to essentially anywhere in the country or, matter of fact, the world, so in the State's view, his profession weighs toward flight risk rather than away from it. As I stated earlier, the SLED paperwork regarding his arrest only crossed my desk shortly before this hearing, so my office has yet to fully review this case. But that being said, I am in a position to advise Your Honor that we are actively looking at additional and potentially even more serious charges."

That was alarming news. I had to cut it off at the pass.

"Your Honor," I said, "even if we didn't have all these folks behind me waiting their turn to be heard, it would not be appropriate for us to spend time discussing hypothetical charges that might never be filed. We're here for one reason: to determine Mr. Carter's bond, given the nature of the two charges set forth on the arrest warrant. Under section 17-15-30 sub A, that's what we're to take account of. Nothing else."

"Yeah, I've got to agree there," Porcher said. "Mrs. Barnes, if the court were inclined to set a bond, does the State have an amount that it would recommend?"

"Yes, Your Honor." She shuffled through some papers. "For context, I do have some information that's pertinent to that. Section 17-15-30 sets forth a number of issues to consider in setting the conditions of release, and those include family ties and financial resources. So what I have here is, first off, the assessed value of the home that the accused owns, which is $843,000. In addition, there's the value of his business, which I wasn't able to determine in the short amount of time I had, but perhaps the accused or his counsel could speak to that. And one more point, which perhaps Your Honor might want to take testimony on from Mrs. Carter there, is that my office has reason to believe she has considerable means of her own, which may be held out of state."

On-screen, Bobby said, almost shouting, "Leave her out of this! She's got nothing to do with this!"

Ms. Barnes shot back, "Nothing to do with what, Mr. Carter? Are you saying she didn't assist you in committing the arson?"

"No! That ain't fair! You can't do that!"

I wished I could hit a pause button on Bobby. Yelling in court was never a good idea. Any other judge would've banged his gavel and called for order, but Porcher was a little slow on the uptake.

I said, "Your Honor, I think we all understand that Mr. Carter is upset at having his wife dragged into this. And again, to avoid getting needlessly complicated and taking even more time away from the folks waiting their turn, the United States Supreme Court told us more than seventy years ago in *Stack v. Boyle* that all we're looking for here is a bail amount that's reasonably calculated to ensure the presence of Mr. Carter at any eventual trial, if there is one. We're not to punish him for being successful or for having a wife who's successful. That is not the law."

Ms. Barnes said, "If I may, Your Honor, the amount that ensures the presence of an accused at trial is the amount that he's not willing to lose. It's got to be significant for him personally, taking account of his assets."

"Your Honor, I hope Ms. Barnes isn't suggesting we can base bail amounts on speculation. The only asset we've heard an actual number on yet is the family home, and that number doesn't take into account any mortgages. And, Ms. Barnes"—I looked at her, and out of the corner of my eye, I saw Porcher did too—"I'm not accusing you of anything untoward. I understand SLED didn't get the paperwork to you until the last minute, so you had very little time to get this figured out. I just don't think we ought to be speculating about what assets might be worth."

I wouldn't have said that so politely if it had been Ruiz opposite me, or any of the men who worked for him. But it never looked good for a male lawyer to be aggressive toward a woman in court.

"Now, Mr. Munroe," Porcher said, "you're not telling me it's speculation to say your client clearly has some fairly significant assets, are you?"

The only way around that question was to bicker about exactly what "significant" meant. I had yet to meet a judge who liked pedantic arguments, so I let that lie.

"Your Honor, I'll gladly admit that the decade-plus of hard work Mr. Carter's put into his business has left him pretty comfortable. I'm just warning against an excessive or speculative bond, which the law forbids."

"Of course. Now, Mrs. Barnes, do you have a number to propose?"

"Yes, Your Honor. The State recommends, as I said, that Mr. Carter not be released, given his record and the nature of the crime. But if the Court prefers to release him, the State would request that bond be set in an amount that reflects both his financial means and the fact that the crime in question cost a young woman her life. So we would request a bond amount of one million dollars."

That would mean Marianne had to pull a hundred grand out of a hat just to get Bobby released from jail. We'd talked that morning about what she had access to, and that was not going to fly. The pizza business had lost half its revenue since the fire destroyed the downtown location, and if they had to pay anything close to what Ms. Barnes was suggesting, they wouldn't have enough left to pay for his defense. And, like any other middle-class couple, they were much too well off to qualify for a public defender.

"Your Honor," I said, "that's far in excess of the full assessed value Ms. Barnes stated for the Carters' family home, which they bought only eight years ago on a thirty-year mortgage, so they've got very little equity. It's almost by definition excessive, since I don't know how the Carters would find a bail bondsman willing to take collateral that's worth far less than the amount of the bond."

Porcher pursed his lips and nodded as if he saw my point.

I wished I could argue for release on personal recognizance, meaning no cash required, but with Bobby's record and the fact that a young woman had died, asking for that would make me look unreasonable. A judge who thought a lawyer was being unreasonable would stop listening. And I needed Porcher to keep listening to me, so Ms. Barnes couldn't lead him down her path.

"And, Your Honor," I said, "we've got to consider the nature of the charges. The perpetrators we see getting million-dollar bonds are the worst of the worst. Mass murderers, drug lords caught with enough fentanyl to kill a thousand people—that's the kind of people we impose that kind of bond on. It is an insult to their victims to impose that type of a bond on a local business owner who's accused of setting a fire in what everyone thought was an unoccupied building in the middle of the night. These are serious charges, but I think we need to be proportional—"

"Okay, I hear what you're saying. I don't think we need to keep going on and on about this. Mrs. Barnes, you indicated your office does plan to take these charges before the grand jury?"

"Based on what I know today, Your Honor, yes, we do, at a bare minimum. But as I said, we are still reviewing the facts, and very realistically, the charges may well be more serious than what's stated on the arrest warrant."

The only more serious charge than arson causing death was murder. How Ms. Barnes thought she would get from accidental death to murder, I didn't know. And not knowing was a bad place to be.

"Okay," Porcher said. "That's fine, but all I can rule on is what's in front of me. And I do think what you're seeking is excessive. So I'm going to set bond for Mr. Carter at $400,000."

That was still too much. I kept my poker face on and said, "Thank you, Your Honor."

On the screen beside the bench, Bobby looked stunned.

9

APRIL 4, 2022

Terri and I were driving up a little street on the edge of town, downhill from the fancier North Side. Century-old oaks grew along the road, and the Spanish moss hanging from them made them look a little shabby and decayed. It was a look I'd always liked. I never felt quite at ease in a manicured yard.

"It's that one right there," I said. "With the magnolia."

I pointed to the two-story brick house I'd toured with Chance over the weekend. The tree in the front yard was covered with pink flowers.

"I'd almost buy the house just for that magnolia," she said. "But he must be sad you came downhill—he's watching his commission shrink right before his eyes."

"Yeah. He's partial to bigger places too. More expensive ones. Last week he showed me a house with a master bath I could park my car in."

She laughed. "Even this one looks kind of big. Wouldn't it be a little weird, rattling around in there by yourself when Noah's gone?"

"Yeah, thanks," I said, and laughed. "Thanks a lot. I'm trying to compartmentalize."

"Oh. Sorry. Yeah, my sister's going through that too, or starting to. Her oldest is leaving for college in Georgia this fall."

"Oof. Well, I'm sure she's fine whenever she manages not to think about it."

I wondered again why Terri had never married or had kids. I'd led conversations toward that topic several times, but I'd never asked outright. It wasn't my business, although I wished it was.

I took the car out of park and headed up the street. We had an appointment in Charleston to get to, with an arson expert.

In a brighter tone, like she was purposely changing the subject, Terri asked, "How are the Carters doing? Bobby happy to be back home?"

"Oof again. He didn't actually get home until Saturday around lunchtime, because it took a while for his wife to get the bond together. I drove her over to get him, and he—I mean, physically he was fine, but he wasn't in good shape mentally."

"Mm-hmm." She shook her head. "I don't even want to know what he's seen. Over in Iraq, I mean."

"Yeah. Man." I stopped at a red light. "It's a problem, though," I said. "If this does get charged. If it doesn't get dropped or end in a plea. How do I put a guy like that on the stand? Cross-examination is hard on a person. And he's got all these, you know, fault lines. I mean, he yelled at the prosecutor at the bond hearing just for mentioning that his wife might have some money!"

"Mm-hmm. And a good prosecutor would, like, poke him where it hurts. Maybe he's the kind of defendant you don't put on the stand."

"Yeah, but you know juries hate that." I turned onto the main road. "They want to hear the defendant talk. They want to decide for themselves if he's telling the truth."

She nodded. "Yes, they do," she said. "And so do you."

"I hate to say it, but yeah. I don't know why I haven't got a clear read on that yet."

"Well, step one is, stop letting his wife hypnotize you!"

I laughed, but she had a point.

We were about halfway to Charleston when I got a call from Jacob Drayton's dad. Terri tried to turn off the radio for me, but she tuned it to static instead. My new car's controls weren't familiar to her yet. I turned it off and picked up.

"Afternoon, Mr. Drayton. What can I do for you?"

He chuckled. "Well, you could get my son's case thrown out. That's what he's paying you for, isn't it?"

"Yes indeed. But these things take time. Listen, sorry if there's background noise, but I'm on the highway right now."

"That's fine. Listen, I didn't want to call you on a Sunday, but I was real concerned yesterday to find out you're taking up that arson-murder thing."

The *Patriot's* Sunday edition had put Bobby Carter's bond hearing on the front page, above the fold.

"Uh-huh. Well, I sure don't mean to cause any distress."

I wasn't about to get into an argument with him. He already knew I couldn't discuss his son's case with him beyond the most basic and public facts, and I certainly wasn't about to discuss Bobby Carter's.

He chuckled again. "Listen, Leland, I know Bobby Carter's managed to get himself some money, but you're allowed to have standards, aren't you? If there's anything I've learned in business, it's that some customers aren't worth the trouble. You've got to pick and choose."

"I appreciate the concern," I lied. Drayton and I were not on first-name terms, and I wasn't a fan of his artificial friendliness. It was condescending. He'd first tried it a couple of months earlier, when he was angling to get me to drop Jacob as a client so he could direct the kid toward the lawyer of his choice.

"Yep," he said, "well, we've got to do something about this. My concern is—well, it's twofold. First off, I wouldn't want another big case to take your time or attention from my son—"

"It won't. That I can promise you."

"Well, good. My other concern is that all the publicity around this arson thing might put a spotlight on my son's case. Up to this point, we've managed to keep it pretty much under wraps, and that's how I'd like it to stay."

I didn't know what he thought I was supposed to do about the local media. "Well, I'd like that too."

"Good. Do you have a plan for how to accomplish that?"

Drayton was not my client, wasn't the one paying the bills, and was often in the mood to share his opinions about my legal strategy, even though he wasn't a lawyer. I'd had about enough. I turned the radio back on and held the phone up to the static. "Mr. Drayton?" I said. "Dray... you're cutting out..." I let him hear another second of static, and then I ended the call.

When I folded my phone shut, Terri cracked up.

I smiled and said, "My God, that man is irritating."

"What'd he want this time?"

"He wants me to drop Bobby Carter and, I guess, come up with a plan for keeping Jacob's case out of the news. How am I supposed to do that? I'm not the one who's friendly with Fourth. He is!"

"Which is why it hasn't been covered so far."

"Right? If you're Fourth's friend, ask for favors and ye shall receive. It's the same reason Ludlow's boy got away with what he did to Noah. And Ludlow got away with... being Ludlow."

The local news hadn't said a word about why Ludlow had left his position as district solicitor, simply that he'd "passed the baton" to Ruiz. Having the baton pried from his clutches by the state ethics board somehow hadn't come up in the coverage.

"They couldn't really publish anything about Brandon, though," she said, "since he wasn't charged."

"Yeah, but we know why that was. If you're Ludlow's kid, you could probably drunk-drive a stolen car through the front door of the court-house and not get charged."

"Well, that used to be true," she said. "I hope it's changed."

I thought about Ruiz. He was a by-the-book guy, but I wondered if he'd go that far. He hadn't done anything about Brandon Ludlow's adventures with fentanyl. Although I supposed he didn't have any evidence to work with, since the local police hadn't collected it.

Approaching the bridge into Charleston, we had the windows down to enjoy the wind coming in from the ocean. The faint salt tang mixed with the sulfurous scent of pluff mud was the smell of home to me. Once we crossed the water and got into downtown, it was windows up and back to business. As we passed a sign pointing the way to the municipal court, Terri asked, "Did Varner ever get you those crime-scene photos?"

"No, and I'm glad he didn't. Last week, I filed a motion to dismiss the arrest warrant."

"You can do that?" She sounded highly skeptical.

"In Charleston County you can, if the solicitor doesn't turn everything over within sixty days of the warrant. A few years ago they amended the rules to streamline how criminal cases were handled."

"Is crime getting that bad there? Courts all backlogged?"

"Not really. Cases just weren't moving through the system fast enough."

I signaled my turn, easing around a parked delivery van. "If the judge grants my motion," I said, "Varner will have to petition for a new arrest warrant. And convince the judge that he had good cause for not turning over the photos."

"You think the judge will grant it?"

"Depends on the judge. Mostly, I just want to see the damn photos, so I filed the motion to make him cough them up. Varner's a pretty organized guy—things don't slip through the cracks—so I have to wonder if there's something in there he doesn't want me to see."

A few minutes later, I parked across the street from the slightly shabby two-story office building my GPS had brought us to. I wasn't sure we were at the right place until we found the expert's name on the intercom: Stefan McDonald, Certified Fire and Explosion Investigator. As I rang his buzzer, I said to Terri, "That's a hell of a job title."

"Yeah. I'd hate to be *that* guy. He sounds so boring in comparison. Or that one," she said, pointing to the names above and below McDonald's: an accountant and a compliance consultant, whatever that was.

McDonald buzzed us in, and we went down a fluorescent-lit hall that smelled like burned coffee. Before I could knock on his door, he swung it open and invited us in. He was a lanky guy, sixty-five or seventy, wearing some kind of rumpled uniform that was a few shades darker gray than his hair.

We all sat down, him at his desk and us in front of it. Behind him on the wall were a few diplomas and certifications, along with a whole lot of framed newspaper headlines about fires and jury verdicts.

"So," he said, "this is not a good report— Let me rephrase." He set his hand down solidly onto what looked like a printout of the fire investigation report that Ginevra Barnes had emailed me over the weekend. "The report is good, methodologically. It's not good for our guy."

"Yeah, I wasn't thrilled by what I read either. You're not seeing any methodology issues? Nothing that they might've done wrong?"

"Not on an initial read. You got to keep in mind I only read it this morning. And I'd like to see higher-res photos of a few things. But as for the basic conclusion, that it was intentionally set... I mean, yes. It was. And not spontaneously or sloppily either. This took some preparation."

"You're sure?"

He shrugged and shook his head like this was self-evident. "Look, I'm a third-generation fireman. After I had my family, which was going on thirty-five years ago now, I stopped being an active firefighter and went over to the investigation side. And if I had these facts before me"—he gestured to the report—"there's no other conclusion I'd come to."

I sighed. "Okay. Well, the facts are what the facts are. So do you agree with what it says about where it started?"

"Well, I'm certainly inclined to agree it didn't start in the kitchen." He flipped partway through the report, then stopped and pointed to a photo. "I mean, sure, that's by far the most severe fire damage right there, which could mean it burned the longest—but this was a restaurant; they've got kitchen grease. That's going to cause a lot of damage. The only accelerant in the kitchen was by the door to that hallway there."

"What type of accelerant was it?" Terri asked. "I haven't had a chance to read that yet."

"Petroleum-based liquid. And I would agree that the fire was caused by a number of incendiary devices, most likely some type of plastic bottle that would've been filled with the accelerant and then stuffed with a wick of some kind. Fabric, usually."

"You're saying a Molotov cocktail?" Terri said, surprised. "Really?"

"Yep, several of them, placed or thrown after being lit. But like I said, only one in the kitchen, and it was by the door."

Terri thought for a second. "Would a pizza restaurant have kitchen grease?" She looked at me. "Did they have fried food on the menu?"

"I don't recall. We should ask Bobby."

McDonald went back to flipping through the report. "From the damage to the kitchen, yes, they did. And there was your typical large commercial stove, with a fryer and the vent hood," he said, turning the report around to show us the blackened appliances. "They didn't just have a pizza oven. So assuming they used this equipment, they'd have some type of cooking oil on hand. And they must've, given how it spread. There would've been grease on the underside of the vent hood, and it would've went up."

"You're saying, because that's how the fire got into the ductwork?"

"Right. On a restaurant hood, you'll always—I mean, as long as it's been in use for a while, say a year or two, there's typically a whole lot of old grease on it and inside it. And that'll catch real easily, and then the ventilation obviously draws the air inward. I couldn't even count how many kitchen fires I've seen that spread that way. Residential and commercial."

"Yeah, that makes sense," I said. "Do you have any thoughts on the, uh, placement of the Molotov cocktails, or the order of events?"

"Well, this isn't so much forensics as... I'm not going to say psychology, it's just common sense. If you know there's cooking oil in a kitchen, and you're tossing what are essentially firebombs, you certainly don't want to be in the room when it goes up. And you don't want it to be between you and the door. So my best guess is the kitchen was the last place he hit. He tossed that last one on his way out, and he was probably in a hurry because several other fires had started in the other ground-floor rooms. He didn't stop long enough to carefully aim that last one, is what I mean. It could've bounced off of one of the appliances, and that's how it ended up near the door."

I thought for a second. "I wonder if that goes to motive. Because most of the value of our guy's insurance claim was probably in that kitchen. The rest was, what, tables and chairs? A pantry?"

"Mm-hmm," Terri said. "Those appliances must've cost a fortune."

"Right. So why not just burn that? Why set fires all over the place and only hit the kitchen on the way out, and not that carefully?"

McDonald nodded like that wasn't an unreasonable line of thought.

I said, "Because from the arsonist's perspective, if you just toss one single Molotov cocktail in there, if you don't wait to see where it lands... I mean, you might *think* it'll all go up in smoke because of the grease, but can you be sure?"

McDonald shrugged. "Not sure, no. But can I ask... who else have you got? I know you said your client rented the premises. Have you looked at the property owner?"

"Yeah, just the preliminaries," I said. "He's a big local landlord. No criminal record."

"I would've wanted to know about *his* insurance," he said, "if I'd been investigating that."

"I'll see what I can find on that, but apparently, there's no indication he's got financial problems, so..."

"Okay." He leaned back in his chair. "Well, it's not common, but once in a while somebody hits his own building for a motive other than money."

"Like what?" Terri asked.

"I saw a woman once, destroyed her own garage while her husband's favorite car was inside. Obviously, they were having marital problems of some kind. And a guy who burned down his vacation home so his wife couldn't get it in the divorce. So, in your shoes, I'd try to get some information about how the owner's personal life is going. And his relationship with the tenant—was there any bad blood between them?"

"That's possible," I said.

"You ask Bobby," Terri said. "I'll ask around. See what his other tenants think of him."

"How old is this property owner?"

"Late sixties," I said.

"Oh, okay."

I could tell from his tone that the landlord's age had made him abandon a hypothesis.

"If he were younger," I said, "would that matter?"

"Oh, some arsonists do it for the attention. They like the sirens and the TV cameras, and, if they're the owners, they might like everybody feeling bad for them. But I've never seen that start when a man was that age. There's normally a history."

I looked at Terri. She shook her head. If Boseman had had a history of fires at his properties, that fact would've been somewhere in her vast mental record of the lives folks lived in Basking Rock.

We came out of McDonald's office thoroughly deflated. As I started my car and pulled away from the curb, I said, "If Bobby did this thing… if he set that fire and killed that girl, I don't think I'm going to be able to fight any too hard for him. I'll have to refer him to some other lawyer."

"Maybe Travis Girardeau's looking for work?"

We cracked up. Girardeau had been a flashy criminal defense lawyer who bent the law a little too much and got in trouble for it. We'd had some dealings with him a couple of years earlier, and since then, he'd become one of our running jokes. He was headed for prison now, I thought, if he wasn't there already, but we still remembered his alligator shoes and his Lamborghini, which had looked ridiculous on the quaint streets of Charleston.

"Seriously, though," I said. "I sometimes wish I didn't care so much. I'd just take Bobby's money and fight for him. But that girl was only twenty-two years old."

"I know." We drove a ways in silence, and then she said, "I guess either you've got to refer him to somebody else real soon, or we've got to figure out if he's telling the truth."

10

APRIL 11, 2022

It was a glorious afternoon. I was standing on an oceanfront golf course on Kiawah Island, looking at the sunlight glinting off the water. Golf wasn't a big interest of mine, but it was a nice place for an afternoon stroll.

Roy selected a club from his bag and said, "You got to watch Hank's game. He's got a feel for the wind. That's why he's buying us drinks about an hour from now."

At the third hole, Hank Manigault had hit a hole in one. Golf etiquette, I'd been informed, required him to treat us to a round at the clubhouse.

Hank said, "I've got a feel for not losing. If that means taking account of the wind, then that's what I'll do."

As Roy stood over his ball, shifting his weight from foot to foot, he said, "Well, Hank, neither of us is losing today. Right, Leland?"

I smiled. "That's what you brought me along for."

Roy laughed. As they were both aware, I didn't know my ass from my elbow when it came to golf. Unlike lawyers in private practice, the prosecutors I'd spent eighteen years working with didn't use the sport as a bonding exercise. They were too busy in court and too cheap from years of making do on state-government salaries.

"You'll learn," Roy said, "if you care to. But no, you losing today is just a side benefit. The point is, I want Hank to hear what you know about the Ludlow boy. He's got a soft spot for that kid—"

Hank said, "Somebody's got to make a man out of him. And his daddy isn't doing it, unfortunately."

"His daddy also isn't trying to teach circus tricks to feral cats," Roy said. "For good reason." He whacked his ball down the fairway. We watched it fly.

Hank, who owned a local chain of grocery stores, had hired Brandon Ludlow to work in one of them. Roy had told me the idea was for Brandon to rotate through every entry-level job in the store—so far he'd been a cashier and a stocker—then work his way up and eventually get into management.

It wasn't the expected path to adulthood for a young man in Brandon's position. For the past three generations, men in his family had served as district solicitor, responsible for meting out justice over thousands of square miles in the Lowcountry and beyond. At his age, Brandon ought to have been weighing offers from multiple law firms or clerking for a federal judge. But he'd flamed out of pretty much all the options normally available to kids like him.

As we headed down the fairway, Roy said, "So, Hank, I wanted Leland to share his perspective on the kid. Not to tell you that you shouldn't try to help him, but just so you go into it with your eyes open."

"I mean, I appreciate it," Hank said. "Don't get me wrong. I know your job is to look out for liability issues. I just don't worry about risk as much as you do. To get anywhere in business, I don't think you can."

Roy turned to me. "You should hear his stories. The things some of his competitors have pulled, it's just this side of *The Sopranos*."

"Oh, yeah," Hank agreed. "The grocery business is… basically mud wrestling. It's *all* below the belt."

I laughed.

"Oh, by the way," Hank told me, "Speaking of folks who've got wayward sons, I was talking with Oz the other day. Osborne Drayton. He told me about that motion you filed to kick the warrant out."

"Did he?" I was surprised at the idea that Jacob had told his dad about it. The two of them didn't talk much. The motion was a public filing, though, and his dad might be keeping tabs on the case.

"Yeah, Oz thought that was a real aggressive move on your part. He approves."

Roy said, "Leland knows when to punch hard."

That won a nod from Hank. "Sure, and he's got to. A man can't get anywhere if he doesn't know that."

"Yep," Roy said.

"Shame about that other case, though." Hank paused and took a golf stance over a wood chip he'd spotted in the grass. "I don't see why he cares—way I see it, if you get through life without any bad publicity, you're not taking enough risks, which means you're missing out." As we stood watching, he whacked the wood chip off to the side. "But, you know, he's got his panties in a wad about the coverage."

We started walking again.

"Yeah, it's a pain," I said.

I had appeared in the *Southeast Patriot* again in connection with Bobby Carter's case. The worst photo I'd ever seen of myself was right at the top of their home page, under the headline "Munroe Makes Hay with Ward Family's Grief."

Roy said, "I understand his concerns, but yeah, Oz doesn't have your appreciation of the rough-and-tumble."

Hank laughed, shaking his head. "Hell no, he does *not*."

"Speaking of, though," Roy said, "there might be a little more rough-and-tumble than you were anticipating in your current plans. Leland's got some insights into the Ludlow kid that most folks don't have. Stuff that's kept a little under wraps around here."

Hank snorted with cynical laughter. "As in, everything? Nothing bad about that family's ever going to be in the news. Old Dabney makes sure of it. But I knew that. Give me the juice, though. What'd he do?"

Roy and I had discussed beforehand what he wanted Hank to know.

"I think the main concern," I said, "in terms of liability, is the drug dealing. If that pharmacy expansion you're working on goes through, your stores will have whole shelves full of the type of drugs that could, uh… pose a problem with him."

"Wait, you're saying drug dealing as in pharmaceuticals? Not street drugs?"

"Yeah. Fentanyl. Opioids."

"Huh." He gave a brisk nod. He saw my point.

I spotted Roy's ball, a dot of white in all the green, like the dots of white sails out on the blue water. My pull cart of rented clubs rolled behind me as smoothly as a good suitcase on a hotel carpet. Working with Roy had given me the sense that for a successful lawyer in private practice, the whole world unrolled with equal smoothness. Life was a sunlit golf course. I wasn't used to it yet, and I didn't know if I was ever going to be.

Hank said, "You know what, though? It's a calculated risk. Like anything else. So I've got to do the calculations."

"Yep," Roy said. "And that's your call. I just wanted you to have the information."

"Appreciate it."

I handed him a business card. "That's my cell, there. Give me a call if you've got any more questions."

"Oh, thanks." He took the card, stopped walking, and pulled out his phone. While I watched Roy, who had arrived at his ball and was playing air golf with one of his clubs, strategizing his next shot, Hank texted me his own number.

As we headed toward Roy, Hank took a golf ball from his pocket and started tossing it in the air. "I guess I might want to rethink letting Brandon rotate through working in security. That gives him a little too much access. It's a shame—he's got the size I like to see in a security guy." He dropped the ball and reached down to grab it. "So anyway, you won't fire me as a client? If I proceed with the plan?"

"Hell no!" Roy told him. "If it goes your way, that's great. Although if it doesn't, I might need to increase your retainer."

They laughed.

"Well, thanks for the info," Hank said. "Helps me come up with a game plan. Somebody hit that kid into the rough, and I don't see why I can't get in there and hit him back out."

. . .

We played nine holes and then had a caddie drive us back to the clubhouse. Hank could only stay long enough to finish the round we drank to celebrate his ace. After he left, Roy and I ordered a late lunch. We were in a corner booth, with a view over the whole restaurant if you looked that way, and the ocean if you looked outside.

As he handed his menu back to the waitress, Roy said, "You should bring Noah here sometime."

"Oh, he knows even less about golf than I do."

"He ought to learn. It'll serve him well. He still around?"

"Yeah, he's not moving to Charleston until probably next month, or whenever he's got a job offer in hand. He's had a couple of interviews, thinks they went pretty well."

"That's good. Well, you should sign him up for lessons in the meantime. Not here—there's much cheaper places back toward Basking Rock. I sent my girls to Oceanside. Made sure all three of them learned how to play when they were still in high school."

His daughters were all in their thirties now.

"What, for the sport? Or the connections?"

"Both. I mean, I'm sure you could meet good people playing tennis or running marathons or what have you, but you can't really *talk* to them while you do it."

"Oh. Yeah." I looked out at the rolling green course. The point of golf had just clicked for me. "It's the perfect sport for a lawyer, isn't it. Because you can talk freely, right? Since you're not out of breath and there's nobody else close enough to overhear."

"Exactly, and that's good for any kind of business. Not just the law." Roy finished his gin and tonic and set the glass down. "And apart from that, a game's a good litmus test. I've had folks I decided not to work with after we hit the links."

"Clients? Really?"

"Yeah. Either they weren't a good sport, or they took it way too serious... Ten or twelve years ago, I was out here with some real estate guy who wanted me to handle a condo conversion or something, and he got so mad about a bad shot that he whacked a tree with his club and broke the damn thing."

"Good Lord. That's just sad."

"Yeah, not to mention dangerous. The head came flying off. Could've hit somebody. And I was just... I'm not working for a grown-up toddler. Life is too short."

"Yes, it is."

The waitress returned with our appetizers and Roy's glass of wine. He thanked her and got a pretty smile in response.

"Miss," he said, "can I ask you something?"

"Yes, of course. Anything you need, you just let me know."

"Oh, no, we have everything we need. My question is... my friend who just left, who bought the first round—would you mind telling me what tip he left you?"

Her smile flickered uncertainly.

"I'm a member," Roy said, sounding relaxed and genteel. "I invited him here today, and I just want to know if he's civilized." He smiled to let her know he wasn't angry at anybody.

"Of course, sir. Well, he did write in a tip, which we always appreciate, of course. It was, uh, ten percent."

"Oh, my. His momma didn't raise him right, did she, now."

She laughed politely but didn't say anything. I figured she wasn't comfortable criticizing a customer.

"Well, thank you," he said. "I'll make up for it. We're all good here for now."

She went away, and he sighed.

"That another litmus test?"

We'd already asked for separate checks for our lunch. I made a mental note to leave a 20 percent tip instead of my usual fifteen.

"Yeah," he said. "He's pretty good company, and a good golfer. But everyone's got their problems. His is that, for whatever reason, he really likes getting one over on people. Sticking it to the man, sort of, except that everybody other than him is the man." He gestured toward the kitchen. "Even a waitress who can't be much more than twenty years old."

"Well, that's a shame. He a good client, otherwise? You've been working for him for a good while."

"Oh, he's no problem in that regard. He takes a risk, he runs into trouble, my bill goes up, and he pays it. You'd be amazed how many problems a grocery store can have. Just about everything short of serial killers happens there. I think that's why his wife kind of handed the reins over to him when it came to the stores. He loves getting right down in the muck, and I guess she doesn't."

I laughed and shook my head. "And here I thought business law was so genteel. Doesn't sound all that different from criminal defense."

"Oh, it's not. Apart from spending a lot less time in court."

"And a lot more on the golf course."

"Yep. And I'll drink to that." He raised his glass of wine, and I raised my San Pellegrino.

I started in on my shrimp cocktail, and we ate for a minute in silence until I said, "You mind if I ask you a question about a case?"

"Course not. Shoot."

"You know that one I'm on, about the, uh, incident?"

"The one up in Charleston?"

I dipped a shrimp in the cocktail sauce. "No, back in town. The higher-profile one."

"Oh, uh-huh."

Only about a third of the tables in the restaurant were full, and nobody was nearby, but we weren't about to name names in public.

I said, "I understand you know the property owner?"

"The property where it happened?" Roy nodded as he took a bite of beef tartare. "Not real well. But professionally, sure. We were on the zoning board. He's still on it. We're not what I'd call friends."

"Huh." That surprised me. Roy was on friendly terms with every successful man in town, as far as I knew. "Why's that?"

He thought for a second and then said, "Put it this way: I'm a conservative. You know that. I think the reason we've got rules and traditions is because they work pretty well, and I respect that. But he... I mean, he and I probably vote the same way, but not for the same reasons. He strikes me as the kind of guy who thinks freedom is him getting to do whatever the hell he wants. Like, if he's got a river running through his land, he's got the right to dam up that river, and if you've got a boating business or a mill or something downstream, well, too bad."

"Oof. Sounds like a great guy to have around."

Roy laughed. "Yeah, and that's why despite his success, I haven't sought him out as a client. I don't need to give him the golf course test to know he'd fail."

"Makes sense. Well, unfortunately, I got some questions I need to ask him. Any tips on the right approach?"

"Well, I can tell you right off the bat, don't go to his house. I had a client sue him five or six years ago, and we sent out a process server. At a perfectly reasonable time of day, I should add. The guy set dogs on him."

"Goddamn! Big dogs? What happened?"

"Oh, yeah. His wife breeds German shepherds. About the last thing you want chasing you. Fortunately, the process server was a young guy. Good sprinter. He was fine."

"Damn. Okay, let's see. I'm guessing he doesn't bring his dogs to work?"

Roy chuckled. "I've never seen them in town. But he doesn't come in to the office too often. He's semiretired. Probably the only place you can reliably predict he'll be at a specific time is church on Sunday morning."

"I doubt he'd appreciate me approaching him on his way out of church, in front of everybody."

"If you're asking him questions to find out if he had something to do with the incident, there's nowhere he's going to appreciate that."

"I guess not."

Roy speared his wedge of baguette with a fork, cut off a piece, and mopped it around the plate. "Oh, one thing." He stuck the bread in his mouth and chewed. After a gulp of wine, he continued. "You might want to keep your PI behind the scenes on this one. Don't bring her with you when you go see him."

Not having Terri there would be a handicap. She'd spent the weekend researching Boseman, to supplement the information she'd already picked up about him from a lifetime in Basking Rock. I'd been hoping she'd be available to throw in a few well-informed questions.

But, given what else Roy had said about Boseman, I didn't have to think too hard to figure out what the problem might be. "He wouldn't like her?" I asked.

"Yeah, he's... old-school about certain things. *Real* old-school, if you catch my drift."

I caught his drift. I wasn't sure exactly where the line was between "real old-school" and formal membership in the Ku Klux Klan, but the message was clear enough.

11

APRIL 13, 2022

Terri and I were in my home office, sitting side by side, looking at my desktop screen. In response to my motion, Cody Varner had folded; that morning, he'd sent me a link to a Dropbox containing the crime-scene photos from Jacob's apartment. Flipping through them was like watching a stop-motion film of the search: first the front of the building, then the lobby, the elevator, the hallway, the officer's hand—meaty, male, with a black cuff buttoned at the wrist—knocking on the door. We could see that upon entering, they'd isolated Kyle Parr and then searched the living room, a bedroom, and the kitchen.

As we clicked through, I said, "That a grid search?"

"Yeah, looks like they gave a zone to each officer and then they did grids in their zones."

There were four search methodologies that law enforcement commonly used, each one named for the shape of the path that the searcher took through the space. From the sequence of the photos, I could tell these cops knew what they were doing: they'd chosen the right method to search an indoor space for objects that might be small and hidden.

One series of photos tracked the cop in Parr's bedroom, who found the joint in the nightstand. The photos taken by the cop searching the kitchen brought us to the next illicit item, the hash pipe, in a silverware drawer. An evidence tag—a yellow square of paper with "1" printed on it—sat next to it on a mess of plastic forks and ketchup packets.

"That's not a normal place to keep a hash pipe," Terri said. "He might've tossed it in there when the police knocked."

"What's a normal place?"

"Oh, your pocket, your backpack… or your nightstand, like the joint. Somewhere personal. That's almost always where I used to find them. Maybe he put whatever drugs were in the pipe down the garbage disposal right before the cops burst in and didn't have time to hide it anywhere else."

We kept clicking until we saw what the officer had testified to at the preliminary hearing: the other bedroom—Jacob's room—had been locked. A cop's hand gripped the doorknob, but in the next photo the door was still closed. Then came a picture of a cop shouldering through it. The cheap, hollow-core thing looked to have splintered instantly. The next photo, taken from the doorway, showed the cardboard box on Jacob's desk, where the drugs were found.

"From the box, at least," Terri said, "that could be more than ten pounds. Not *much* more, but still."

The snapshots then took us on a straight path to the box, which was loosely closed, not taped. A shot from above, with it open and an evidence tag placed beside it on the desk, showed several sandwich-sized plastic baggies of weed sitting on what looked like more of the same. The officer then proceeded through a grid search of Jacob's room, finding a locked gun case—the one I'd managed to get back for him—plus a few boxes of ammo, and nothing else of interest to the police.

Another cop was photographed going to the desk and, over the course of two dozen photos, removing the baggies from the box and placing them in rows of ten on the floor. He was itemizing what they'd found and making sure there wasn't anything else in the box. When he finished, it was clear from the pattern and the numbered evidence tags beside each row that there were 157 baggies.

Terri started flipping through the crime-lab report on her lap. When she got to the page she was looking for, she yelped in excitement and showed it to me.

I read it. "A hundred and sixty-four baggies? Holy crap!"

The crime lab had somehow received more baggies than were depicted in the photos of the search. I blew the photo up on screen and started counting the baggies on Jacob's bedroom floor.

"You don't need to do that," Terri said. "Look. They're not even the same kind of bag."

On the page she had the crime-lab report open to, I could see that seven of the baggies were a different brand or style. The seam where they sealed shut was green. On the other baggies, the seam was blue.

I looked back at the screen. It sure looked like every seam in the picture from Jacob's bedroom was blue.

"A hundred and fifty-seven ounces," I said, almost to myself. Three ounces less than ten pounds.

I'd learned within probably the first week of my prosecutorial career that a baggie typically held an ounce of weed. The extra seven bags in the crime-lab report took the haul from Jacob's room over the ten-pound limit. That difference stripped the judge of his discretion: if the jury returned a guilty verdict, the judge would have no choice but to put Jacob in prison.

"This kind of thing is why I quit the force," Terri said.

I looked at her. She was quietly, deeply angry. I gave her a quick nod and said, "Yeah. In your shoes, I'd have done that too."

The idea of being in her shoes, looking at things from her perspective, made something occur to me.

"Hey, if you were one of the cops executing that warrant," I said, "how would you have understood it?"

As I looked through my binder for a copy of the warrant, she said, "What do you mean?"

I found it and skimmed the pertinent parts. "Well, it identifies the target as Kyle Parr, and it describes him. And it says the scope of the search is 'the residence of Kyle Parr situated at 624 Bouquet Street.'"

"It says that?" She leaned over and read what I was pointing at.

"I didn't think about it before," I said, "because I was focusing on the probable cause aspect, and I knew the apartment's just one dwelling unit."

"Right, so they can search the whole place." We both knew the normal rules for search warrants.

"Uh-huh, even if he's got roommates. But—"

"But Jacob's door was locked," she said, nodding with enthusiasm. "And Parr told them he didn't have a key. And if they didn't know he was subletting to Jacob—"

"Which that detective testified that they didn't—"

"Right, so what made them think Jacob's room was within the scope of the warrant?"

"You're seeing what I'm seeing? This sounds like a viable argument?"

"I mean, I don't know what the case law is. But if I was executing this warrant, yeah, I would have some doubts."

"Hot damn," I said. "Between this and those extra baggies, I think we got ourselves a motion to suppress some or all of the evidence."

Then my lawyer brain alerted me to a problem. "Hang on," I said. "Is the box empty?"

I clicked through the next dozen photos, until we were back out in the living room. There was no photo showing the box empty. No actual proof that the 157 baggies lined up in rows on the floor were the only weed they'd found.

"Dammit." Technically a defense lawyer didn't have to prove innocence, but in practice, juries usually acted like we did. "This is good, but I still can't *prove* there weren't more baggies in there."

Terri stood up so fast her chair shot three feet away on its little wheels. Stalking around my office, looking like she wanted to punch someone, she said, "They did that on purpose. They photographed every damn sock in his drawer, but not the empty box? They do not miss a *trick*."

"Maybe not," I said, "but on the other hand, they can't prove there *were* more baggies in there, and the fact those seven baggies look different is real interesting. I can get a motion to exclude drafted and filed by next week. Even excluding those baggies alone would bring us under ten pounds, so the judge would have the discretion to sentence him to no jail time. Which, for a first offense, and his background…"

"It sure is good to be a rich boy with a trust fund."

I looked over at her. She was standing at the window with her arms crossed, shaking her head. Outside, the palm tree was blowing in the wind, its green fronds rising and falling.

"Every time we find something like this," she said, "you know, something that could change our client's future... half of me feels great. But the other half thinks about all the people who fall through the cracks. The folks with public defenders who've got forty cases going at once and just can't put in the *time* that we do."

I knew what she meant. I said, "The only way I ever found around that problem was to think about it as something like driving at night. You turn your headlights on. Your high beams if you can. You light up that part of the road, and that's where you look. Everywhere else, it's dark, but you can't look there—"

"Yeah," she said with a slow nod, still watching the palm tree. "Because if you look there, you'll crash. I like that."

After a minute, she added, "And if you see somebody driving with their lights off, you flash yours. You remind them to turn theirs on. Yeah. I like that a lot."

Around dinnertime, a few hours after Terri left, I drove into town to meet up with her again. She'd arranged for us to talk to a young woman who we thought might be able to tell us something about Dixie Ward and the landlord she and Bobby Carter had shared. Terri told me this woman, Kaylee Sumter, had been a good friend of Dixie's—possibly her best friend. Terri had found her on social media and talked to her on the phone.

I parked half a block from the coffee shop where we were meeting. Walking past a taco place, I got a whiff and briefly wished we'd arranged to meet there. From experience, though, we knew this coffee place was ideal: the guests and baristas talking, the music, the growling of espresso makers and hissing of milk steamers, and the noise-amplifying exposed brick walls and concrete ceiling made it easy to talk without being overheard.

Terri and the girl were sitting at a table I figured Terri must have picked, up on a riser in a back corner of the café. The other two tables on the riser were empty. Kaylee looked to be in her early twenties, with a sullen but pretty face and long dark hair. They already had drinks, so I got mine and went to join them. Terri made introductions, and as I sat down, seeing Kaylee close up, I realized her expression wasn't sullen. It was sad, with an overlay of defensiveness.

"Miss Sumter," I said, "first off, I want to say I'm real sorry about the loss of your friend."

She nodded fast, her face tightening like she was trying not to cry.

"It's a heck of a blow at your age," I said. "And a girl that young, it's just awful."

She nodded some more, apologized, and dabbed at a couple of tears with a napkin.

"Kaylee was just telling me how the news coverage is making it worse," Terri said.

Kaylee made a face. "It's like they're talking about a different *person.* Or just—the *same* person every time, you know? Every time a girl my age dies, in the news it's always 'She was bubbly, everybody loved her, she had the most beautiful smile'... It's like they turn her into, just, this generic dead girl!"

"Oh, I hear you," Terri said. "They do that a lot. I've noticed it too."

I nodded, remembering the—thankfully minimal—news coverage of my wife's death. *Devoted mother, sparkling hostess.* It had felt hollow at the time, and it still did.

"Their true personality gets left out," I said.

"Yeah, exactly!" Kaylee looked at me. "It's like, she's *really* gone now, because we can't even remember who she actually was!"

"What do you remember about Dixie?" I asked.

"She was, like…" She looked toward the ceiling, shaking her head as if there was too much to put into words.

Terri said, "You had mentioned her sense of humor."

"Oh, yeah, she was funny as—excuse me, but funny as hell! Like, sarcastic, but not in a mean way. It was—I mean, even going to the *laundromat* with her was fun, back when we did that."

"Oh, I love that kind of person," Terri said.

"Right?"

"Yeah, that's great," I said. "Did you stop doing that, though?"

"Oh, just the laundromat. We still did other boring stuff that was fun because of her. Like, she got me a job last summer at her hotel, and we cleaned rooms together. Which should've sucked—some people are pigs—but it was fun."

"How'd she make it fun?" Terri asked.

"Oh, she would—if I say it like this, it sounds weird, but, like, she would find whatever weird stuff was in the guest's room and just, I don't know, make up stories about it. Whole routines. It was freaking hilarious."

"That is truly a gift," Terri said.

"It is," I said. "Is that why y'all stopped going to the laundromat? Because you used the machines at the hotel?"

"Oh, no, that was later. After she moved. Her apartment had the nicest washer and dryer I've ever seen. No, the ones at the hotel were, like, industrial strength. You might as well wash your clothes in boiling water."

"Ouch," Terri said. "Not a good plan. Do you mean... I'm sorry, but, her *last* apartment? The one over Bobbino's?"

"Yeah." Kaylee looked away, deflating. "Yeah, she was real excited about that."

I nodded sympathetically. "So it was a nice place?"

"Oh, yeah."

I was curious why she was suddenly less talkative.

I said, "It was like a home-design show, wasn't it. With the, what was it, the blue Bahia granite in the kitchen?"

She looked at me with a hint of surprise and said, "Yeah."

"Ooh, that's one of my favorites," Terri said. "I watch way too many of those home shows. Did she like that granite too?"

"Yeah," Kaylee said, turning to her. "It was her favorite color."

"Did she get to choose it?" I asked.

Kaylee jabbed her straw around in her iced coffee and then took a sip, not looking at either of us.

I let her take her time. I was starting to wonder about the nature of Dixie's relationship with the landlord.

Kaylee let her eyes rest on the table as she said, "I didn't—I wasn't up on the exact details of her, like... *life*. We didn't have that kind of, like, you're my sister, I tell you everything relationship. That wasn't how she was."

"I get that," Terri said, nodding. "What *was* she like?"

"She was more… logical? Like, she didn't agonize over stuff. She didn't really need a shoulder to cry on, or whatever." An expression flitted across her face, gone so fast I almost missed it: resentment.

Maybe she'd wanted a deeper friendship than Dixie was willing to give.

I wasn't about to ask her that. I said, mildly, like I was half-curious but more just politely asking because she'd brought it up, "Did you ever get the sense *she* was doing the renovation? Making the choices, like, with someone doing it for her?"

"Oh yeah." She nodded like that almost went without saying. Then she grabbed her drink, stabbed the ice again with her straw, and took a long drink, looking in three or four directions, none of which was toward me.

"Huh," I said idly, watching folks lining up at the register. I'd pushed a little too far, and I needed to back off now if we ever hoped to talk to this girl again.

Terri, with her usual grace, said, "This is such a great little café. I love how you can see the water from here."

"Mm-hmm," I said. Out the front window, across the street, the ocean glinted in the sunlight.

"I should probably go," Kaylee said.

"Okay, honey," Terri said, watching her sweep her earbuds and a spare packet of sweetener off the table and into her purse. "Thanks so much for meeting with us."

"Yeah, thank you," I said.

Kaylee stood up and glanced at her chair like she was making sure she wasn't forgetting anything.

"Oh, you know what," Terri said, reaching into her bag. "I'm sorry, I was just wondering if you could give me the number for…" She flipped through her little notebook. "Asher. Dixie's fiancé?"

She must've noticed the same flash of worry in Kaylee's face that I had, because she added, "Never mind. You know what, I can see how telling me that might put you in a weird position." She smiled, all reassurance. "I'm sorry, forget I asked. I can just go talk to him at his work."

Kaylee looked more than worried. She looked like she'd just opened a door and seen a tornado and the imminent loss of everything she held dear.

Terri said, "Honey, if there's anything you're concerned about, you let me know. You've been through a lot, and the last thing I want to do is make anything harder for you."

Kaylee relaxed a little bit. Then she found her voice and said, "Just—could you—maybe not ask him about that stuff? The remodel, I mean? Like, why that happened?"

"Oh, honey," Terri said.

"He lost… more than I did," Kaylee said.

"Yes. Honey, I understand. How's he doing?"

"He's… I mean, it's really hard. He doesn't need to hear about… any of that right now. It's too early."

"Of course it is," Terri said, nodding. "We won't mention that at all. You have my word."

12

APRIL 24, 2022

Shortly before eleven thirty on Sunday morning, I parked in the lot outside Victory Baptist, turned off the engine but not the AC, and sat back in my Subaru, waiting to see if Clyde Boseman walked out after church. I'd been here once before, a few years earlier, to a basement Bible meeting that a high-flying local businessman I was friendly with had invited me to. If Boseman went to that meeting instead of coming straight out after the service, I'd be waiting more than an hour.

Victory Baptist looked as traditional as it was: a big, white church building with simple lines, a front porch like something off a Greek temple, and a sharp white steeple pointing at the sky. It sat on a well-manicured lawn, with live oaks alongside it draped in Spanish moss. The parking lot was framed by palm trees and had nearly as many BMWs in it as the one at Roy's golf club.

Eight or ten minutes after I parked, folks started coming out. Families and older couples, mostly. I flipped through the folder of photos Terri had sent me of Mrs. Boseman from her dog-breeding website and the society pages of the *Southeast Patriot*. If I spotted her, I'd know to look for her husband nearby.

She was plump, with shoulder-length silver hair, and in the clothing department there was a clear liking for florals and pastels. Half the women coming out of the church fit that description. I decided to get out and walk closer.

When I'd told Terri that I'd been advised not to bring her with me when I questioned Boseman, she seemed surprised that the topic even needed to be discussed.

"Oh, it never crossed my mind to come," she said. "I know what Boseman's like. We all know."

It was clear that I wasn't part of that "we." Not because she was trying to exclude me, but because despite all the time we'd spent together, our life experiences were not the same.

I shut my car door, went over to the bottom of the broad walkway leading to the church, and stood there reading the bronze plaque detailing the history of the place. Every few seconds I glanced up at the folks coming out. I saw a couple of lawyers I knew, half a dozen well-known businessmen, and beside the door, talking enthusiastically with the pastor, Judge Chambliss, who'd heard a couple of big cases of mine.

Mrs. Boseman stepped out the door. The pastor turned to her to exchange a few words. I stuck my hands in my pockets and moseyed up the walkway, nodding hello to folks as I passed.

I was about halfway to the church steps when Mr. Boseman came out. He nodded to the pastor and kept going. His wife said a hasty goodbye to the pastor and scurried after her husband. She still hadn't caught up by the time he got within range for me to say hello.

"Mr. Boseman!" I said. "Morning. Leland Munroe." I held out my right hand.

He stopped but kept his hands at his sides. "I know who you are," he said. "You following folks to church now?" He was white-haired, pushing seventy, but still a powerhouse of a man. Looking him in the eye meant looking up.

"Well, I didn't think it'd be right to bother you at your home. A man's home is his castle, and I respect that."

He gave me a deadpan look and said, "Yeah, most folks know we got dogs."

His wife caught up to him and smiled at me, waiting to be introduced. He didn't do the honors, so I said, "Mrs. Boseman, a very good Sunday morning to you. My name's Leland Munroe."

"Well, good morning, thank you."

"I am so sorry to intrude upon y'all's day, but as I was just explaining to your husband, I had a question or two for him, and I didn't want to impose on you at home."

He explained, "He's afraid he'll get bit."

"Aw, no!" she said. "My dogs are sweethearts!"

"Oh, yes, I'm sure they're very well trained. Now, to make sure I don't take up too much of y'all's time, let me just say, by profession, I am an attorney, and at the moment, I represent your tenant Bobby Carter."

"Oh, my goodness," Mrs. Boseman said, bringing her fingertips to her chest as if his very name pained her.

"Mr. Munroe," Boseman said, "as I'm sure you can appreciate, my wife's been terribly upset over the tragedy that occurred—"

"That poor girl," she said.

"Yes," I said. "It's a horrifying loss. For her family and everyone who knew her."

A searching look cut through Mrs. Boseman's bland sweetness like a ray of light through fog. I got the sense she realized that I meant it—I wasn't just spouting platitudes—and she was trying to make sense of me.

"This guy," Boseman told her sarcastically, "feels so bad about it that he's representing the arsonist."

"Well, hold on, now," I said. "Innocent folks do get accused of crimes sometimes, and that's its own kind of tragedy. Nothing like as terrible as what happened to Miss Ward, of course."

"No, of course," Mrs. Boseman said.

"Are you saying that man's *innocent*?" Boseman retorted.

"Are you saying he's not?" I asked. "Were any of us there that night?" I turned to his wife. "Are we there in his heart?"

"Sweetheart," she said gently, turning to her husband.

He opened his mouth and then closed it again. For her sake, I could see, he was trying to keep a lid on his anger.

"I know this must be real hard for y'all," I said. "And the last thing I want to do is make it worse, but I've got to do what I can to understand what happened. I'm still trying to fill in the blanks on some very basic questions. Like, for instance, what sort of tenant was Mr. Carter? He pay his rent on time?"

Boseman sighed. His wife was still gazing up at him, and it seemed he wanted not to disappoint her.

"Yep," he said. "In cash, but yeah."

"Cash?"

"Restaurant tenants do that a lot. And I'm a little old-school. I'm fine dealing in cash."

"Uh-huh. Any complaints?"

"From me? Or the public?"

"Either way."

"I mean, noise complaints sometimes. Mostly weekends. I don't think I ever had a lower-end restaurant tenant that didn't get those once in a while, though."

"Nothing excessive?"

"No."

"And did you two have a good relationship, personally?"

He shrugged, indifferent, like that wasn't something he paid attention to.

"My husband's not the social one," Mrs. Boseman explained, with a *you know how that is* smile. "That's more my job."

"Uh-huh," I said, returning her smile. I looked back at him and said, "Why'd you spend so much renovating Miss Ward's apartment?"

His eyes turned hard. He said, "I run my business how I want to."

His wife looked up at him, confused.

I said, "The blue Bahia granite? What's that, a hundred dollars a square foot?"

She looked at me, eyes wide with surprise. "A hundred dollars a *foot*? Oh, my, no, I don't think…" She turned back to him, silently asking him to clear this up.

A smile flickered at one corner of his mouth, and the hard glare he'd leveled on me softened. He looked quietly triumphant as he told me, "I'm afraid you've been misinformed. That apartment just needed a little updating. It's a shame it's not still there for you to see. If it was, I'd give you a tour of it so you could see I didn't do nothing special."

It was a pile of half-burned rubble in the junkyard, of course. And from what he'd said about cash and his old-school ways, I took him to be the type of person who made sure not to create paper trails. Miss Ward's luxury apartment had literally gone up in smoke.

"Yeah, that's a shame," I said.

He gave me another second of his smug little smile before saying, "Nice chatting with you, Mr. Munroe, but we've got to get on home."

"Bye, now," his wife said. "You have a blessed day."

They continued down the walkway toward the parking lot. Above them the sky was bright blue, cloudless, like someone had scrubbed it squeaky clean. Down at the bottom of the walkway they turned right, and Mrs. Boseman glanced around. When she saw me still standing there, she smiled and waved.

I waved back, but she'd already looked away.

I had no evidence of anything. You can't go before a jury and tell them about the hardening in a man's eyes or the smug way he pointed out that a fire had destroyed the evidence that he'd spent outlandish sums to remodel a young woman's apartment.

But I could tell that his wife didn't know about the remodel, and that he didn't want her to.

Late that afternoon, in my office at home, I sat back with my feet up on the side table and looked at my corkboard for the Carter case. Next to a snapshot of the building before it burned, I'd pinned a photo of Dixie and one of Bobby. Hers was beside the second floor, since that's where her apartment had been, and his was right below. Green strings linked both of them to Boseman—green for money, since they were his renters—and red strings ran from each of them to photos of their partners: Bobby to Marianne, and Dixie to Asher, her fiancé.

My corkboards helped me think. They brought out patterns and connections.

I wondered if there ought to be a red thread running between Dixie and Boseman.

I was going to need to find out more. The question was how. As a prosecutor, I'd worked with law enforcement. I reviewed their warrant requests, and I got to see whatever evidence the warrant brought in. Phone records, cell-tower data, surveillance, DNA. As a defense attorney, I didn't have those powers.

What I had was Terri. And my own ability to persuade folks to talk. That was it.

My phone rang, startling me out of that line of thought. It was Chance, my realtor.

"Hey, Chance."

"Hey there, Leland."

We caught up for a second, and then he said, "So, I hate to be the bearer of bad news, but something's come up. I got a call from the seller's agent on Grass Lake Run."

The house with the magnolia in the front yard. I'd put in an offer on it the day before.

"Yeah? They want more money?"

"Uh, no." His voice had a tight, awkward sound.

"Well, what is it?"

"So... full disclosure, I've never had this happen, so I'm kind of at a loss here. But what she said was, they're rejecting your offer because there's concern about your, uh, profile. The Carter case, the whole criminal defense thing..."

"What? They're leaving! Why would they care what my profession is?"

"That's exactly what I said. And what she told me is, they've got friends and family in the neighborhood, they're not moving that far away, and they don't want to get blamed if... like, an undesirable element..."

"Wow. Really?" I knew where the sellers were moving; they'd bought a disused old firehouse downtown to convert it into lofts.

"Yeah," Chance said. "Basically, they're concerned you might bring criminals into the neighborhood. As clients or, I don't know, opponents seeking retribution?" He gave an irritated sigh and added, "I feel ridiculous even saying that. I mean, this is real life, not a TV crime show. But that's what she told me."

Chance, I realized, didn't know I'd been through a home invasion a couple of years earlier, perpetrated by a top dog in a criminal cartel. He didn't know about my home security system or the reason I'd bought it. What he thought was TV crime show material was my real life.

I didn't feel like getting into that, so I said, "Well, that's disappointing. I really did like that place, but I guess we've got to keep looking."

After we hung up, I sat and thought about what might've spooked the sellers. They'd known who I was for a couple of weeks; they'd been there both times that I'd toured the house. Dabney's coverage of the

Carter case had gotten personal recently, with a rising tide of innuendo and insults directed my way, but there'd been nothing in the last couple of days.

I looked up at my corkboard. Boseman was a well-known guy, and a powerful one. A big landlord, head of the zoning board, one of the richest men in town.

The sellers, I realized, would need permission from the zoning board to convert the firehouse they'd bought into residential units.

Had he called them? Was that his response to my showing up outside his church that morning?

I got the sense that if I tried to show all the ways that Boseman was connected to my case and my life, the strings running out from his photo on my corkboard would look like a multicolored spiderweb.

Half an hour later, Terri rang my doorbell. She was coming over to review what I'd received the day before from Ginevra Barnes: Dixie Ward's autopsy report.

As we said hi, I looked over her shoulder at her Forester. The paint was so glossy I could see perfect reflections in it of the palm trees that framed the parking lot.

"If I didn't know you better," I said, "I'd think you got yourself a new car in the same color."

She laughed. "No, I will drive that thing into the ground. But yesterday I took it to the shop where Dixie's fiancé works. I got it detailed and hung around trying to talk with him."

"Oh yeah? He have anything interesting to say?"

"No, he shut down as soon as he figured out I'm working for Bobby Carter. As far as he's concerned, I'm trying to help his fiancée's killer."

I winced. "That's hard." I stepped aside to let her in.

"Yeah." She held out a cardboard tray with two takeout coffees and said, "Got you a latte."

"Oh, thanks. Head on into my office—I'll get some cookies."

I grabbed them from the kitchen and followed her back.

As we sat down, she said, "I don't think normal people read autopsy reports over coffee and Oreos."

"I'm not sure either of us would know what normal people do."

She laughed and said, "And that's why we get along."

I pulled the report up on my screen and made it big enough for both of us to read. It kicked off with a summary of the facts and the conclusion. Like most fire victims, it said, Dixie Ward had been killed by smoke inhalation, not by flames. She had soot in her airways, consistent with having been alive during at least the initial part of the fire, and her blood levels of carboxyhemoglobin, or COHb, also indicated that.

I scrolled down and saw the first photo of her dead body, mostly unburned, lying in the partially charred remains of her bed. The firefighters had managed to put the fire out just as the flames reached her.

I shut my eyes and sighed.

Terri said, "You hate this part, don't you."

I nodded. "I never liked it back at the solicitor's office, either, but at least then, it meant something. My job was to go through these things with a fine-tooth comb looking for everything I could possibly use to find out who'd done it and bring him to justice."

"Mm-hmm. It's different on this side, isn't it. I feel that way too."

"If I was Travis Girardeau, I'd go through this thinking about nothing but how to get my guy off." I shook my head, reached for my coffee, and took a swig. It was good and hot. That always helped bring me back a little.

"If you were Travis Girardeau," she said, "I wouldn't be sitting here."

"Thanks."

It meant something to hear her say that. But it didn't solve my problem.

"Thing is," I said, "it's written down in black and white what my ethical duty is. As a prosecutor, the duty was to seek justice. Meaning, figure out who took this girl's life, nail him to the wall, and also make sure I don't lock up the wrong person. But now the duty is to zealously represent my guy. Protect his rights. The victim doesn't come into it."

"Is that really the problem, though?" she asked. "I mean, I hear what you're saying, and that's always going to be an issue in any case you take, now that you're on this side of the aisle. But is that what's bothering you about this particular case?"

I looked at her and shook my head. "No, it's not. You're right."

I took another sip of my coffee. The big problem here wasn't some legal conundrum. It was that the facts didn't point toward innocence at all.

I said, "I got to tell you, I really do appreciate the fact that you always call me on my crap."

She gave a little laugh. "Your crap, or just your human nature? Nobody wants to look at the truth when it's ugly as hell."

"You mean like when my guy's been accused of arson and manslaughter, and the fire is unquestionably arson? And then the autopsy says the fire is what killed a twenty-two-year-old girl?"

"Yeah. Like that."

13

MAY 2, 2022

When I got out of the shower, I had a voicemail from Ginevra Barnes. It was eight thirty in the morning, and I was standing in my kitchen in my boxer shorts, rubbing my hair dry. The message said Ruiz had asked her to set up a meeting with me, today. She didn't say why.

I called back. She wasn't available. Her assistant suggested I swing by at ten.

I called Terri and put her on speakerphone while I buttoned my shirt and told her what was going on.

"I don't like it," I said. "It's raising my hackles. Have you heard anything?"

"No. And I guess you can't call Ruiz. He's on the campaign trail. What day is his thing, again?"

We'd been invited to a gala cocktail party launching his campaign. He was shooting to go from acting solicitor, named to serve out the rest of Ludlow's term, to duly elected solicitor.

"Wednesday night. But even if he wasn't busy, you know how he is."

Ruiz operated as if there was a book called *The Scrupulously Proper Prosecutor*, several hundred pages long, whose rules he was bound by. Somewhere in that book, I was sure it said that if he told his assistant solicitor to meet with me, it would be inappropriate for him to go behind her back and talk to me about it in advance.

"Is there anything she could be calling about other than the grand jury coming back on Bobby Carter?" Terri asked.

"Not that I can think of. God, I wish Ruiz hadn't taken himself off my cases."

"What difference would that make?"

"He's a known quantity." I took the phone over by the coffee maker and started brewing a pot. "I understand how he thinks, and I respect him. His minions, not so much."

"Barnes shouldn't be too bad to deal with," Terri said. "At least she ought to know what she's doing."

Terri had looked up Ginevra Barnes's background and told me that, before marrying Dabney's brother five years earlier, she'd served ten years as an assistant solicitor in a rural county in the mountains.

"I don't know. At that bond hearing, she went a little overboard. I can understand righteous indignation and tugging on the heartstrings in front of a jury, but most folks tone that way down when it's just the judge."

"Ugh. You think she's a true believer?"

Some prosecutors were crusaders, convinced of the absolute rightness of their case. They were impossible to reason with.

"She might be. I guess I'll find out."

"You think she had anything to do with the press showing up at Bobby's house when he was arrested?"

"She could've. Or they could've been listening in on the police scanners."

"For SLED?"

"Oh. Right."

Our local law enforcement didn't use encrypted scanners, but SLED did. For Dabney's reporters to have been on the scene so quickly, somebody must've tipped them off that Bobby was about to be arrested.

I was going to have to watch my step with Ginevra Barnes.

"Oh," Terri said, "I was going to tell you, I pulled the permits for Dixie's remodel." I'd told her about my strange interaction with Boseman. She'd gone straight to the same theory I had: that it sounded like there might've been more to his relationship with Dixie than he wanted his wife to know.

"Yeah? Find anything interesting?"

"Well, it was the big kind. An over-$50,000 project." Basking County required different permitting paperwork depending on whether the remodel cost over or under fifty grand.

"For the kitchen in a rental apartment? Damn."

"Yeah. And they've got the name of the contracting company on them, so that's someplace to start."

"Well, good," I said. If I hadn't been preoccupied by Ginevra Barnes's voicemail, I would've been more enthusiastic.

Terri must've noticed my tone, because she said, "It's an uphill battle, isn't it."

"It always is." I sighed. "Man, even Ruiz probably wouldn't listen to my alternate theory this time. 'My client didn't accidentally kill Miss Ward, because her landlord's making me think that he might've been her sugar daddy, and that for some unknown reason he might've killed her on purpose.'"

She laughed. In a gruff voice, her joking imitation of a judge, she asked, "And what's your evidence, counselor?"

"'He acted weird when I asked him about a remodel.'" It sounded so ridiculous that I cracked up. "'He spent a lot on her kitchen.' God, we're doomed, aren't we?"

"Well, we would be if he was going to trial tomorrow. But remember how you and I roll. We'll keep digging. We'll set some traps. It takes time to bring the big ones in."

"Lord, I hope you're right."

At around a quarter of ten, I parked outside the courthouse and headed in. There was a commotion in the security line; a man was face down on the floor with his hands on the back of his head, submitting to a pat-down. The guard standing at the X-ray machine, an old Black guy with a face that had seen everything, told me the guy had shown up for a hearing with a switchblade in his pocket. The guard motioned me through the metal detector, shaking his head at the folly of humankind.

Up in the solicitor's offices, I explained my presence to the receptionist. Ruiz ran a tight ship, and I couldn't just walk down the hall to someone's office anymore. I waited in the lobby for Ms. Barnes to come get me.

One minute before the appointed time, she appeared, looking like a seasoned lawyer on a TV show, with her navy pinstripe suit and perfect helmet of blonde hair. She gave me a big Southern smile as we shook hands.

"Good to meet you properly at last," I said. "Ruiz has spoken highly of you."

"Well, thank you."

What I'd said wasn't true—Ruiz and I hadn't discussed her at all—but I wanted to start on a good note.

She led me to her office, offered a cup of coffee, and phoned her assistant to bring it in.

Like every deputy solicitor's office, hers had a wall of legal books behind the desk and cherry veneer filing cabinets. In all other respects, it looked like she'd had the place redone by an interior decorator. Understated artwork—a watercolor of a flower garden, a sailboat on the ocean—hung on the walls, and her window was accented by some sort of multilayered drapery, which was half open, apparently to let the sunlight reach the potted pink orchids on the sill. Her desk was spotless, with nothing on it but her computer and the mouse. My own desk, strewn with Post-its, pens, and packets of takeout cocktail sauce, did not compare favorably.

She hung up the phone and said, "Now, Mr. Munroe, thank you for coming on by. I called you today at the special request of Mr. Ruiz. We wanted to let you know personally that the grand jury came back late yesterday with a true bill against your client, Mr. Carter. We're proceeding with an indictment on charges of first-degree arson and felony murder."

There was no point hiding my surprise. "Felony murder? That's what you put before the grand jury?"

"Why, yes."

SLED had arrested Bobby for first-degree arson—in other words, intentional arson resulting in death. That was the charge I'd expected the solicitor to put before the grand jury. It was a felony that carried a potential sentence of thirty years to life.

Felony murder carried the same potential prison term. The only difference was that it could also get the death penalty.

I'd never heard of an arson case being charged that way when the defendant didn't know the building was occupied.

I asked Ms. Barnes, "So we're clear here, has something changed in terms of the factual allegations?"

"I'm not entirely sure what you mean."

Her big blue eyes were wide and blank, but it was an act. Nobody in her position could've failed to grasp what I meant. I was asking why they'd sought an indictment on more serious charges than the ones Bobby had been arrested for.

"Well, let me rephrase," I said. "In SLED's arrest warrant, they alleged that there was probable cause to believe my client had purposely set fire to the building at approximately 3 a.m. on February 24, and that the resulting fire caused the accidental death of Miss Dixie Ward. Is that the theory you took to the grand jury?"

"Yes, of course. Based on all the evidence, I have no doubt that that's what occurred."

The phrase "no doubt" gave me pause. In a case like this one, where there was no DNA or camera footage to show that they had the right guy, that level of certainty was a strong hint that she was the true-believer type. I hadn't even liked working with that sort back in Charleston, when I was on their side.

"And do you charge all fatal arsons as felony murder?" I asked. She blinked but didn't reply.

She knew—there was no way she didn't know—how unusual it was to charge an arson that way.

Normally, a murder charge required proof that the defendant had intended to kill the victim. But under the felony murder rule, any felony that resulted in death—even an accidental death—could be charged as murder. The prosecutor simply had to prove that the defendant intended to commit the underlying felony—in this case, arson.

If they proved that, the defendant would be sentenced as if they'd killed the victim with malice aforethought.

"Is your office planning to seek the death penalty here?"

"As I'm sure you can appreciate, at this early stage, that's not a decision that's been made."

It took my brain a second to process what she'd said. She was keeping the door open to a possible death penalty.

Nothing about that made sense.

Something new had to have come up to convince her office to escalate to felony murder. And no matter how ardently she believed in seeking maximum punishment for crimes, I knew she couldn't have gone that route without Ruiz's okay. If he was willing to bring more serious charges than SLED had initially recommended, there had to be a reason.

But I had no immediate right to find out what it was. I normally kicked the tires of the State's case at the preliminary hearing, but since the grand jury had already looked at Ms. Barnes's evidence and decided that she had probable cause, we had no right to such a hearing.

It was horrifying. It was wrong. But pounding on her desk and telling her that wouldn't help Bobby any.

I had to find out why this made sense to her.

"So... let me just explain where I'm coming from here," I began. "I appreciate that felony murder charges have their place. For instance, up in Charleston, when I was in your shoes, working as an assistant solicitor, that's what we'd charge if a violent attack inadvertently led to the victim's death. So if a victim died in the course of a rape or a mugging, or any other truly despicable crime, that's what we'd do."

"Oh, I'm sure we'd do that here too," she said, nodding. "I don't know anybody who'd disagree with that use of the felony murder rule. Fortunately, as a small town, we don't get much of that kind of crime down here. We're very blessed in that regard."

"Uh, yes, we sure are. And, of course, we also don't have much of the other types of crime that would merit such charges. Gang killings, for instance, or any other group crime, where we couldn't prove which of the bad guys had pulled the trigger. If they were all committing the same burglary or carjacking or what have you, and somebody died, we could get them all for felony murder. That way we'd keep the public safe, getting every one of them off the street."

"I certainly agree with that too," she said, smiling, all polite Southern charm. "That being said, I'm sure you understand better than just about anybody that this is not Charleston. Y'all must've had some truly terrible crimes to deal with up there. It's a very dark place in some regards. A lot of folks who are not walking the right path. And so y'all probably had a very different perspective on things."

"No doubt we did," I said. "But you don't need any special perspective to see that the situation we're talking about here is nothing like that, is it. Here we've got a decorated veteran who, even in your worst-case scenario, had no reason to think anybody was in the building at the time—"

"Mr. Munroe, I promise you, we all appreciate the sacrifices your client made for this country. That's something every one of us in the solicitor's office respects. But we can't base a charging decision on his service. It might go to sentence mitigation, of course, but I don't think it does justice to Miss Ward to grant leniency to her killer right off the bat."

She was still smiling at me. I noticed her lipstick was sparkly pink. It felt like I was trying to have a boxing match with a cloud of cotton candy.

"You know what," I said, "can I ask what you've done thus far in terms of investigating the landlord?"

She tilted her head and looked at me like a puzzled kitten. "How do you mean?"

Her airhead routine was getting very old, very fast.

"I'm referring to how in most arson cases, the perpetrator is the property owner. Usually for insurance. Or sometimes to spite his spouse, or what have you."

"Oh, well, as I believe you'll have seen in the SLED report, the property owner was out of town that night."

I waited for her to continue. She didn't.

"Uh-huh," I said. "And does your office have reason to believe Mr. Boseman lacked the means to hire somebody to do it for him, if he so chose?"

She smiled. "I think we both know that Mr. Boseman has the means to do a *lot* of things. However, let me see. To the extent I can speak to you about this… well, as I'm sure you'll appreciate, a man who's that well established, with a level of financial security that most folks can only dream of—it's hard to see much motive there, isn't it."

"Doesn't the same go for Mr. Carter? Not to the same degree, perhaps, but he's doing fine." Recalling Bobby's cell phone records, I added, "And besides, what's the evidence *he* was anywhere near the scene of the fire?"

She looked at me with her blank, polite smile for long enough that it got into Stepford wife territory. I maintained my own polite smile. I had long ago realized that the best way to conceal my thoughts was to look a little bit bored—it made folks think that as far as you were concerned, nothing stressful or important was happening—so that's what I did.

Finally, the silence got awkward enough that she spoke.

"Mr. Munroe... Listen, y'all will get this in discovery eventually, and I like to play fair. I'm not the cloak-and-dagger type. So I don't see any reason to conceal from you that we have an eyewitness who places your client at the scene a matter of minutes before the fire."

I didn't flinch. "I don't see how that's possible."

"I guess we'll cross that bridge when we get to it. As of now, Mr. Ruiz and I are going to try to get this trial scheduled for November."

I nodded like I was thinking about how that would work with my schedule. I was relieved on Bobby's behalf that it wasn't that far off. In most of South Carolina, prosecutors, in consultation with the courts, were in charge of scheduling. I'd learned over the years that in other states it wasn't like that—courts there controlled their own dockets—and also that most states considered our system a little backward, since it put a whole lot of power in the prosecutor's hands. One prosecutor I knew had purposely scheduled a trial two years out because he knew the defendant couldn't make bail and he thought the prospect of sitting in jail for two years might make the man cave and plead guilty. It had.

"Well," I said, "I do appreciate that y'all are aiming to handle this efficiently."

"Yes, that's one of Mr. Ruiz's priorities. I'm not sure if you're aware, but he pushed hard to get the backlog cleared after the pandemic, and we did actually manage to do that."

"Well, that's something, isn't it."

I heard a faint buzzing, and she looked at her watch.

"Oh," she said, "I apologize, but I have a hearing at eleven that I've got to get ready for real quick. But I do need to cover one last thing with you. As I mentioned, I asked you here this morning at the specific request of Mr. Ruiz, to let you know all this in advance. That way, you can arrange to have your client turn himself in, rather than going through another situation where there's police vehicles up and down his street and officers dragging him out."

"Uh-huh. Well, please tell Mr. Ruiz that I appreciate that."

"Of course."

"Apart from the police vehicles," I said, "our other concern is the presence of the press. Is that something you'd be willing to help us avoid?"

"I understand that concern, but unfortunately, that's not in my control."

She must've known I wasn't asking her to personally control what reporters did. She'd been a prosecutor for over a decade. I shouldn't have had to spell out what I meant. But apparently I did.

"What I'm referring to," I said, "is whether you'd agree not to disclose to the press where or when my client will be turning himself in."

"I hear you on that. But of course," she said, "I would have to run something like that past Mr. Ruiz. There's procedures we've got to follow."

"And is that something you'll have time to do before whenever it is that you'd like my client to turn himself in?"

"I'll do my best."

I had zero confidence in that. Her pastel-pink politeness made me think of the clouds of ink that octopuses sprayed to confuse their predators.

"In the meantime," she continued, "can you have your client turn himself in here at the courthouse at 5 p.m. today?"

"I'll have to check with him. I imagine that's as good a plan as any other. Oh, and would you also have to check with Mr. Ruiz to see if we could come to an agreement on bond?"

"Bond? For a murder charge?" I hadn't realized her eyes could open any wider than they already had.

"Ms. Barnes—"

"Mrs., if you don't mind. I do take some pride in that."

"Mrs. Barnes. Of course. As I'm sure you've noticed, my client's been out on bond for a month now without any issues. He's got no history of violence—"

"Are you suggesting my office should agree not to oppose bond on a *murder* charge?"

"Yes, Mrs. Barnes, I am. Mr. Carter doesn't pose any danger to anybody—what you're alleging here is an *accidental* killing—and he's not going anywhere. His presence in the community is directly responsible for keeping a number of people employed—"

"Mr. Munroe, I trust you'll understand that I can't go to Miss Ward's parents and tell them that in order to keep a pizza shop open, I let their daughter's killer remain on the streets."

I could picture her saying that on the courthouse steps. Every heart-tugging thing she said was crafted to make a good headline, and she delivered it all with charm, looking like a very polished and professional mom.

If Dabney Barnes had handpicked a solicitor to destroy Bobby in the press just as thoroughly as she aimed to destroy him in court, he couldn't have found a better one.

―――

14

MAY 2, 2022

Terri and I were sitting in the Carters' living room with Marianne. Bobby was down at the pizza shop helping with the lunch rush and hadn't yet heard my news.

"I know how shocking this must be," I said. "If you need a minute—"

"It's not me I'm worried about."

Marianne was on the couch, her elbows on her knees and her fingers steepled under her chin. I could hear the slow, smooth rhythm of her breath.

She chuckled, and then she said, "I have this wild urge to grab our passports and run for the border."

"I think most folks would have that urge, in your shoes," I told her. "Although, obviously, that's illegal. It could get Bobby convicted in absentia, and your assets could be seized."

She gave a slow nod, looking off into space. Then she said, "I hate that we're reduced to wanting such… *small* things now, but if we can't get out of the big problem, can we at least avoid the media somehow? Bobby's got enough to deal with without people sticking mics in his face and yelling questions."

"Yeah, we don't have a ton of great options, but I was going to recommend that we head over early. If Ms.—Mrs., she prefers that—Barnes is tipping off the press, she'll be telling them that it's happening at five."

"So we go over at four?" Marianne laughed. "Get to jail early! Beat the crowds!"

Terri and I smiled. It was bittersweet. Marianne was picking up quickly on our habit of trying to find humor anywhere you could. It was the only way I'd ever found to get through a crisis like the one she and Bobby were facing.

A little while later, we headed to the pizzeria. Marianne went in to get Bobby, and then we all crossed the street and went for a walk on the beach. The tide was coming in, covering the rocks where teenagers liked to sit and smoke. Bobby took the news wordlessly—it was a gut punch, and then he seemed to recover. He stood a few feet up from the waterline, looking out at the ocean. I could see the muscles in his jaw clenching and unclenching. On the other side of him, Marianne was looking at the water, too, holding his hand.

After eight or ten minutes, Marianne leaned back so she could see me and said, "Would you two be able to come meet us at our house in an hour or so? And then we can drive over from there? We just… I think we need a moment."

"Of course."

They headed off across the parking lot. When they'd gotten into their Volvo and shut the doors, Terri said, "You think they're even going to *be* there in an hour?"

I looked around to make sure nobody was close enough to overhear. "Or are they heading to the airport, you mean?"

"Mm-hmm. I don't know. If I was facing charges like that…"

"You'd run?"

"If I'm looking at the death penalty as a worst-case scenario? And, what, half a million in legal fees as the best case?" She shook her head, thinking about it. "Yeah. I really might."

I nodded. "It's a big ask, isn't it," I said. "I mean, the legal system asking folks to trust it with their lives."

"*Too* big, sometimes. For me, anyway."

Forty minutes later, after quick trips home to walk our dogs, I drove by Terri's place to pick her up and get back to the Carters' house.

As I turned the corner toward the main road, she said, "I've been looking into Dixie's fiancé, Asher. He's not a big social media guy, but he is on LinkedIn—"

"At his age?"

"I guess he's an ambitious kid. He's already assistant manager of that car shop, and it said he's doing a part-time MBA."

"No priors, I assume?"

She chuckled. "You know that's the first thing I would've told you."

"Yeah. So he looks okay?"

"As spotless as a Ken doll."

"He does kind of look like a Ken doll, now that you mention it." I'd seen his picture in the news.

"Well, I do put some thought into my analogies."

"You do. Any thoughts on how to build rapport with him?"

She shook her head. "I mean, they were engaged," she said. "So he's basically a family member. And you know the victim's family never wants to talk to the defense."

"Uh-huh. And, of course, neither do the perps."

"Yup. Well, except for the psychopaths who think they're smarter than everybody else. They're happy to talk. It's a game to them."

"So I guess we at least know he's not that type."

"Yeah, I don't think so," she said. "That young man's grief and rage seemed absolutely genuine."

When we got to the Carters' house, their Volvo was parked out front.

"I guess he wants to stay and clear his name," I said.

"He must have some faith in the system. I hope he doesn't learn the hard way not to."

As I pulled into the driveway, my phone rang, and Marianne asked me to drive around to the back. When we got there, she beckoned us into the kitchen.

"I've got my armor on," she said, gesturing to her outfit. It was a lot like what she'd worn to court for Bobby's preliminary hearing.

"Looks good," I said. "Where's Bobby?"

"He's relaxing."

She pointed toward the living room. Through the doorway, I could see him lying flat in his recliner, feet up, eyes closed, with little white earbuds in.

"He doing a hypnosis thing?" I asked.

"Hypnotherapy. Yes, just something to make this as… tolerable as possible for him."

"Okay. So… I can't tell from here whether he's wearing a watch or anything."

"No, he took it off. And his phone's in my purse." She sighed and looked at the floor. We had talked earlier about not bringing his valuables.

"I'm so sorry, Mrs. Carter," Terri said.

Marianne nodded. Then she looked Terri in the eye and said, "He didn't *do* this. That's what's killing me. It's not even physically… I mean, he's not the best sleeper, so he takes melatonin and sleeping pills. There's no way he got up and drove across town in the middle of the night."

"Uh-huh," I said. I was sure I'd asked her, when Bobby was first arrested, if he was on any medications, and she'd said no. "Do you have his pill bottle? With the prescription sticker on it?"

"Oh, yeah. I should have thought of that."

"Why don't you go get it," I said. "The correctional nurse ought to be able to give it to him on whatever his regular schedule is. And I can ask if they'll allow the melatonin."

"That'd be great," she said, heading for the stairs. "He takes the melatonin every night, but he's tapered down the prescription stuff to every other day."

In his recliner, Bobby was taking slow, deep breaths. His eyes were still closed.

Quietly, I asked Terri, "You remember those cell phone records? His phone never left this house that night, right?"

"Right."

"Did you check hers?"

"In case they traded phones, you mean? I can do that."

"Good. That'd be a nice one-two punch for the jury. Not that it proves he didn't do it, but it never hurts to point out that Barnes can't prove he was there."

The phone records also couldn't prove that he *wasn't* there—he could've left his phone at home—but I wanted to be sure I could tell the jury that there was no cell phone evidence placing Bobby anywhere but his own house that night.

"Mm-hmm."

I'd told her what Ginevra Barnes had said about the eyewitness. We were curious about who had allegedly been in the vicinity at three in the morning and how they'd identified our client, but we knew it'd be awhile before we got those details. In the meantime, we had to do what we could to shore up our argument that Bobby wasn't there.

"Oh, when she brings that pill bottle down," I said, "could you snap a photo of the label? I should talk to his doctor."

"You should get your own smartphone, is what you should do. Stop living like it's 2003." She smiled when she said it, but I knew she had a point.

When it came time to go, Marianne took charge.

"I'm thinking we should split up," she said, "and take different routes. Caravanning over there might attract attention. Your Subaru has tinted windows, right?"

"It does."

"Okay, so let's say when Bobby gets up, he rides with you." He was still in his recliner. "Terri, would you mind riding with me?"

"Not at all. You sure you don't want those last few moments with your husband, though?"

"I do, but not if it means some reporter catches on and harasses us. Actually, Terri, why don't I give you my keys? It might help confuse whoever's keeping an eye on us if it's not me at the wheel. And we can leave a few minutes later than them."

She went over to the recliner and talked quietly to Bobby, holding his hand. He listened, nodding. Then, with a sigh, he brought the recliner up straight and got to his feet, and the two of them embraced.

I went out the back door, turned my car around, and reached across to throw the door open for him. When I glanced back at the house as we turned the corner, Terri and Marianne still hadn't come outside.

Bobby didn't say a word the whole ride. I didn't force it. Everybody dealt with this kind of thing in their own way, and I wasn't about to interfere.

Downtown, I circled the courthouse to see which entrance looked best before dropping him off at the back.

"Just go on through security," I said, "and if it takes me a minute to park, step into the men's room that's off to the right. I'll meet you there."

It took me about five minutes to get parked and inside. I went through security and texted Terri to let her know where I was. The men's room looked empty. As I glanced down to see if Bobby was in a stall, he stepped out of one and gave me a nod.

I pushed the other doors open to make sure we were alone. Then I said, "If you've got any questions before we go up to the solicitor's office, ask me now. If questions occur to you later, once you're booked you ought to have access to a phone. You've got the right to call your lawyer."

He gave a curt nod. His posture, I noticed, had lost its usual ease. He was standing like a military man. It made him look even taller. "I got one question," he said. "What are the rules here?"

The rules filled a book. "I'll see if I can get you a copy of them. For now, the main thing is, follow orders."

"I can do that."

"That's how you deal with the staff. When it comes to the other prisoners, there's two rules: don't trust them one iota, and don't take any shit."

He nodded. "I wasn't going to."

"Good. Yeah. With prisoners, you don't want to be anything but top dog. But I know you've dealt with far worse than this."

He squinted off at the corner of the room like he was thinking that over. After a second, he said, "Yeah. Hard rules are better than no rules, I guess."

"Yes, they are."

"Oh. I forgot something." He looked down and twisted his wedding ring until it came off. "Can you take this? When we're all done here tonight, give it to Marianne."

"Of course."

I'd never seen a ring that big. It felt as heavy as a silver dollar. To keep it safe, I pulled out my wallet and tucked it inside.

When Terri and Marianne arrived, we all took the elevator to the solicitor's office. The Carters sat together, holding hands, while I dealt with the receptionist. She called Mrs. Barnes, who spoke loudly enough that I could hear her tone through the receiver, although not her actual words. I got some satisfaction out of the surprise and irritation in her voice.

She didn't come out right away. I wondered if she was calling her brother-in-law and telling him to get those reporters over here sooner.

She eventually emerged with some paperwork and without her usual smile. I got the signatures done quick, and she went back to her office to call for the van to bring Bobby over to be booked into the county jail.

I knew the van didn't have tinted windows. It was the opposite of dignified.

I asked the receptionist for directions to the nearest restrooms, although I knew where they were, and the four of us stepped into the hall. I hit the elevator button, and when it came, I was glad to see it was empty. I got in and nodded for the others to follow me.

When the doors closed, I said, "Bobby, I'm driving you over to the jail myself. Get you out of here before the press shows up. I'll tell Mrs. Barnes I misunderstood what she said."

"Is that... okay?" Marianne asked.

"I'll deal with it. What's she going to do? I misunderstood. Let her try to prove I didn't."

Terri smiled. "I didn't hear her say anything about a van. Did you?"

Marianne shook her head. "No, now that you mention it, I didn't."

"Maybe she should've talked louder," I said. "Made herself a little clearer. But that's on her."

Downstairs, they all waited inside the back entrance while I brought my car around, and Bobby got back in.

. . .

An hour and a half later, after he was booked, I returned to my car. I'd missed a few texts from Terri: *Marianne talking to press! Killing it!*

That reminded me that I had Bobby's wedding ring. I gave Marianne a call, got voicemail, and left a message offering to bring it by.

When I got home, Noah's beater was in the driveway. These days, it usually wasn't; I mostly expected him not to be around. I wished I'd called to see if he wanted me to bring back some takeout. Dinners together had become few and far between.

I pushed the door open. He was in the living room watching TV.

"Hey there," I said. "You want to order pizza or something?"

"Sure, whatever. Look at this!"

He pointed to the television. Marianne was on the screen, and I could see Terri off to the side. In her gray suit and lilac blouse, with her chin lifted defiantly and the sparkle of tears in her eyes, Marianne looked pained and elegant and utterly righteous.

To the half-dozen microphones in front of her, she said, "We are *Americans*. We care about the truth. We care about justice. We owe that to Dixie Ward, and we owe it to my husband too."

"That's your case, right?" Noah said. "Where were you?"

"Smuggling my client out the back door so the press wouldn't bother him."

"Stealth. I like it."

On-screen, Marianne said, "Nobody should accept this. Nobody should accept that an innocent young woman died such a terrible death. And nobody should accept that an innocent man is getting railroaded for a crime that I know for a fact he did not commit. Is that what this country is about? Is that what we've become?"

Somebody in the crowd yelled, "No!"

"No!" she said, nodding toward the voice. "No! We can't accept that, can we! That's not who we are!"

"She should run for mayor or something," Noah said.

"She's a pretty compelling speaker. How long's she been on?"

He thought about it for a second. "I don't even know," he said. "Five minutes? Ten? I kind of lost track of time."

"Interesting," I said. "Yeah, she has that effect."

"You know what she'd be good on," he said. "That podcast. She's, like, a storyteller."

"*Carolina True Crime*, Shannon Pennington's thing? Hoo, boy. I don't think that's a good idea. Nothing Mrs. Carter says is going to change this prosecutor's mind, and it could give them an argument that we're trying to taint the jury pool."

"I mean, I don't know about the legalities," Noah said. "I was just thinking, you put her on that show, she could get the whole damn *world* on her side."

15

MAY 3, 2022

After dinner, I picked Terri up to take her to Ruiz's campaign event. The primary elections had taken place that day, and what passed for the glitterati in our small town were invited to a hotel ballroom to watch the results come in and raise a glass to Ruiz whenever his victory was declared. It felt odd to be celebrating barely twenty-four hours after Bobby had been locked up, but staying home in a hair shirt wouldn't help him any.

Terri stepped out onto her porch, looking stunning, and turned to lock the door. She had on a cocktail dress, or an evening gown—I'd never been sure where the line was between the two—with a fitted gold top and a full black skirt.

I got out and went around the car to open her door.

"Thank you," she said, gliding past, trailing a warm scent in her wake.

I went back to my seat like an automaton and drove us down the street. At the stop sign, I realized I hadn't said a word to her. "That's a hell of an outfit," I said. "And here I am looking like I slept in my suit."

She laughed. "Like Columbo."

"I share his powers," I said. "He can wrinkle a suit just by *thinking* about putting it on."

"It's his own special magic." She watched the town go by for a second and then said, "Oh, speaking of magical detectives, if I may say so myself, I got something that might help out with Jacob Drayton. I finally convinced that girl to talk to me—his roommate's ex-girlfriend."

"The informant?" Kyle Parr's ex had given the police the information they used to get the search warrant. "What'd she say?"

"Well, her main thing is, she wants to see Kyle put away. That's why she went and told the cops about the drugs in the first place. He was your standard stalker ex, and she'd run out of options for getting him to leave her alone."

I shook my head in annoyance at Cody Varner. He was firing on all cylinders to make an example of Jacob, when Parr was who he should've been focusing on. Varner did not have his priorities straight, and I wondered why. I'd always thought he was smart and clear-sighted. "What'd she say about Jacob? Anything?"

"She never saw him dealing, never saw drugs in his room. And she said something interesting. Apparently, Parr knew that ten pounds is the threshold for a mandatory prison sentence, so he made absolutely sure he never had that much on hand. He even made her leave once, when he found out she had a dime bag in her purse, because he was that obsessive about controlling the exact amount of drugs in his apartment at any given time."

"Wow. I wish I'd known that before I filed my brief to get those extra baggies thrown out. I suppose I might be able to get her in at the hearing on that, as newly discovered evidence, if she's willing to testify."

"Yeah, I don't know about that."

I glanced over. She was shaking her head.

"She's staying as far under the radar as she can," she said. "Because Kyle Parr is still a free man. If he gets put away, she might be willing to help Jacob—she did say she feels bad he got caught up in the whole thing. But she's keeping her head down for now. She's terrified of what Kyle might do to her."

I stopped at the light across from the fanciest hotel in town, where Ruiz's shindig was taking place. A sign on the parking garage informed us that normal parking wasn't available; it was all valet.

I swung into the half-circle drive, and we both got out. Terri grinned at me as she gestured to the other cars around us. "Good thing you got rid of that Malibu. Don't think it would have fit in."

I looked around and had to agree. Granted, the same was probably true of my Outback.

Kaylee, Dixie's friend, was staffing the valet stand. We chitchatted for a second. She was wearing a black-and-white server's outfit, and she explained that she'd been asked to fill in for a few minutes when one of the valets had to break up a scuffle and drag someone off to security.

"My goodness. Well, you stay safe, now," I said, giving her my keys. She handed them off to a young man in the hotel's uniform.

As we turned away, I told Terri, "I feel like an ass. I can park my own car."

She shrugged. "It's a pretty good job for them, though. They'll be making bank tonight."

"Fair point. Oh, speaking of good jobs, Noah got an offer today from some PI firm in Charleston."

"He did? Fantastic!"

I followed her through a revolving door and into the hotel lobby.

"So he's really on his way," she said. "Do you know which firm?"

"No, he was telling me this morning, but right then, the FedEx guy got there with my new phone."

"A smartphone? Hallelujah! Welcome to the twenty-first century!"

I laughed. "Yeah, and welcome to my kid not being a kid anymore. I was still signing for the delivery when Noah headed out to apply for his concealed-carry permit for the new job."

"Just so you know," Terri said, "at his experience level, it's going to be a good while before they send him on any jobs where he might actually need that."

"I sure hope so. It feels like only last week that I was teaching him to ride a bike."

We headed over to the security table outside the ballroom to check in for the event, then went in and started weaving our way through the crowd. A cheer went up, and I looked around for a TV screen. The first results had come in. Ruiz had a little over 60 percent of the vote so far, with three other candidates splitting the rest.

Through an opening in the crowd, I spotted Roy standing with Ruiz and Ginevra Barnes. We waved and headed over. Folks in the Basking Rock legal community made a point of being collegial. Our courtroom sparring might resemble a blood sport at times, but for social occasions, we laid our weapons down.

That was another way small-town life was different from Charleston. Business lawyers like Roy were friendly with everybody up there, too, but the folks on the prosecution side never would've socialized with the defense bar.

We said our hellos, and I soon realized that all of them were well into their drinks. They were lively, talking louder than they normally would.

"Hey, Ruiz," I said, "how's it feel to be a politician?"

"Oh my Lord," he said, looking wide-eyed toward the ceiling. "I hate this campaign stuff. I just want to get back to my desk and do my job."

"I hear you."

Some businessman came by to shake his hand. As they made small talk, I glanced past them and saw Dabney Barnes on the far side of the room, chatting with Hank Manigault. They looked to be enjoying themselves.

I turned a little so that if they looked this way, they wouldn't see my face. I knew getting Fourth's support had been huge for Ruiz, and given the man's dislike of me, I didn't want to remind him that Ruiz and I were friends.

Beside me, Terri murmured, "There goes Kaylee again. I guess things must've settled down at the valet station."

I followed her gaze. Kaylee was heading toward the kitchen, balancing a silver tray of empty glasses.

"I suppose most of the kids in the local hotel industry are working this gig," Terri mused. "It's bound to be good pay and good tips."

I agreed. "It's strange to think that Dixie Ward probably would've been here tonight, if she hadn't…"

"Yeah."

There was another flurry of hellos and back pats for Ruiz. This time the well-wisher was Osborne Drayton. Roy welcomed him loudly and called a waiter over to get him a fresh drink.

Another cheer arose, and we all looked at the nearest screen. Ruiz was up to 67 percent.

While folks were celebrating that, Drayton stepped closer to me and said, more quietly, "I saw that motion you filed. Good one. I have to say, I wasn't expecting the aggressive approach, but I like it."

Then he gave me a nod, took a sip of his gin and tonic, and went back to talking to Ruiz. Our conversation was over. His son's legal predicament was not a topic he wanted to spend more time on or let anybody overhear.

The motion he was referring to was the one I'd filed seeking to throw out the extra baggies of weed. The hearing on it was coming up. I wondered if he'd find the time to show up for that one.

As Ruiz was taking a sip of what looked like a Bloody Mary, the numbers on the screens updated. He was now at 69 percent.

"Oh, look at Lawrence Tucker," Roy said, reading one of the other candidates' names. "Three percent. That's embarrassing."

"Yeah, he's kind of a weird one," I said.

Tucker had been an explosive, case-altering witness in one of my trials the previous year. I'd been grateful for his testimony but was glad he was losing. He was another true believer, and humorless to boot. In my view, the farther he stayed from the solicitor's office, the better.

"What I don't understand about him," Drayton said, loudly enough for us all to enjoy, "is his decision process. I mean, who figures it's a good idea to run for office barely a year after getting arrested under the Sea Island Bridge with your pants around your ankles?"

They all exploded in laughter. I couldn't help but join in. On top of being a moralizing bore, Tucker was a hypocrite who got caught— very publicly—cheating on his wife.

"I tell you what, though," Ruiz said, "that incident did make my campaign manager's life easier."

Mrs. Barnes drained her glass of wine and said, "Oh my goodness. I'm sure that made it a cakewalk."

Another local dignitary stopped to congratulate Ruiz.

As they talked, Roy said, "Oh, Leland, quite the high drama going on in your arson case, am I right?"

"Oof, yeah, it's a situation."

To the others, he explained, "I was out on a little fishing trip until this morning. Haven't had a chance to catch up with him. Or you, Ginevra."

"Oh, yes, indeed," she said. "Well, you know how when a case finally starts moving, it's like an avalanche."

I asked her, "How are Miss Ward's parents doing?"

"Oh, I mean, terrible, of course. Just how you'd expect."

"I can imagine."

"They were actually kind of mad at me the other day, and I count that as *your* fault." She pointed a pink-nailed finger at me, teetering on her high heels. She was clearly somewhat drunk.

"Oh? How so?"

"Well, speaking as a solicitor—you'll understand this; you used to be one. Didn't you find that victims or their families want to see the suspect being arrested? It gives them a sense of, you know, justice being done."

"It does," Ruiz agreed, stopping a passing waitress to set his empty glass on her tray.

"I do remember that, yes," I said.

"And they didn't get to do that in this case. It didn't happen. Because, am I mistaken," she said, looking at me with her puzzled-kitten expression, "or weren't we going to meet at five o'clock? I had everything ready for y'all to get there then, and I know I had ordered the van to come by at quarter past."

"Oh, man, I don't even know what I was thinking," I said, shaking my head, trying to look mystified. "You know how it is when you look back at something, and it's just so obviously a misunderstanding, but in the moment it was happening, you thought it made sense?"

"Well, bless your heart," Mrs. Barnes said, looking at me like I was in need of special care. "I guess it was just one of those things."

Roy nodded and said, "We've all been there. Happens to the best of us. I don't even want to *tell* y'all about some of the mistakes *I* made when I was starting out."

A minute later, when Ruiz had moved on to glad-hand somebody else and Mrs. Barnes had walked off with Terri to show her where the food was, Roy grinned at me and said, "Misunderstanding, my ass! What the hell happened?"

I laughed. "In confidence, I *may* have had some concerns about her media connections."

"Oh, yeah. Damn right. She's real tight with that SOB." He didn't need to explain that he was referring to her brother-in-law.

"And as a result, it might've seemed prudent to get there an hour or so earlier than she was expecting."

He laughed. "An hour, that's perfect. I would've told her I thought it was Daylight Saving Time. Or my phone was on the wrong time zone. That could happen to anybody." He winked at me and took a sip of his drink.

"I also may have sensed that she intended to get a couple of officers to put my client in cuffs and shove him into the jail van in front of the photographers—"

"After a good long perp walk outside," he said.

"Right, that would've been step one. Parade him before the cameras. Anyway, if she did mention that the jail van was coming, it must've been when I was preoccupied. All of a sudden, all four of us needed to use the restroom at the same time, and I was just trying to coordinate that."

"And then, I take it, you had to coordinate a quick trip to the ground floor," he said, "and the parking lot, and the jail. My God. Hang on a second."

He stopped a waiter passing by with a tray of drinks, selected a small bottle of Perrier, and handed it to me.

"I did not see one single photo of your guy in the news," he said, raising his half-empty whiskey glass to me. "Which I'm sure is how he wanted it."

I smiled and raised my Perrier, and we clinked.

"You protected the hell out of your client," he said. "And that's exactly what they pay us for."

We sipped our drinks. I looked around, enjoying the moment.

Terri was twenty feet or so away, near the jazz band, holding a little plate of food and bobbing her head as they played. A pearl choker glowed at her throat, and the gold bodice of her dress highlighted her shape.

"Not to intrude," Roy said, "but you've got a thing for that girl, don't you."

I looked at him. His smile was fatherly. "So much for my poker face," I said. "Thanks for the reminder to rein it in."

He raised an eyebrow. "You do anything about it yet?"

"Oh, hell no. What a mess that'd be."

For some reason, that cracked him up. "My God, boy, don't be a jackass." He shook his head. "Life's too short."

That phrase gave me a chill. I dealt in shortened lives; that was my job. Some were curtailed by crimes or accidents, and others were spent buried alive in prison cells.

I looked over to Terri again, but she was gone.

As the evening was winding down, Terri and I headed for the door. As we passed the check-in table, which I was surprised to see was still staffed, we saw a young man arguing with one of the women who'd been checking ID.

"Sir," a security guard said, "I'm going to have to ask you to leave."

The kid's body was stiff with anger, and his fists were clenched at his sides. As we got closer, he turned to gesture, and I recognized Brandon Ludlow.

"That girl right there," he said. "She's right there! I got something to say to her, that's all, and y'all need to let me in!"

"Oh my," Terri said. "Is he pointing to Kaylee?"

Kaylee was frozen in the doorway to the ballroom. She looked like she'd walked in on something awful and couldn't think of how to extricate herself.

The lady at the table said, "Young man, let's not cause an incident here."

"Yeah, let's not!" he yelled. "Let's let me go have a damn conversation!"

The security guard's right hand moved to rest on the butt of his holstered gun.

"Oh, Brandon!" I said cheerfully, walking toward him. "Hey, how've you been?"

He looked at me, startled. We hadn't laid eyes on each other in nearly a year.

Up close, he stank of alcohol.

"So, listen," I said. "Kaylee's working right now. You can talk to her later. But I'm glad I ran into you." I lowered my voice like I was sharing something confidential and said, "Can we step outside? I got something I wanted to tell you about Hank Manigault."

I made that up on the fly, thinking the name of his employer might get his attention.

Brandon looked back at the ballroom doorway, and I followed his gaze. Kaylee was gone.

"They've been running her off her feet all night," I told him. "She's got to earn her keep. Come on. I only got a minute."

Looking dazed, he let me lead him toward the exit. I let him go first through the revolving door. As he did, I handed Terri my phone and said, "Can you text Hank? If he's still around, see if he can meet us out front here."

Hank's presence, I thought, might remind Brandon to behave himself. If it didn't, hopefully the goodwill Hank had for the kid would result in a fatherly talking-to.

I followed Brandon outside, wondering what I could possibly say to him, and found him leaning back against the front wall of the hotel. His eyes were closed.

I heard the swoosh of the revolving door again and looked around for Terri. Somebody else had just come out; she still hadn't.

Brandon looked… sad. His eyes were still closed. After a second, he started moving his head forward and back, tapping his skull repeatedly against the stone facade.

His mood shift was familiar to me. My late wife had done that, too, when she was in her cups. After half an hour or so of mania, which could be deranged laughter or intense anger depending on the day, she'd subside into a weepy, self-hating state that could only be cured by sleeping it off.

"Hey there," I said, setting a hand on his shoulder. "You'll feel better in the morning. You got a ride home?"

His face crumpled like he was barely managing not to cry. He opened his eyes and looked at me. "What the hell, dude. After what I did to your son? What the hell!"

I stared at him. He'd knocked the words out of me. The previous summer, Noah had nearly died from an accidental overdose at Brendan's apartment, thanks to Brendan's habit of storing fentanyl patches in a NicoDerm box.

Because of who his daddy was, Brendan had suffered no consequences from that incident. And I'd assumed Brendan had inherited his father's lack of conscience.

"Noah okay now?" he asked.

"Yeah, he's good."

He gave a sigh that was heavy with relief.

"How about you?" I asked.

He shook his head, looking off into the distance. "Oh, I'm just screwing up," he said, starting to bang his skull against the facade again. "And screwing up, and screwing up."

The revolving door thumped again, and I heard Hank Manigault say, "What's up, Leland? Oh, my goodness."

Brendan looked over at him, and fear flashed across his face. "Aw, shit," he said, and took off running. He lurched around a Mercedes piloted by one of the valets, ran down the hotel's curved drive, and disappeared around the corner of the next building.

"What was that about?" Hank said.

"Oh, he had a bit too much to drink," I said. "I thought maybe you could come talk some sense into him."

"Yeah. I'll talk to him. Maybe tomorrow." He flashed his big toothy smile at me, said, "That boy needs a firm hand," and went back inside.

I was alone for a second, except for a valet a few yards away who was talking on his phone.

The door spun again, and finally Terri emerged, a vision in black and gold.

"That door makes me think of a vending machine," I told her, "or one of those machines at casinos. It spun, and out you popped, like a prize."

She gave me a weird look.

"I... That came out wrong," I said.

She laughed. "You're out of practice, I guess."

I grappled with the possibility that she had recognized my inept comment as an attempt at flirting. Before I could get my thoughts organized, she changed the subject.

"I went back for a minute to see if I could talk to Kaylee," she said. "She really appreciated you stepping in. Seems there's a whole story between the two of them and her, uh, friend."

I knew she meant Dixie Ward.

16

MAY 19, 2022

I t had been nearly four years since I'd last set foot in the solicitor's office in Charleston. I parked on the edge of the French Quarter, crossed the street, and went into the lobby, heading for the security desk where visitors got their passes. The sounds of echoing conversations and my leather shoes on the stone floor brought me back to my last night here, when I'd scuttled across the lobby in the other direction, carrying a cardboard box of my family photos and the few other personal items from my office. It wasn't a good feeling.

I set it aside.

The guard on duty was a big-bellied guy I didn't recognize.

"What's your purpose here today, sir?" he asked.

"Meeting with Cody Varner, up on the fourth floor."

While he looked up the list of the day's preapproved visitors on his computer, I slid my ID across the granite surface of the guard post.

He found me on the list and pushed my ID back, along with a binder and a pen.

"Sign in there, sir," he said. "Date, time, and who you're meeting with. And you'll need to sign back out again when you leave."

I signed and then rode the elevator, waited in the upstairs lobby, and took a few sips of the bad coffee the receptionist gave me. I didn't recognize her, either; a lot of folks here were new.

When Varner finally came to get me, after treating me to a fifteen-minute wait, he didn't offer his hand. I didn't either. Our hearing on my motion to dismiss was that afternoon, and we both knew I was in a pretty good position. I wasn't about to break that spell by chasing handshakes he wasn't inclined to give.

In his office, I sat across from him and said, "Nice place you've got here. Better than that old closet they had you in before."

"Yeah, things are good. Can't complain."

He was clearly not up for a trip down memory lane. I took a cue from his let's-get-on-with-it tone and said, "So, what do you think? Can we work something out, or do you want to keep our appointment with Stickman?"

This was his last chance to get a plea deal in place before Judge Stickman, who'd recently been assigned as our trial judge, ruled on my motion and threw out whichever part of Varner's case he liked the least. If I was lucky, that could mean all of it.

"Well, first of all," Varner said, "just to frame the conversation, things have moved on here since you left. We've had a rule change, since last year, to where we're no longer offering overly harsh sentences in plea deals. We don't come out of the gate trying to strong-arm defendants with something punitive."

"Yeah, I'm aware of that." I still had cases in Charleston County; I knew the rules.

"Okay, I'm just mentioning it to set expectations. Whatever we offer now, it's what we realistically expect we could get at trial."

"And that is what?"

"Before I get into that, are we still looking at no information from your guy?"

He meant, was Jacob still unwilling to testify against Kyle Parr.

"Well, so... here's the thing," I said. "Our concern is that you got Mr. Parr there, who's got multiple priors and, as I'm sure you're aware, has known gang connections—"

"Look, I'll tell you right off the bat that as of now, I've got no admissible evidence on that. We're aware of the likelihood, but he's managed to keep himself looking pretty clean. That's why we're asking if your guy has any information."

"I don't know how my Olympic athlete studying for a business degree is supposed to know more than Charleston law enforcement does about Mr. Parr's gang connections. How would he know which of Parr's associates are gangbangers or local drug lords? He's not the one who's got files full of their mug shots."

"Leland, I hear you on that, but I simply do not believe that a man in Mr. Parr's position would get himself a new roommate who had no connection to or interest in his narcotics operations. I think your guy's holding out on me."

"You think a kid from Basking Rock who spent the previous three months in Germany training for the Olympics, and never had so much as a citation for possession for personal use, was—what, part of Parr's gang? Are you serious?"

He shrugged. "I just need to know if he's got something he can bring to the table."

"Well, let's say he did. Just for the sake of argument, let's say he had photographic evidence that known gang members used to come hang out with Parr and count their drug money on the living room couch. Why would he trust you to do right by him? It doesn't exactly inspire confidence to see your office hitting the kid with no priors and no gang connections with felony intent to distribute, while the guy who we both know is a lowlife is only facing a misdemeanor for the joint in his nightstand."

"Are you telling me your guy's got a chip on his shoulder about—"

"What I'm telling you is… how many informants or witnesses do you expect to get if they think that, at most, you might put Parr away for a few years, and in the meantime, all his associates are still on the outside, very possibly willing to take those witnesses down?"

"Are you telling me how to do my job?"

I could've said a few choice words on that point, but that wouldn't help Jacob. He wasn't paying me to have a pissing contest with Varner.

I sat back with a sigh and shook my head.

"Cody, listen. We both would love to see Mr. Parr behind bars. And so would my client, and Mr. Parr's ex-girlfriend. But that's the problem with fighting gangs: if you only take one member down, the rest are still free to take revenge. My client only lived with Parr for a month— I very much doubt he knows anything more than what's already in your files—and he's afraid for his life. And he knows I'm about to go in there and argue, I think pretty convincingly, that the cops here took a few baggies out of the evidence room to bring their haul over the ten-pound threshold. And on top of that, they searched a locked room that they knew belonged to somebody who wasn't the target of the warrant—"

"Yeah, I read your brief," he said, with more than a hint of snark. "You don't need to recite it to me as well."

"Fine. So how about you tell me what you're offering as of now. And what you could offer if, let's say, my client had some information you wanted *and* you had some way of convincing him that sharing what little he knows wouldn't put his life in danger."

"Like I said, our policy is to offer what we realistically think we could get in court, plus a little sweetener to get the deal done."

"Uh-huh."

"So, realistically, if we stay over the ten pounds, it's a felony with a mandatory five-to-ten-year sentence. But I'm authorized to propose just one year."

"Uh-huh. And if we're under the ten pounds?"

"Felony possession, no jail time. One year of probation."

"Okay, let me tell you what we need. You know Mr. Drayton's a world-class target shooter, and obviously a felony conviction would end that, since under federal law he'd never be allowed to own or possess a firearm again."

"Are you asking me to take ten pounds, or nine and a half pounds, of weed"—he was gesturing with his hands, framing a shape about the size of a couch cushion in the air—"and turn that into a misdemeanor?"

"I'm telling you that's what my client needs."

"Well, if shooting sports are so important to him, maybe he shouldn't have gotten himself a dealer for a roommate. Maybe he shouldn't have stashed half a bushel of weed in his room."

"Cody, it wasn't his. He didn't put it there."

"You're arguing out of both sides of your mouth, though, aren't you," he said. "At the preliminary hearing, you said Mr. Parr must've locked the weed in there before he let the officers in. Now you're saying the room was under your guy's control, not Mr. Parr's, so the officers didn't have the right to search it. Which is it?"

"Listen, we could argue about this all day. Or we could come up with a deal. My client might well accept a short spell in prison, a month or two perhaps, if you can send him there on a misdemeanor instead of a felony. He'd prefer that over a felony with no prison sentence. But what you've offered up to now, we cannot take."

He shrugged. "I've offered what I can give."

Judge Stickman only gave us half an hour for the evidence suppression hearing, but it went pretty well. Varner's only real argument on the search of Jacob's locked room was that there was no controlling case that required the evidence found there to be excluded. On the seven baggies that magically appeared at some point between the apartment and the crime lab, he said what I'd anticipated: that since there was no photo of the empty box in the apartment, those seven baggies might've been hiding inside it when the other 157 bags were photographed.

Still, it didn't sit right with me that the judge told us he'd "pray on it" and let us know his answer later. Most judges ruled on evidentiary matters then and there.

I put that concern out of my mind and drove back to Basking Rock to visit Bobby.

At the jail, I waited in the private room reserved for lawyer visits. There was a clock on one wall. I remembered what Marianne had told me and switched chairs so Bobby would be sitting where he could easily see it.

Within a few minutes, a guard who barely came up to Bobby's shoulders, escorted him in. The guard walked loosely; he looked relaxed. Bobby was giving off gentle-giant vibes, and the guard seemed to trust that he wasn't going to pull anything.

After the guard locked us in, Bobby took a seat. I saw him focus on the clock behind me and take a deep breath.

"How's it going?" I asked.

"I'm following the rules," he said, looking at me like he was checking to make sure I caught the reference. "And not trusting nobody, and taking no shit."

I smiled. "Good."

He looked back at the clock and said, "I was taught to just state my name, rank, and serial number. Sit tight and wait until I could get out. I guess, in a way, I trained for this."

"That's a good way to look at it."

He looked around and said, "Big room. Wish they'd let Marianne visit me in here."

"Yeah. I'm sure it's good to see her."

He nodded. I could tell from his expression he had mixed feelings.

"It's real weird," he said, "only being able to see your wife twice a week. I don't see how they get to limit that."

"Yeah, it doesn't seem right. You try the video visits?"

The jail's visitation policy was two in-person visits per week, limited to forty-five minutes apiece, and up to three thirty-minute remote ones. They could talk on the phone daily, but calls cut off automatically after ten minutes.

"Yeah. We do what we can." He sighed. "Thanks for bringing her my ring."

"Of course."

"She was real upset about the coverage, though. I guess I could even say, angry."

"Oh. What Fourth said, you mean?"

The *Patriot* website had published an unflattering photo of Marianne speaking to reporters on the courthouse steps, along with an article that misquoted what I'd heard her say on TV.

Bobby cocked his head at me like I wasn't making sense. "Fourth?"

I realized that, unlike me and my fellow lawyers, a guy who ran pizza shops probably wouldn't need to—or care to—know the names and positions of the local coterie of rich old men.

"Sorry," I said. "Dabney Barnes the Fourth. He owns and edits the *Southeast Patriot*."

"That's his name? Dabney Barnes the goddamn Fourth? Man." He was shaking his head, his face screwed up like he'd smelled something bad.

I smiled. "Yeah, I know."

"What's his brother's name, if he's got one? Chauncey?"

He sounded so disgusted I had to laugh. Bobby and I were definitely from the same side of the tracks.

"I like that one," I said. "Maybe I'll start calling Fourth that. Yeah. So, Chauncey runs the paper as a way of helping out his friends and messing with folks he doesn't like."

Bobby looked a little bit at a loss. "Why doesn't he like me? Or Marianne?"

"I'm trying to figure that out. It could just be his default mode, which is favoring the rich boys—the ones who were born rich, I mean. But if there's more to it, I'd like to know."

"Yeah. I mean, I would too. She was real upset."

I nodded and then leaned down to get my legal pad and a pen. "Okay," I said. "So, there's a few things I wanted to ask you about."

"Fire away."

"Tell me about Boseman."

I liked asking open-ended questions. Folks sometimes answered them by telling me something I would never have thought to ask about.

Bobby exhaled heavily, like there was a lot to say and he wasn't sure where to begin. After a second, he said, "I guess Boseman falls into the rich-boy group."

"Yeah. How'd you meet him?"

"Oh, I saw the beachfront space advertised, and I rented it. He shows his own spaces. I guess he doesn't like paying for an agent. So that's when I met him. At some point after I got up and running there, he could see things were going well, and—it might've been one time when I brought the rent over. We got to talking, and he mentioned he had the other space, but it wasn't fit for occupancy. It was just a shell."

"You brought the rent over in person? At his house, or where?"

"Sometimes his house, sometimes his office downtown. Just what was convenient for us that month."

"So… how'd you pay? Cash? Check?"

"Cash. I was an all-cash business for the first probably four or five years, because I didn't want to deal with the fees and charge-backs and whatnot for credit cards, so that's the habit we got into."

"And he gave you, what, rent receipts?"

"Yep."

"Okay." I noted that down. "And what's your impression of him as a person?"

"As a person? You know what, he always reminded me a little bit of my first commanding officer in Iraq. Just a real take-charge, no-nonsense guy. The opposite of indecisive. Real strong character."

"Huh. Did you like your commanding officer?"

He blinked a few times and looked thoughtfully at something above my head. Maybe the clock. "Yeah, uh… He was a hard-ass, but some of us owed our lives to him. He, uh, he didn't come home."

"I'm sorry."

"Yeah."

For half a second, I saw the entire war in his face. Then he came back to the present, looked me in the eye, and said, "You got an interest in Boseman? You think it could've been him?"

"I mean, it usually is. Unless you've got a firebug or someone's trying to, I don't know, teach someone a lesson or something, arson's usually about insurance, so it's either the owner or a well-insured tenant."

"I guess that makes sense. Although I kind of figured he's too rich to care about one little building."

"That's how the solicitor feels too."

"Oh, that's why they aren't after him?"

"Yeah. But I actually have a different take. So I wanted to know, do you recall when Dixie Ward moved in?"

"Oh. Uh… Well, it would've been last summer when we saw them carrying that granite countertop in. So I guess it was probably around then."

"Right after that?"

"I guess that makes sense. When the remodel was done."

"And did you ever see or hear anything between her and Boseman?"

His eyes widened in surprise. "Oh, my."

He looked off to one side like he was trying to recall.

"I mean, he came over sometimes," he said. "To pick up my rent and, I guess, hers. I assumed that's what he went upstairs for. Man, is that where you're going with this? You hear something about him?"

"Well, I'll tell you what. I went over to Boseman's church on a Sunday to catch him and his wife on the way out and have a little chat. And he was real cagey about that remodel. I got the strong impression he didn't want his wife to know how much money he'd poured into making Miss Ward's apartment look good."

"He did put a lot into it. Especially considering I had built it out myself a few years earlier, and it was fine. It's not like it needed anything before he could rent it."

"I remembered you saying something like that. It's part of why I wanted to ask him."

"But—wait, are you saying… Are you thinking they had a thing going on, and then for whatever reason, he… killed her on *purpose*?"

"It could've been that. Or maybe he didn't realize she was there that night, and he destroyed the place so he could get rid of her as a tenant without having to evict her. He could've been afraid of what she might tell folks, or say in court, if he served her with an eviction notice and things got hostile."

"Damn."

I let him absorb that for a minute. Then I said, "But I also wanted to ask, what was *your* relationship with her?"

A look of alarm flashed across his face. I got the sense he felt cornered.

He didn't say anything, so I continued. "That first night I came over to meet you and Mrs. Carter, you said something about that to me as we were walking to my car."

He shut his eyes and sighed.

"The reason I'm asking," I said, "is so that I can defend you. I've got to be ready for whatever comes up."

"Yeah. Uh, well, there was… I felt… temptation."

"She was a real pretty girl," I said.

"I did not take it anywhere," he said. He still wasn't looking at me. "I didn't cheat on Marianne. I didn't touch that girl."

I nodded slowly and relaxed back into my chair. I wanted to put him at ease. I'd found the truth spilled out better that way.

"But I had her number, you know, because Boseman would some-times text both of us to notify us of things going on with the building, and… there were some messages I sent," he said, "that were maybe… more affectionate than they ought to have been."

I pictured Dixie Ward's phone lighting up with one of those.

"Messages from you?"

He nodded.

I wondered if anybody else had seen them. Her fiancé, her sugar daddy? New motives for the fire and her killing came to mind.

"And these were just regular text messages?" I said. "Not any of those, like, disappearing instant messages or whatever?"

"Oh, I don't know anything about that. Texting's about the most high-tech thing I do."

"Did she ever reciprocate?"

"Oh, of course not. After the last one, she wouldn't even look me in the eye anymore." He blew out a breath. "I was a damn fool. I should've left those thoughts in my head where they belonged—I mean, not that they belonged there either. Anyhow, I don't know why I ever figured she might want me to talk to her like that."

Ginevra Barnes must've seen those messages. Miss Ward's phone had been destroyed in the fire, but only a piss-poor prosecutor would fail to subpoena whatever they could get from her phone company. And Mrs. Barnes was good at her job.

17

MAY 26, 2022

Terri called right after breakfast, and what she told me made me postpone my drive up to Charleston. I'd been planning to help Noah move into his new place and then go meet with the fire expert.

"Kaylee needs help," Terri said. "She wants to talk to both of us, but she doesn't want anyone to overhear, so she wanted to meet somewhere out of the way."

"She could come to my office. Laura's the only one there—Roy left early for his Memorial Day trip."

"Yeah, I suggested that," she said, "but she wasn't comfortable with it. So I asked if she was a churchgoer."

Terri gave me the address, and I was mildly surprised to learn that Kaylee was Catholic. My late wife had been raised in that faith, but then, she was from Louisiana. There weren't a whole lot of them around here; they only had one church.

I drove across town to Saint Francis. It was a beautiful brick-and-stone building, close to two hundred years old, with a tall, square bell tower that always made me think of Italy.

I parked by a stand of palm trees and went through one of the huge wooden doors, trading the bright, sunny day for an interior so dimly lit that, for a second, I was blind. The place was at least ten degrees cooler than the outdoors, and since it was a church on a Thursday morning, it was almost silent. As my eyes adjusted, I saw stained-glass rainbows high above. When I lowered my gaze to ground level, I saw Terri in a doorway, beckoning. I followed her down to the basement meeting room.

Kaylee was waiting for us in the semidarkness. Terri shut the door and turned the light on. The room was furnished like a living room, with chairs and couches and low tables. Kaylee was on one couch, hugging a multicolored pillow on her lap.

I said hello and took a chair. Terri sat on the love seat across the coffee table from Kaylee.

"Thanks for coming," Kaylee said. A smile flickered across her face, and she added, "I'm sorry if this is weird. I'm probably being paranoid, but…"

"Better safe than sorry," Terri said. "So, what's going on? How can we help?"

"Well, okay, first, I want to thank y'all for helping with Brandon that night at the hotel."

"Oh, no problem," I said. "I'm just glad we could. He was a little out of hand."

Her slow nod spoke volumes. I got the sense my statement did not begin to capture how that situation had felt to her.

Terri said, "If you don't mind my asking, what's the story there?"

"Oh, it's… it's a *story*." Kaylee hugged the pillow tighter. "I made a big mistake. I dated him for a little while, last year. And he was—he had a lot of problems."

"Uh-huh," I said, recalling what I'd learned about him last summer. "Yes, he sure did."

"So, you know, I bailed," she said. "Or I tried to. And Dixie was *there* for me, you know? I mean, she pointed me to all these resources, and, like, she went with me to magistrate's court…"

"Oh, you got a restraining order?"

"I tried to. I went there three times, twice with Dixie, but it just—it was confusing, and nobody there would help me. I filled out the same paperwork every time, and it kept getting… like, *lost*? That's what they said. Like, sorry, there's no record of it, fill it out again. And, I mean, he's Solicitor Ludlow's son, you know? So I was, like, are they just putting this straight in the trash when they see his name? After a while, I gave up."

"I am so sorry," Terri said. "That's infuriating."

"Yeah," I said. "I can tell you, though, in case it's any help, that the guy who replaced Solicitor Ludlow is a good guy. And no friend of Ludlow. I can talk to him about it, if you want to try filing again."

"I don't know." Kaylee shook her head, eyes closed. She looked exhausted. Then she looked at me and said, "I mean, thank you, but I don't know if it's worth it at this point."

"Has he been calling you?" Terri asked.

"Oh yeah. On and off. There'll be a couple weeks of nothing, and then I guess he'll get it in his head again and leave all these messages."

"He say anything threatening?" I asked. "Or inappropriate? We could use that as evidence against him."

"No, not like… I mean, it's weird. It's mostly just the sheer number of messages. But, you know, he's a lawyer's son. No offense, Mr. Munroe. I just mean that he's smart enough to know what not to do."

"Sometimes men like him call just to hear your voice," Terri said. "So the advice is to have somebody else record your outgoing message."

"Yeah, I actually did that last fall. And it did help. He called a lot less after that. But once in a while I see him outside my work, like, looming in the shadows. Letting me know he's there. And he still kind of loses it, sometimes."

"Is he the reason we're meeting here?" I asked. "Hiding out, I mean."

She nodded hard. "Yeah. Yeah, exactly. Because there was, like, a lull for a few weeks, but then it was right after we met up in that café last month that he kind of went off again. And then that night at the ballroom. He doesn't like me talking to the two of you. I don't know why."

Terri took that in for a moment. "I guess, on the one hand, it'd be interesting to ask him why. But on the other, you're probably trying to avoid talking to him at all."

"Yeah, exactly."

"Mm-hmm. And that's the right call. When somebody won't leave you alone, everything you give them, every word you say... it's like more fuel to them."

"Yeah, yeah. That's what it said in the book Dixie gave me. It was called *The Gift of Fear*, and she gave it to me and was, like, follow this! She was doing *so* much to help me, you know? More than family."

"I'm so sorry you lost her," Terri said.

"Yeah." Kaylee covered her mouth and squeezed her eyes shut for a second.

When she'd recovered, I asked, "And you can't talk to us at your home either?"

"Oh, my roommate would… We were all friends, so she's, like, why are you betraying Dixie? You know, because y'all are working for the guy who… You know." She hugged the pillow tighter and shut her eyes.

"I can understand that," I said. "Just so you know, I do not think he did it. That's my belief. And I'd truly like to figure out who did, both to help my client, of course, and to see justice done for Miss Ward. But I appreciate you must be in a real difficult situation."

She nodded. A moment later, she took a loud breath and squared her shoulders like she was psyching herself up for something. "Okay, so, there's something else. It might be nothing, I might've just lost my mind because of everything that's—everything I've been through lately. But there's something I've been wondering, and something that I… I think ought to be said."

Terri murmured, "Yeah, you've been through a whole lot. And, child, I'm here for you."

Something in her voice—sincerity and understanding, woman to woman—changed the spirit of the room. A space opened for the girl to unburden herself.

Kaylee said, "I knew Dixie real well. And I don't want to— There were things in her life that she didn't want her parents to know."

"Mm-hmm."

"But if it might help… I want *someone* to know, someone who's trying to figure this out, what she told me. The thing is, not even two weeks before she—before it happened, she told me she was pregnant."

I stopped breathing.

Terri gave a slow, sympathetic headshake. "Oh, that was hard for her, I'm sure."

"It was *so* hard." Kaylee leaned forward, got a Kleenex from the box on the coffee table, and blew her nose.

"What a thing for you to be carrying, all by yourself," Terri said.

"Yeah. Yeah. It's a lot."

"Did she tell you how her fiancé took it?"

"That's... that's... No. That's the thing. I don't know if she ever told him." Kaylee blew her nose again and said, "She never— I've got nothing to base this on, I never asked her and I might just be making things up, but I always wondered if the baby might not be his."

"Mm-hmm." Terri had a way of listening that I'd never seen in anybody else. It was limitless, a sense of her infinitely absorbing or embracing everything a person told her, with no judgment, nothing but deep sympathy. No sharp edges, everything gentle and slow.

In her presence, people felt safe.

And they talked.

"Because the thing is," Kaylee said, "if it was his, why was it this huge disaster, right? Why was it complicated? They were engaged. Her parents liked him. She'd finished college. They would've been okay."

"Yeah," Terri said. "I hear you. I would've wondered the same thing, in your shoes."

I was wondering why the coroner hadn't run a pregnancy test. And whether there was any way to do one now.

After we said goodbye to Kaylee, Terri and I drove up to meet with the fire expert again. He'd reviewed Dixie's autopsy report and reread the fire inspector's report, to see if anything in it hit him differently now that he'd read up on her cause of death.

Mr. McDonald had printed out paper copies of both reports for all of us to look through together. The fluorescent tubes on his office ceiling buzzed as we talked. Every few minutes, they flickered. It was distracting to me, but he paid them no attention. Maybe his years as a firefighter, and then the decades he'd spent reviewing reports of hideous death on the daily, had made him impervious to such minor discomforts.

He dropped the fire report onto his lap and said, "So, the one thing that stands out to me, now that we're sure she was alive when the fire started, and what toxicology they were able to do shows she wasn't blackout drunk or on drugs, is that she was found just lying there in bed. I don't like that."

"She shouldn't be in bed at 3 a.m.?" I asked.

"Oh, sure," he said. "She was probably asleep when the fire started. But this was a recently renovated building, with all the right permits on file, up to code and so forth. It had fire alarms." He smacked the report with a knuckle. "It says so right in here. A couple of them were melted, and another one came through intact because the fire was extinguished before it reached it. So—"

"Oh, my goodness," Terri said. "She should've heard the alarms and woken up!"

McDonald pointed a *you-got-it* finger gun at her. "Right," he said. "When I see people who were alive during a fire, people whose autopsies show they died of smoke inhalation, and they weren't under the influence, they're not normally in bed. They die trying to escape." He spun his chair around and gestured to one of the framed newspaper clippings behind him. "Like that one," he said. "Subject was found prone beside the bedroom window. And that one, she was on her side in the hallway. That guy there was in his bathroom, with a towel stuffed under the door. That's what I'd expect to see."

"Because people who are conscious try to escape," I said. "God*damn.*"

McDonald turned back around and said, with a hint of dark humor, "Oh, no. I wouldn't say this was God's fault."

"Mm-mm," Terri said with an emphatic shake of the head. "Not at all. This is the sin of a man."

Afterward, we walked out to our cars. Terri was going home, and I was heading over to Noah's apartment to see what I might still be able to help with. Since she was checking her phone, I checked mine. I had an email from Charleston County's electronic case filing system.

"Ooh," I said, opening it. "We got a decision on my motion in the Drayton case."

"Oh! How badly did Varner get beat?"

I stopped walking and read the document. Then I read it again to make sure I hadn't missed something.

I looked at Terri. "Denied," I said. "Stickman denied it on everything."

It took her a second to process that. Then she said, "Everything? Are you kidding me?"

She stepped closer to look over my arm and read it herself. I turned my phone sideways to make the court's order bigger.

"All the drugs are staying in? Even the seven baggies that magically appeared at the crime lab? How does that make sense?"

"It doesn't."

I scrolled back up to read it from the top again, to see if the words had changed.

They hadn't.

We'd come out of McDonald's office fired up, ready to ride the path of righteousness to bring down the man who'd killed Dixie Ward. We were now all but certain that she'd been murdered, and that her killer was doing his best to make Bobby Carter take the fall.

All that energy had drained away. Hundreds of hours of our work had turned to nothing at the stroke of a judge's pen.

"I've got to call Jacob," I said, "and tell him he's going to trial."

"When does it start, again? How long do we have to prepare?"

"Two weeks."

18

MAY 26, 2022

I was sitting on a stool in Jacob's kitchen, sipping a glass of water and watching him stalk back and forth, swearing. I'd gone to his new place to give him the bad news in person. He lived alone—I doubted he'd ever have a roommate again, now that he'd learned how much damage a bad one could do.

"Can we just *talk* to Varner?" he asked. "Is there any way to make him understand?"

I remembered hearing someplace that there were five stages of grief—or was it six? Either way, I was pretty sure the stage he was at was called "bargaining."

"Unfortunately," I said, "with the way the judge decided this, we don't have a lot of leverage right now."

"How'd that even happen? I thought you said we'd get it thrown out!"

"I did think, bare minimum, he'd toss the seven baggies and take you under the ten pounds."

"So why didn't he? What's the law say? Can we appeal?"

I thought for a second about how to explain this. How to make it simple, and truthful, but not too depressing. The last thing I wanted, with trial two weeks away, was to have Jacob fall apart. We had a lot of work to do together to have a shot at winning, and I needed him to be in the best mental shape he could.

"Probably the best way to understand what happened," I said, "is to picture the law like this: you got the black, the gray, and the white." With my hands, I marked out the three imaginary colors in a row on his kitchen counter. "Some things are black or white. The judge has to rule a certain way, or he's wrong. The law on those things is clear."

"Oh." He seemed to deflate. I could tell he could see what was coming.

"And other things are gray," I said. "The judge could go either way. That's where we were. And what's common is, if you've got a few different issues that are all in the gray area, you'll see the judge more or less split the difference. He decides some issues one way and some the other. Which is why I thought he'd probably toss the seven baggies, at least."

"So why didn't he?"

"I don't know. I've been before Stickman several times, when I was still working up here in Charleston, and he wasn't what I'd call hard-core on drug cases. He was a reasonable guy."

He absorbed that for a minute, and then he said, "Okay. Still, we can appeal, right?"

I wished he hadn't asked that again.

"We can," I said. "But not until the trial's over. If you lose, that's when we can appeal."

"If I… You mean we have to go through the whole trial first? With all this evidence?"

I nodded.

"And then, if I... If the jury... If I lose, then we appeal? How long does all that take?"

"A criminal appeal? At least a year, maybe two."

He sat down hard on the other kitchen stool, like he didn't have the energy to keep standing up.

Most of my clients took a long time to realize how much trouble they were in. He was no different. TV crime shows got through the investigation, the trial, and the verdict in less than an hour. In real life, nobody—or at least, nobody who wasn't part of the criminal justice system—ever realized up front just how long their misery was likely to last.

After a minute, he said blankly, "I guess that's it, then. No Paris Olympics."

"Well, I'm still talking to Varner about a misdemeanor plea, so..."

He looked at me like I wasn't making any sense. Then he shook his head. "That's right, I didn't tell you yet. Oh, man." He sighed, his back slumped in defeat. "I talked to my coach about this some more, like in more detail, and he said that wouldn't be enough. I might be okay for Nationals, but for the Olympics, there's this thing called accreditation. If you get convicted of a significant drug crime, it's usually twelve to twenty-four months before the IOC will let you participate."

"So... that's separate from winning whatever events you need to win in order to qualify?"

He nodded. "You've got to qualify as an athlete, but also, I guess... as a good human being?" He let out a bitter laugh. "And that's where I fail. If I get convicted, anyway."

He'd just blown a large hole in my strategy, but with the state he was in, I couldn't tell him that. I put on an upbeat voice and said, "So I guess we've just got to win."

"How can we, though? When they found a big old box of weed sitting on my desk?"

"Well, it comes down to reasonable doubt, and with a known dealer for a roommate, and him being the only one there when the police arrived—"

"Okay, but—I mean, this sounds like Russian roulette! Just pull the trigger and hope we don't get a juror willing to convict me!"

It was a relief to realize he must not have paid attention in civics class. I might be able to cheer him up a bit.

"It's not quite that bad," I said. "Varner needs all twelve of them to agree to find you guilty."

"Oh. Yeah, I guess I did know that. But still, how hard is it to get twelve jurors to say, yeah, that box of weed was mine?"

"Well, the key is to get at least a few folks on the jury who are either a little more skeptical of the police than most, or who are real hardcore libertarian types. And of course, anybody who's ever been betrayed by a friend ought to be able to see what Kyle Parr did to you."

"You can ask them that?"

"We can ask them some things. As for what we can't ask, or we don't want to ask in front of Varner, Terri, my PI, will be pulling up the potential jurors' social media accounts and letting me know which ones we want or don't want hearing your case. She's a magician with that stuff."

He nodded. I could see he was weighing his options. After a minute, he said, "Okay, but there's still room for a plea, right? If I help him?

Because I'm starting to feel a little… like, trapped. Like there might be no way out. Is there anything we've actually got that he wants?"

"Well, like he's always said, if you could help him close the net on Kyle Parr—"

"What do I know about that, though? I only lived with him for a month before this went down. I met some of his friends, but they were… I don't know, man. I didn't like them. I mostly stayed in my room."

"Yeah, I'm sure. But have you looked through your photos or your texts to see if there's anything useful? And did you find anything on his social media?"

"No, he blocked me after I got charged. He's not stupid."

"No. He's got a record, he knows how things work."

"Dammit." He got up and started pacing again. "Yeah, that's why he knew what to do when the cops knocked on the door."

"Uh-huh. So, listen, how about I ask Varner if you can take a look at the mug shots he's got? Maybe that'd trigger something for you."

He shrugged like he doubted it, but we might as well. He'd walked into the living room—his apartment was small—and leaned back against the wall. After a second, he asked, "Is this, uh… is this drug thing the only crime Varner's interested in?"

I didn't answer for a second. I had the sense that any sudden moves on my part might spook him. Then I asked, in a casual tone, "How do you mean?"

"What if I knew about something else?" He was looking at me warily, with his mouth shut and his arms crossed over his chest. Withholding something, if I was reading him right.

"Well, that would depend."

"On what?"

"For starters, where this other crime happened."

"What if it happened on Kiawah Island?"

"Well, that's in Charleston County, so it's in Varner's bailiwick."

"Does that mean he might be interested?"

"Yeah, he might. Especially if it was something significant."

I gave him another minute to spit out whatever was on his mind. He didn't say a word.

"Listen," I said, "what's with the secrecy? I'm your lawyer. I'm not allowed to tell anybody what you say to me, and I need to know everything I can, if you want me to be able to do my job and help you."

He just kept on looking at me like a beat-down dog that didn't know what was safe.

I shrugged. "Well, you can tell me whenever you feel able to." I went over to the sink and refilled my glass.

I'd drunk about half of it before he spoke. His voice was quiet but clear. "I really don't know what all happened. I'm not sure of the details. But I think somebody died."

I took another sip. I didn't say *What the hell do you mean, you* think? And I did my best to keep that reaction from showing on my face. Shock or impatience would only shut him up again.

Eventually he said, "I was hanging out with a friend of mine at the time. Smoking weed, drinking. Like, all day. We were wasted. And that's probably why I don't really remember things all that clear."

"Sure, that'll mess with your memory." I kept my voice low, calm.

"Yeah, and, uh… I guess I don't really *want* to remember it. Or I didn't want to. But now, maybe…"

I nodded and got myself some more water while I waited for him to continue. I didn't know what kind of horror he was about to hit me with, but it felt like a big fish on a deep line, and I knew those had to be brought in real gentle and real slow.

"The thing is," he said, looking off someplace above my head, "I'm not a hundred percent sure that what I saw is connected to the… to what happened later. I don't want to name somebody as a murderer when I'm not even sure of it. Because I know what that's like, being accused of something you didn't do."

That word hung in the air: murderer.

"Yeah, that makes sense," I agreed.

"How do you figure out if something really happened the way you remember it, though? Because it's not like… a movie, you know? In my head. It's not like watching a movie. It's more like flipping through the photos on your phone, except a lot of them are missing, so…"

I left him another good long pause. He stayed quiet, but the secretive vibe was gone; his arms were loose at his sides.

"Well," I said, "one thing that might help work that out is if you had some sense of *when* it happened."

"Oh, that's not the hard part. It was the summer before junior year of high school. The last summer we hung out. After that, his dad sent him to"—he flashed me another wary look—"uh, to a different school. So we didn't really hang out after that."

I could tell he knew perfectly well what school his friend had gone to. He just didn't want to spill anything that would let me figure out who this friend was.

"Okay. And who was it that you think was killed?"

"A girl that his dad was seeing."

"Uh-huh. What do you recall about her?"

"She was real pretty. Saw her in the swimming pool there, and—yeah, she was gorgeous. Blonde, about college age."

"You got a name?"

"It started with an M. I remember because we were joking about it— like, watching her and saying *Mmm!* And it was a longer name, like… it had a rhythm to it."

"More than one syllable, then."

"Oh, yeah. More than two, I think." He looked at the ceiling again, shaking his head real slow, like he was trying to make out something that was too quiet to hear.

I believed he'd seen something, but as it stood, it was useless. With an unidentified victim, uncertainty as to whether any crime had happened at all, and Jacob admitting he'd been too wasted to be sure of what he saw, I couldn't even mention any of this to Cody Varner. He'd question my judgment and my common sense, then laugh me out of his office.

But I couldn't say that to Jacob. He was in a bad state, and the only remedy for that was hope.

An idea came to mind. Even if it didn't help with this vaguely remembered possible crime, it might be useful for identifying Kyle Parr's friends.

"Listen, Jacob. If there was something that might help refresh your memory, and maybe also help you, uh, manage stress right now, would you be interested?"

"Yeah, of course. Why wouldn't I?"

"Well, what I'm talking about is, uh, hypnotherapy. And some folks think that's a little weird—"

"Oh, no, that's cool. I did that once, in Germany, for my training. Because, you know, for competition, you got to be in the right mental state."

"Oh yeah? It work?"

"Pretty good, yeah. But can that actually make you remember things?"

"I don't know. I'll ask."

After that, I drove across town to help Noah and a friend of his carry a couch and a mattress into his new apartment. It was a cheap studio; he'd be living on his own. Without naming names, I'd told him what had happened to Jacob Drayton. That, plus the habit of discretion he'd decided he was going to need in his new line of work, had made him swear off roommates.

After finishing moving him in, we shared the pizza and beer that he'd provided as payment for our services, and I headed home. It was a quarter past nine when I left his place, and darkness was falling. I was looking forward to a shower and bed. I'd call Marianne in the morning and see if she could help with Jacob.

A few minutes after I'd crossed the river and gotten onto the road out of town, my phone lit up. It was Terri.

"I think I have your answer," she said. She sounded upset; she hadn't even said hello. "The reason Stickman kept that drug evidence in."

"What is it?"

"This wasn't in the news until yesterday, but the day before your hearing, his nephew overdosed."

"Oh, God. That poor family."

I had some sense of how they felt. I remembered sitting beside Noah's hospital bed last summer, not knowing if he'd ever wake up. And I remembered burying my wife.

"Yeah," she said. "He was sixteen. They're in hell on earth right now. And I wonder if that's why he didn't give you a decision at the hearing. It was fentanyl, not weed, obviously—the kid took one of those fake pills that look like prescription painkillers—but maybe he realized he wasn't in a good state of mind to decide anything in a drug case."

"That's awful. Yeah, I wouldn't be surprised if that's how he thought about it. He's a good judge, normally. Whenever I was before him back in the day, he always tried to do the right thing."

She sighed, part sympathy, part resignation. "I guess he didn't give himself enough time to think it through."

"Right. One week? That's not enough."

"I know. The poor kid's funeral hasn't even happened yet."

We talked for another few minutes and then signed off. I was heading southwest, and the lights of Charleston were a faint glow in my rearview mirror. Soon even that disappeared. The road was dark, with almost no traffic, and out my window was the starry sky. The words "kid's funeral" were still ringing in my head. Two words that should never be together.

The trees to my left hid the ocean, and they hid Kiawah Island too.

Playing golf there on a glorious spring day had shown me one side of that place. It was a wealthy suburb of Charleston with less than two

217

thousand residents. I pictured them strolling around in $500 shoes, enjoying the sunshine, the absence of folks who weren't like them, and the constant sound of waves.

But anywhere I'd ever gone, there was always an underbelly. Jacob had reminded me of that, with his confused flashes of a half-remembered crime that might've left a young woman dead.

Kiawah Island was beautiful, but I didn't think there was any place on earth—at least, no place that human beings had lived—that didn't have blood in the soil.

19

MAY 31, 2022

I was in my home office, drinking my third coffee of the morning, when Marianne called. I hoped she didn't need to change our plans. We'd arranged to meet at her house that night, with Jacob, to see if she could help him.

"Morning, Marianne."

"Leland," she said, "I am so sorry if this disrupts anything for you, but can you do me a favor?"

Something was wrong. Her voice had a strain in it that I hadn't heard before.

"Most likely. What's going on?"

"It's Bobby. I think he's kind of losing it—the news coverage last night really did a number on him—and with the visitation rules, there's only so much I can do."

Half an hour later I was walking through security at the jail. Visitation rules for lawyers were different. We had to call in advance, but as long as we did, and there wasn't a lockdown or a disturbance going on, we could have a half-hour visit with our clients any time from eight in the morning to nine at night.

When they brought Bobby to me in the meeting room, I could see Marianne was right. He was agitated and did not look well.

I stood up and shook his hand. "Hey there," I said. "I got some updates for you, and I wanted to hear your thoughts."

Marianne had asked me not to tell him she was worried about him. She'd explained that he took his cues from her, and knowing she was concerned would only make him more so.

We sat down. While I pulled some papers out of my briefcase, he drummed his fingers on the table for a second, put his hands in his lap, and then started picking at one of his fingernails.

I set the papers on the table and said, "I'm not going to ask if things are okay, since this is a jail, so I know they're not. But there's a lot I can help with, so if there's a problem, just let me know."

He started rubbing his wrist like it hurt and looked off past my shoulder. "It's not—it's not— There's a problem, but it's not the jail."

"Oh?"

"I done what you said. Be cool with the guards, take no shit from the other guys, and all that. And I was trained to get through being a POW if I had to. I can handle this, for a while anyway, although I'm not sure Marianne can."

"She's holding up, so far. But, yeah, it is hard on families."

That was obvious. "Sure," he said. "But the thing that's kind of sticking in my mind is... I don't know how things work in court. I know there's rules, but I got no idea what they are. And there's..."

He got up and started pacing around.

"Let me rewind a minute," he said. "Just so I'm clear. Is this— Are we going to trial for sure? Or is there any way to get the charges dismissed?"

"Dismissed? No. They've got what they need to proceed. At this point we're looking at either a November trial or some kind of a plea deal."

"You mean, plead *guilty*?" He looked incredulous. That apparently had not crossed his mind.

"Yeah, the kind of thing where you'd plead to some charge that's less than what they've got you in here for."

"But I'm *not* guilty." He spread his hands, palms facing me, like he had nothing to hide. "I didn't set that fire. I can't plead to what I didn't do."

"Yeah," I said. "I hear you."

"And November's close to half a year away. Now, I know there's men in here who…" He looked away again. After a second, he found the words: "There's men here who've got it way worse than me."

He let that drop and looked me in the eye. I didn't need more description. He wasn't in the overnight lockup with local boys picked up on DUIs anymore. Once he'd been bound over for trial, he went to a different wing, with a more dangerous population. We both knew what tortures he was talking about.

"And there's men," he added, "who don't have a woman to come visit them. A woman to go home to when they get out."

"You do have that."

"Yeah. But not if I lose."

I nodded. Losing at trial would most likely mean a sentence of thirty years to life. Marianne was a good woman, but I knew that, statistically, to have a spouse stick around after a sentence like that would be a miracle.

"I'm the type of guy," he said, "if something bad's coming up, I want to get it over with. Rip the Band-Aid off. So unless there's a reason we want to sit and wait, I'd like to know if there's some way to get this trial done faster."

He didn't understand that six months was already fast for a murder trial.

But to get the best out of him, to get the help from him that I needed to have a decent shot at winning, he had to be in as good a state of mind as possible. I had to give him at least a glimmer of hope.

And Ruiz was apparently prioritizing moving cases along.

"Well, the truth is, we've got a pretty good schedule already," I said, "but if you want, I can talk to Mr. Ruiz and see if he's amenable to fast-tracking this."

"I'd appreciate that."

"Bear in mind, though, that gives us less time to investigate and prepare."

"Oh. Yeah." He thought about that for a second. "Is the extra time going to make the difference?"

"It might. It might not. Speaking of things making the difference, though, my PI and I found out some interesting stuff. That's what I wanted to talk to you about."

He came back to the table, sat down and said, "Shoot."

"Okay, we're going to run short on time if we go through all the details"—I gestured to the pile of papers I'd set in front of me—"so I'll sum it up. There's three things. First off, my PI narrowed down who we think the solicitor's alleged eyewitness is—"

"Narrowed down? You mean they haven't told us who says they saw me there?" His tone was part shocked, part indignant.

"Yeah, that's—"

"How is that not my *right*? As an American, I don't get to know who's accusing me?"

"You do," I said, "but not yet. In a lot of states you would, but here—"

He was getting angrier, opening his mouth to interrupt.

"Now, hear me out, Bobby. You want to win a game, you got to know the rules."

He paused, then sat back. That was language he understood.

"The rule that matters here is Rule 5 of South Carolina's Rules of Criminal Procedure. So, first thing is, that rule says the solicitor doesn't have to give us the names of the witnesses they're going to call until ten days before trial. And—"

"Ten *days*? How in the hell are we supposed to prepare?"

"Yeah, it's hard, although I got us a little head start, on top of what Terri's doing. But anyway, that same rule says that if we ask for witness statements and so forth, the solicitor's office has got to provide them within thirty days. But there's two big problems. Or three, if you count the fact that half the time solicitors ignore that deadline and drag things out as long as possible. The first problem is a loophole you could drive a truck through: if you want the pretrial statement of a prosecution witness, they don't absolutely *have* to give it to you until after that witness has testified at trial."

"*After* they testify?" He looked confused. "What's the point in that?"

"Well, it's after they testify on direct, meaning right before I cross-examine them. I get to see their pretrial statement at that point, and I scan through it as fast as I can to see if it says anything different from what they said at trial. And if it does, then I get to point out that their story changed."

"That's it? You don't get to see it until a minute or two before you get up in court and do your thing? How is that fair?"

I shrugged. I didn't know what to tell him. I sometimes forgot that most folks assumed the system was at least set up to be fair.

He absorbed that. Then he asked, "What's the other problem?"

"Oh, it's not a problem in our case, because Ruiz is in charge. He's got the right policy: he sent me, or I mean he had Mrs. Barnes send me, the fire inspector's report and the autopsy report without my even asking. If we'd had to ask for them, that might've been an issue."

"How so?"

"Well, once a defendant asks the prosecutor for the evidence he's entitled to, that kind of opens the door. It puts what they call a reciprocal obligation on us, so Mrs. Barnes would have the right to ask us for the results of any tests we had done, and copies of evidence we're planning to use at trial."

He looked astounded. "You telling me the prosecutor can ask for—for —like, the recipe for our secret sauce, and we've got to turn it over?"

"Yep."

He shook his head angrily. "Dammit. This happens in *America*?"

"Yeah. So it basically becomes a strategy question: do they have something we need so bad that it's worth the risk of them taking a look under our hood?"

"Uh-huh." He was listening intently, and I could see he was getting it. "So are you saying we shouldn't ask for that witness statement now?"

"Exactly. If we can figure out who it is on our own, then we can look into their background—even talk with them, if they're willing. Which they sometimes are. If they're not, sometimes their friends are. I've generally found that more useful than getting a piece of paper with the written pretrial statement on it."

"Huh. Yeah, I guess I can see that."

"Terri put her ear to the ground, and it seems folks are saying the witness is some guy that lives in that duplex catty-corner across the street. Which, there's only three tenants, so…"

"Okay. I guess it's good she's running that down." He gave a discouraged sigh.

"Let me tell you about our head start, though," I said. "To get around that witness-statement problem as best we can, I had a conversation with Mrs. Barnes about what's called *Brady* materials. That means evidence in the prosecution's hands that tends to show you're innocent."

"You think she's got some?"

"Oh, she did. It's not a silver bullet by any means, I've got to be honest with you, but she turned over records of the investigation showing that their eyewitness didn't identify you right off the bat. He —he or she, I ought to say; they redacted the witness's name off the records—"

"Redacted?"

"Blacked it out. Anyway, the witness told investigators right after the fire that he'd seen a tall, slim man fleeing the scene—"

"Slim?" Bobby cracked a smile. He was about as wide as a full-sized vending machine. "See, that's it right there," he said. "I'm innocent."

We both laughed. Then it was back to business, since I only had half an hour with him.

"Anyway, it's a minor inconsistency, but I gave Mrs. Barnes a whole speech about *Brady*, and that's what she coughed up in response. So I requested a hearing—"

"Really? For what? You think you can get that witness thrown out?"

With Porcher as our judge, that was not going to happen, even though the rules allowed it. But I didn't want to depress Bobby by focusing on something we couldn't change.

"Well, it's not so much that," I said, "as an opportunity to kick the tires on their star witness. I'll get to meet him, or her, and basically cross-examine them—"

"Oh, before trial? So we'll find out who it is?"

"Yep. And it's way before trial. Porcher disappears every year for most of July and August—I heard he's got a cabin up in North Carolina, in the mountains someplace. So he wants to get as much as he can out of the way before then. He had an 8 a.m. slot next Friday."

Bobby's face had fallen. Something was wrong.

After a second, he shook his head. "So they took May from me already, and I have to sit here however much longer, but the damn judge gets to look forward to a summer in the mountains—"

He stopped speaking. From the look on his face, I thought I must be witnessing what Marianne had described: him spotting a sinkhole and holding still to make sure he didn't fall into it.

He sat back in his chair and said, in an upbeat tone, "So, a hearing real soon, that's good. Okay." He looked at the clock on the wall for a few seconds and then asked, "Was that it for the news?"

"Just one other thing." I tapped on the front page of the fire investigator's report. "If you're up for talking about the fire."

"I got to be, I guess."

"Okay. So, that expert I've been talking to up in Charleston pointed out a curious detail about Dixie. Now, we know this was an intentional arson, and she was alive when the fire started. But he pointed out that the way she was found was unusual, because it looks like she didn't make any attempt to escape."

"Oh," Bobby said. He looked sad all of a sudden. "How come? Didn't she have a chance?"

Another feather landed on the right side of my mental scale. I was already all but sure that Bobby had nothing to do with this, but that stab of grief in his eyes added weight to my sense of his innocence.

"What the expert suggested," I said, "is that she might not have been conscious. But there's nothing in the toxicology to indicate why. Blood alcohol level of zero, for instance."

His face changed as the realization hit him. "You're not saying— Are you trying to tell me… somebody knocked her out?"

I nodded.

"Knocked her out and then… Are you telling me she was *murdered?*"

"It's possible, and if she was, I think we might know why."

"Why? Why would *anybody*—"

He looked away suddenly and breathed like he was trying to get a hold of himself.

I gave him a second.

When he'd calmed down, he looked back at me and said, "You know what, forget it. There's no 'why' for that. There's no reason that counts. All that matters is who. Did you find him? Can we sic the cops on him and put him away?"

"That's what we're trying to do now."

"Can I help?"

"Maybe, yeah. Do you have any recollection of seeing anybody going up to visit her?"

"Anybody? You mean any man?"

"Most likely, yeah."

He looked up, shaking his head, like he was searching his memory and coming up dry. "I mean, there was her boyfriend, but I'm guessing you know about him already."

"Uh-huh. Asher? Young guy, twentysomething?"

"Yeah. Tall blond kid. I saw him sometimes, and some girl about her age, and her dad... I don't recall anybody else. I never saw her throw parties or anything."

"Really? Young girl like that, with a nice apartment?"

"No, not that I saw. Although remember, I was only ever there a couple times a week."

"What about Boseman? You ever see him visit her?"

A look of disgust flashed across his face. "Do you think—"

I shrugged. "He's a suspect. In my mind, anyway."

He stared at me, trying to make sense of that, and then said, "How come?"

I sketched out why: How he was a natural suspect, since he owned the building and had it insured. The oddness of that expensive remodel, and his defensive, almost malevolent reaction when I talked to him about it. My suspicion that he'd retaliated by talking the sellers of the house I'd wanted into not selling to me.

I was about to get into the revelation that Kaylee had said Dixie was pregnant, but before I could, Bobby said, "Hoo, boy," and leaned back in his chair. The agitation had gone out of him. He looked like he was grappling with heavy thoughts.

After a minute, he said, "I ought to tell you something. About Boseman. I don't know if this is connected at all, and I don't want it to come out, but you ought to know it, in case it helps."

I nodded. "Every little thread helps. You pull on it and see what unravels."

He sighed, then shook his head, discouraged, like everything had turned to dirt. "Even if I get off at trial," he said, "I'll probably go down for this. But okay: he and I had a deal."

"Oh?"

"Yeah. On paper, I signed leases with him saying I'd pay him six grand a month in rent. For each place."

"Is that high for a commercial place?"

"A little. Not crazy high. But that's not what I paid."

"Huh. How'd that work?"

"He gave me receipts saying I paid that much in cash, but I really only paid him $1,500 a month. It was his idea, but I liked it."

"Oh, because you could deduct that rent on your taxes?"

He nodded. "Seventy-two thousand a year, for each location. But I was really only paying eighteen."

Tax fraud. No wonder he didn't want that coming out.

"Well," I said, "I can point you to a tax guy if you want to see what you can do about that. But, uh, why'd he suggest that arrangement? What was the upside for him?"

"I guess… I don't honestly know. He said he wanted to give me a break because he wanted another restaurant tenant. I know I shouldn't have done it, but… back then, I just wanted to get my business up and running, and I figured the low rent and the extra write-off might make the difference between succeeding and going under, at least at first."

It was the wrong choice, but that wasn't my problem right now. I pondered what interest Boseman might've had in inducing his tenant to commit tax fraud. "He ever ask you to do any, uh… favors for him?"

"No."

That left only one answer—or at least, only one answer that immediately came to mind. "You ever heard of money laundering?"

"I've heard the words. Can't say I know what it is."

"Well, there's lots of ways to do it, but one of them is to create a paper trail that shows money coming in legally, to help explain how you came by a bunch of money that you actually made illegally. Folks do that to cover up all manner of things. Money from drug running, or human trafficking, or bribery…"

I stopped there. Boseman was, among other things, a public official. A public official whose decisions could make other people a lot of money—or keep them from making it. Exactly the kind of leverage a man needed, if he was inclined to demand bribes.

Bobby hadn't noticed my distraction. "Dammit!" he said. "He tricked me? And I played along?" Then the fire went out of him. "I guess that's the least of my worries. And I don't see what that has to do with

— I mean, Dixie was a young girl working in a hotel, not a business owner with deductions for rent and all that."

He tipped his head back and slapped a hand over his eyes, rubbing them like he was exhausted. When he was done with that, he slumped forward, shaking his head, looking at the floor. "I know how rich men are," he said. "I don't even want to think about what he wanted from her and how he got it. If we can take him down over the financial bullshit he was running on me, I'm glad to help—but I can't see how he could've been… money laundering, or whatever, with her."

A hard rap at the door made Bobby startle. The guard looked at me through the window, and his keys rattled in the lock. Our half hour was up.

After lunch, I drove in to the office for the Zoom call I'd set up with a forensic pathologist. My setup there had a more professional-looking background, and we wouldn't get interrupted by Squatter yapping for attention.

When the call ended, I leaned back in my chair, looked at the ceiling, and swore. Dixie's autopsy hadn't included a pregnancy test. That testing wasn't standard, and nothing in the circumstances of her death had suggested it might be necessary. The blood the coroner had collected from her body had all been used for toxicology, and the pathologist had just shot down the only other idea I'd had for getting proof she was pregnant. He'd explained that, once a woman's body is embalmed, the only way to prove pregnancy would be to locate a visible embryo in her womb. And from what Kaylee had said, Dixie wasn't far enough along for that.

I went out to the reception area and poured myself my fifth coffee of the day.

For the hell of it, since it was breezy and less hot than usual outside, I took my cup and walked around the parking area and down the path that led between palm trees to a bench that nobody but lizards ever sat on. Birds chittered somewhere overhead.

I wished I worked in a world like the one in crime shows on TV, where big-city pathology labs were striking black-and-white spaces full of the latest equipment and smart, engaged scientists with fancy degrees, a passion for their work, and limitless time to dedicate to my case. In that world, I could prove Dixie had been pregnant—and maybe even get a fetal-tissue DNA match to identify the father—all before we cut to the commercial break.

Unfortunately, I lived in the real world. And specifically, in Basking Rock, population eleven thousand. I was lucky a competent autopsy had been done at all.

20

MAY 31, 2022

It was going on 10 p.m. when I drove up the Carters' driveway and parked behind the house. Terri was beside me, and Jacob was in the back seat. We'd all come in my car and waited until after dark, to minimize the risk of being noticed. For the same reason, Marianne had left the back porch light off.

She let us in through the mudroom, and we followed her into the kitchen. The blinds were down, and the room was lit in what I thought of as restaurant lighting, with a pool of gold at the kitchen island where she was inviting us all to sit and warm shadows everywhere else.

After pouring us all glasses of water or sweet tea, she sat down and began.

"What I like to do before a session is kind of sketch out what the process is like and what you can expect." She was looking at Jacob with calm curiosity as she stirred her tea. "But I don't want to waste your time with things you know. Leland tells me you've done hypnotherapy before?"

Jacob nodded. "Yeah, uh, through my coach I was working with in Germany. He arranged it. But it was for, like, flow, you know? Peak performance. It didn't have anything to do with remembering stuff."

"That's so interesting." She put her elbows on the counter and leaned toward him. "This will probably feel very similar. Any hypnotherapist is going to take you to the same place, although we've all got different ways of getting there. What was that like for you, in Germany?"

"Well, he didn't do that thing from the movies, with the, like..." He mimed swinging a pocket watch.

She gave a low, relaxed chuckle. "Oh, I don't think anybody does that."

"They don't? Anyway, he sure didn't. He just, like, talked. I was surprised."

"And did you feel it worked well?"

"I mean..." He sat back, crossing his arms loosely and looking up at the ceiling like he was scanning his memories. He seemed completely at ease in Marianne's presence. I took that as a good sign. "Yeah," he said. "I mostly just remember being super relaxed. I don't know what he said. But it did help, because I was in, like, the exact right state of mind for my next... I don't know, two or three practice sessions? They went amazing."

Marianne nodded, smiling. I could tell it pleased her to hear him confirm that this strange art she'd dedicated years of her life to was real. "That's great," she said, stirring her tea again, her spoon tinkling against the glass. "Because there are some people—not many, but I've come across a few—who can't be hypnotized. It's just how their brains are wired. But clearly, you're not one of them."

"I guess not." His voice was slow. He was gazing at her glass of tea and looking very relaxed.

She kept stirring for a little bit, making a rhythmic tinkling sound. Then she said, "So... I'm thinking, why don't we step into the living room, there? I've got a chair ready for you, really comfy."

"Sure, sure."

She got up and went around the island to show him the way. Terri and I followed.

The living room was lit the same way: one lamp about the color of a candle flame, darkness everywhere else. Bobby's armchair was reclined, almost flat, and she had Jacob lie down in it.

Terri and I sat on the couch, and Terri took a silver microphone the size of my pinky finger out of her bag. She attached it to her smart-phone and set the apparatus on the coffee table.

I'd done some research and found, to my surprise, that across America, there was no blanket rule against allowing a person to testify to facts that they only remembered after being hypnotized. The Supreme Court of South Carolina itself had allowed such testimony in two cases. That didn't seem like much when you realized that hypnosis had been around for more than a hundred and fifty years, but two cases were a whole lot better than none.

The main thing courts wanted to see before allowing posthypnotic testimony was proof that the hypnotist hadn't coaxed the witness into believing something that wasn't true. For instance, if the hypnotist showed you a man's photograph while you were under and suggested he might be the perpetrator, and then later you picked that man out of a lineup, that would not fly. So I'd asked Terri to record tonight's session, in case Jacob provided useful information and we ended up needing to prove that Marianne hadn't planted it.

A few feet away, Marianne stood near the armchair, facing Jacob and talking to him in her low, warm voice, gently suggesting that he bring his attention to his feet. She told him to tense and relax them—I saw his toes point and then go slack—and she guided him through the same exercise for his calves, his thighs, and all the way up to his scalp.

Then she said, "So, here's what we'll do. Why don't you touch your shoulder, right here, like this."

She touched her own shoulder as she spoke, and he mirrored the gesture.

"Because what you want to do," she said, "is just… find yourself, right where you are. In this comfortable chair. And you can touch your jaw, and your ear"—she moved her hand to illustrate, and he did, too—"and your hair, and when your arm gets tired, you can put it down, right there, where the chair's so nice and soft. And then bring your other hand to your other shoulder, right there…"

She took him through the same sequence on that side. Somewhere under her smooth voice I noticed a faint sound, or thought I did—I had to listen closely to find it again: flowing water, as if a shallow creek were running over stones a hundred feet away. She'd put something on her sound system, I supposed, at a volume almost too quiet to hear.

"And whatever you feel is fine, it's fine," she murmured. "Some tense muscles, some slack ones, some knots, some weight. That's the body, your body, that's how things are. The chair is soft, it's fine, it's where you are."

She kept on reassuring him, and I leaned back against the sofa cushion. Her voice was musical, a rich sound, a cello. It made me think of the classical albums my late wife listened to.

Terri poked my arm, and I snapped out of it. I reached into my jacket for my notebook and pen.

Marianne was saying, "And you can just drift back, now, to January, when you were living in Kyle Parr's apartment. You can drift on back and see Kyle's friends, see who you remember. Their faces can come back to you. Their names can come back."

She went on in that vein, and Jacob murmured a few first names and what sounded like nicknames. I wrote them down. Marianne had explained that she was going to give him some prompts to refresh his memory, so that when he woke up perhaps more details would become clear, and it sounded like that's what she was doing.

Then she moved on.

"And you can go back further, now," she said, "to when you were in high school, that summer before your junior year, and you're safe, it's okay. You're back on Kiawah Island, and you're safe this time, and you don't need to do anything, you just need to let it go by and see it, watching it like a movie. And some of it will be clear, and some of it might not be—it is what it is, and that's okay. You remember some things, not everything. And that's fine. That's how it is."

I knew why she was saying that. She'd told me, when I asked her if she could help Jacob remember, that she couldn't make a memory clear if his perception had been blurred at the time. She wouldn't even try; in her view, therapists who did that ran a high risk of creating false memories.

"It's kind of like enhancing a photograph," she'd explained. "I don't mean what people refer to as a photographic memory—not at all. What I mean is that if you take a photo and I'm trying to make it clearer, I can only work with what was in the frame. I might be able to increase the resolution on that. I might even be able to help you remember what that thing was that's over in the corner and mostly outside the picture. But I can't bring back something that was never in the frame at all."

Jacob, in the armchair, murmured something I couldn't hear. His eyes were closed.

Marianne, her voice liquid and warm, asked, "Can you say that again?"

"Hot," he said. "It's hot."

"Oh, uh-huh, it's hot?"

She was speaking much slower than usual, in a tone that suggested any answer was fine with her: nothing mattered, she was talking and listening for the sheer pleasure of it, and time did not exist.

"It's summer," he said. "July Fourth weekend. The Fourth is tomorrow."

As I was scribbling that down, Marianne said, "And what do you feel?"

"The hot, bumpy... He's got these fake wicker chairs around the pool, the black plastic kind, so it was really hot when I sat down. I just got out of the pool, so it feels good. I could fall asleep here." He took a deep breath and relaxed even more, sinking another half inch or so into the overstuffed armchair.

"And is anyone there besides you and your friend?"

"No, ma'am—we've got the place to ourselves, and we are getting *wasted*. His dad's liquor cabinet doesn't even lock. And it is some primo stuff."

He went on about the quality of the alcohol, naming brands— Lagavulin single malt, Havana Club rum, Booker's bourbon—until Marianne gently redirected him. She asked him to describe the room the liquor cabinet was in and, "if you can see this," how it connected to the pool area. He described a hardwood floor stained nearly black, a set of folding patio doors leading outside, and a rock formation at the far end of the pool with a waterfall—an artificial one, I assumed—tumbling down from somewhere higher than his head.

The level of detail made my lawyerly brain light up. He was describing a very specific house, and if his memories of it turned out to be accurate, that would make whatever else he said more credible. That was the other thing courts liked to see: independent evidence that corroborated what the witness said under hypnosis. I glanced at the coffee table. A tiny amber light glowed near the base of the mic connected to Terri's phone. She saw me looking and gave a little nod: it was recording.

His friend, Jacob said, brought some weed out to the patio. They rolled joints and smoked them. He spent a while describing the pulsating geometries of the blue-and-silver pool tiles, which he said he'd slipped back into the water to stare at.

Then they heard a car door. His friend scrambled to gather all the paraphernalia and run it back to his bedroom. Jacob floated around the pool on his back, laughing at the sunshine, until a beautiful young woman walked out onto the patio. The two of them looked at each other, and then his friend came back and said, "Oh, hey, Melody."

I wrote her name down.

Marianne asked if the woman's last name had ever come up. It hadn't. All Jacob remembered was that she was "smokin' hot," and she looked about twenty-two, and she declined their offer of a drink. When she went back into the house, his friend told him she was his dad's girlfriend.

"My mom's out of town," the friend said. "So I guess he gets to play."

They kept drinking and smoked another two joints. As they got more and more wasted, Jacob's narrative fractured, like a jigsaw puzzle dropped on the floor. One piece showed a black sports car pulling up out front. Another piece was Melody crying, with black makeup

239

smeared around her eyes. A third one showed a glass shattering on the stone tile in the foyer, checkerboard tile as shiny as water.

He remembered someone—not his friend, the friend's dad—shouting at the girl for "pulling this shit," for "tricking" him, for being "a goddamn slut."

He saw the girl crying in a deck chair by the pool. It looked like her shirt was torn—a gaping gash at the top of one sleeve? Jacob wasn't sure.

He kept coming back to the glass shattering. There was glass everywhere, he said, all over the foyer, more than that one tumbler could explain. He heard the girl scream, high-pitched and frantic, just once. The black-and-white tiles had blood on them, but he didn't know why. His friend lurched into a nearby bathroom to vomit.

There was a long smear of blood across the tile, up to the door. His friend's dad was serving him another drink. There was blood on the doorknob. It was quiet—nobody was yelling anymore. The girl was gone, but her car, her little light-blue car, was still there. The trunk was open, and he thought he saw blonde hair inside.

He went to find his friend, to ask him what the hell was happening, but his friend was passed out on the bathroom floor. The room stank of vomit. There were orange streaks on the white toilet and on his friend's shirt.

He remembered waking with a headache like a jackhammer ramming the base of his skull. Later he woke again, with the headache dulled enough for him to look around. It was light out. It looked like he was in a guest room. He was clean, as if he'd showered, and wearing someone else's pajamas. He went downstairs, holding one hand to his head, trying to make it hurt less.

Everything was clean. No glass, no blood. No little blue car.

The checkerboard floor was as shiny as glass. Perfect black and white, nothing on it, not one stain.

He found his friend on a couch, moaning, also in pajamas, with an ice pack on his head.

He went into the kitchen and saw his clothes from the night before washed and folded on the counter. He put them on and called his older brother for a ride home.

Jacob stopped talking. As the silence settled in, I noticed the sound of running water again, the creek Marianne had put on the sound system.

"Is there anything else you want to say?" she asked him.

He shook his head. His eyes were still closed.

Marianne started murmuring to him. I heard her say "resurface" and "come back gently." After a minute or so, his eyes started blinking rapidly. He turned his head to the side, looking around. "How do you feel?" she asked.

"Okay, I guess." He sat halfway up and peered over the side of the recliner, trying to figure out how to work the chair. She pointed out the lever, and he brought it upright. He looked at Marianne and then at me and Terri, curious. "Did I say anything?" he asked. "You get anything useful?"

"It was real interesting," I told him. Then I glanced at Marianne. I wasn't sure if it was typical for him not to remember, and I didn't know what I ought to say or do.

She gave me a reassuring smile and said, "This is normal. Some people remember, some don't."

"Uh-huh." It felt a little like she was reading my mind, although I figured most folks watching somebody come out of a hypnotic trance would probably wonder the same things I was.

Jacob looked at her. "Oh, I said stuff?" He turned to me. "Really?"

I started to debrief him, but before I could get a full sentence out, he interrupted.

"Hey, can you… I really appreciate all this, so much," he said. "Especially if it'll help with my case, of course. But I don't think I want to hear this yet. I'm glad I told you stuff, but is there any way y'all could figure out if it made any sense before you tell me what it was?"

Marianne nodded in her calm, reassuring way. "I think that's *very* wise."

Terri was nodding too. "So, we'll research what you said and see if it matches up with any news stories, something like that."

"Yeah, please. Because I know the little bit I do recall, and I don't want a bunch more of that in my head. Not unless it's real and we need it."

"I can do that," Terri said.

Marianne added, "You know, Jacob, most people I've worked with, after a session like this, they notice their memories trickling back naturally over the course of the next few days, or weeks sometimes. Not necessarily everything, but a lot of it. So I don't want you to be surprised if that happens. But I agree, why dump it all on you at once? Let your brain handle it the way your brain wants to handle it."

"Yeah. That works for me." He looked over at me and said, "Don't give me any details, but do you think we got something?"

"Well, if it matches a, uh… a criminal case, and if it does come back to your memory like Mrs. Carter said it probably will, then yeah. I think we could have something Varner might be interested in."

His face fell. "That's all? He just… *might*?"

As a trial lawyer, I knew we had nothing yet. Even if what Jacob had described under hypnosis turned out to match a murder or missing person case, I couldn't put him on the stand unless he actually remembered it when he was awake. But as *his* lawyer, with his trial starting in less than a week, I realized—a little late—how much he needed a reason to have hope.

So I backpedaled.

"It was pretty dramatic, I'll tell you that," I said. "If I were Cody Varner, I'd much rather put the guy you were talking about behind bars than put you there."

Jacob's hangdog expression didn't change. He knew I was throwing him crumbs to make him feel better.

After driving Terri home and dropping Jacob off at his car, I went home and took a hot shower. Usually that helped me get ready to sleep, but I wasn't tired. Hearing Jacob tell that story and then seeing him sit up afterward with no memory of what he'd said did not make sense to me. I understood not remembering your dreams, or forgetting things that happened a while ago. What I could not wrap my mind around was being awake enough to hear questions and answer them, but then not recall a word of it a minute later.

In my pj's, I made myself a snack, then went into my home office and stared at the corkboard I'd made for Jacob's case. Photos of everybody who was involved, or names written on index cards for folks I didn't have pictures of. Different-colored strings running between them depending on how they connected with each other. Pictures and a satellite map of his building. A floor plan of the apartment.

Nothing lit up for me. No new insights came to mind. Unlike in some cases, questions about memory—how it worked, how accurate it was —weren't likely to come up in Jacob's trial. His memory only mattered for a possible plea deal, and there wouldn't be any such deal unless Terri found a case that matched the facts he'd claimed to recall tonight.

I turned and looked at the corkboard on the opposite wall. Bobby's case was different. There, I had a client who was supposedly zonked out on melatonin and sleeping pills when a fire was set across town; his wife, who swore he was in bed right next to her all night; and an alleged eyewitness—whose identity we still hadn't pinned down—claiming to have seen him outside the burning building at 3 a.m.

I was going to have to come up with a hell of a cross-examination outline for that eyewitness. I'd need to anticipate everything he might claim to have seen and every reason his memory might not be accurate. Had he been half-asleep? Drunk? On medication?

For now, I thought, I could at least go find out for myself what a man could see there in the middle of the night. It was past 1 a.m., which I figured was close enough.

I got dressed again and drove over. The streets were empty, no surprise on a weeknight.

I went around the block first, to get the lay of the land. Dixie's building had been nearly cleared away; the doorways I'd noticed before, looming out from piles of bricks, were gone. The streetlight beside the property was out, and the stop sign across the street was bent over like a car had hit it. This neighborhood was rough and not well maintained.

I wondered again why Boseman had installed a $50,000-plus kitchen in an apartment in this part of town. Buying a whole apartment for that price would've surprised me less.

I parked about half a block from the property. We knew the eyewitness was a neighbor, and if he was looking out a window now, I didn't want him spotting my car.

One small apartment building stood across the street from where Dixie had lived, and another—the one I was closest to—was catty-corner from it. That was where folks said the witness lived. I picked my way across its ratty side yard and stood with my back against the building, looking at the place where Bobbino's had stood.

I was about sixty feet from what had once been Bobbino's front door. I didn't see how you could recognize a man's face at that distance, at night, unless you had binoculars and a light source.

A nosy neighbor might have binoculars, but if the building was already in flames when this eyewitness looked out his window, the fire would've backlit whoever he saw, turning the arsonist into little more than a silhouette.

I was composing my cross-examination as I walked around the corner of the building.

As I kicked my way through the unkempt yard, my phone buzzed in my pocket. I pulled it out, hoping Terri was calling to let me know she'd found a murder case that matched Jacob's story. It wasn't her, though. It was a blocked number.

I answered anyway. I always answered; you never knew where good information might come from.

"Hey, Mr. Munroe," the caller said. "Dabney Barnes here. You got a minute to talk?"

It was nearly 2 a.m., and I'd never spoken to him in my life.

I put on my poker voice, a polite and slightly bored tone. "Sure. What's up?"

"Well, it's something I wanted to let you know confidentially. You see, I've been getting a lot of commentary from the public every time we report on that tragic arson case that you're involved in. And I thought you'd want to know that my readers are starting to wonder if you're making a simple case complicated just to rack up your bill—that's what some folks have said—or raise your profile."

"Uh-huh."

"And, in fairness, I thought I ought to give you a chance to respond."

In other words, he was about to publish another hit piece. The fact that he'd never given me "a chance to respond" before made me read this phone call as a warning: back off, or worse will come.

There was nothing to be gained by giving him a quote. He'd publish whatever he liked and twist anything I said to his benefit.

"I'm sorry," I said. "You're cutting out."

He started talking again, so I spoke over him: "What? Sorry, I can barely hear you."

Then I hung up.

As I walked back to my car, it occurred to me that calling at 2 a.m. meant he knew I was awake. Otherwise, he'd at least have pretended to apologize for the late hour.

I looked around. Nobody else was on the street, and the windows of the apartment buildings were dark.

But somebody was watching me.

21

JUNE 6, 2022

On the morning of Jacob's first day of trial, Terri and I dragged our rolling briefcases past the palm trees lining Charleston's Broad Street, heading for the Judicial Center, where the eleven courtrooms of the Court of General Sessions were located. It was a bright blue, cloudless day, still only in the seventies at nearly 8 a.m., but the sweat on my neck told me the humidity was going to get a lot worse.

That wasn't the only thing that might get worse. The trial had been assigned to Stickman, the judge who had denied my motion to throw out any of the State's evidence in our case. His newly acquired harsh views on drugs could be a big problem for Jacob.

My plan for countering that was to demonize Kyle Parr. Stickman needed a drug dealer to hate, and I was going to give him one.

As we reached the white stone columns that framed the entrance of the Judicial Center, Jacob stepped out of an illegally parked Mercedes and said hello. His father, at the wheel, pulled back out into traffic.

"He's coming, this time," Jacob told us. "He told me to text him at the end of, uh, voir dire?"

"That'll be maybe eleven, close to lunchtime," I said. I held the door open so he and Terri could get in the security line. "It takes a little while to pick a jury."

"Oh. Yeah."

The kid looked nervous as hell. A courthouse could have that effect. It reminded defendants that the system was much bigger and more powerful than they were.

To calm him down, I said, "Just to remind you, we've got a plan B. I've had a ton of cases get resolved on the first day of trial. It's a good time for a plea."

He started to ask a question, but I said, "Let's wait until we're up in our war room."

He nodded. He knew from his earlier hearings that we would have a small conference room to ourselves not far from the courtroom door.

He took out his phone, and I could see he was texting his dad. He stumbled through about five different drafts of a short message telling him what time voir dire was likely to end.

I found myself wondering whether his dad's presence would make him more nervous than he would be without him. I was going to need to figure that out. Jurors liked to see a defendant's parents, but I was planning to put Jacob on the stand, and a defendant in a good frame of mind was far more important than a supportive-looking parent in the gallery.

We took the elevator to the third floor. I peeked into our courtroom—only the deputy was there—and then got us settled in the conference room.

Sitting beside Jacob at the table, I said, "So, this is what Terri put together." I turned my laptop toward him. "She got the names of the jury pool from the court clerk last week. We don't know who in the pool got called for today, so she went digging for info on everybody on the list."

"Whoa." He scrolled through the fifty-odd pages of names and charts. For most of the jurors, she'd found photos and enough data to come up with probable religious and political affiliations.

"Some of them I couldn't find any type of social media on," she said. "But I did what I could."

"Oh, dang," he said, reading a Facebook comment from the profile of one sweet-looking, motherly lady in her forties. Under an article discussing the possible legalization of medical marijuana in our state, she'd written, "Anybody who supports this, you can unfriend me right now as you are not right with the Lord! This gateway drug nearly cost me my son's life!"

"Yeah, if she's picked," I said, "she'll be getting a peremptory."

"A what?"

"That's what we call it when we nix a juror without having to explain why."

Terri's psyops mission was particularly necessary because South Carolina was one of only five states that did not let attorneys handle the voir dire. Instead of questioning potential jurors ourselves, responding to their cues and letting the conversation go where it needed to, we had to provide a short list of written questions for the judge to ask.

Terri's other mission over the past week had also been successful. She'd found an unsolved murder that fit what Jacob had described under hypnosis. Marianne had advised me not to spring it on him—she'd said I should wait until he asked me, or ideally until he started remembering on his own. I didn't know the psychology behind that, but it fit with my need not to taint the evidence by suggesting things to him.

However, I was going to need to give his memory a kick under the table if he didn't start talking to me about it soon. I expected more plea talks with Varner today, over lunch or during a break, and I needed all the bait I could get to pull him into a deal that would be acceptable to Jacob.

We got a decent jury more quickly than usual. Jacob frantically texted both his parents during the midmorning recess, letting them know that Varner's opening statement would start at eleven thirty. I wasn't happy about that timing; if we broke for lunch right after that, Varner's story would be percolating in the jurors' minds for a good hour before they heard what I had to say.

Jacob's parents arrived separately, but they made it in time to hear Varner's compelling opening statement.

"We're here today in a modern courtroom," Varner said, gesturing around, "but the story you're about to hear is very old. You've probably read it in Proverbs, which tells us two things. First, that pride goeth before a fall. And second, that the greedy bring ruin to their households." He turned to look at Jacob with profound disappointment. All the jurors turned too.

"The defendant here," Varner continued, "was a champion athlete. Olympic level. World-class. He's a competitive sharpshooter who's won prizes galore."

I wasn't surprised that he'd brought that up. It had annoyed him to see me deploy those facts during the preliminary hearing, and he was doing his best to neutralize them for the jury before I had a chance to speak.

"But that wasn't enough for him," Varner said. "Just like having the support and love of two good parents wasn't enough." He gestured to Jacob's parents.

As he spoke, I jotted a few things down—points he'd made that I was going to have to tweak my own opening for. I wasn't going to argue against anything he said; I didn't want to repeat it and get it stuck in the jurors' minds. The tweaks were more like shifting the song that I'd been planning to play into a different key, to bring the jury back out of the mood he was putting them in.

"Ladies and gentlemen of the jury," he said, "would it surprise you to know that when the Charleston police executed a warrant on the defendant's apartment, they found $40,000 worth of marijuana in his room? Ten pounds and four ounces of marijuana, carefully measured into one-ounce packages, ready to sell on the street."

He looked at Jacob again, shaking his head in dismay, and repeated, "Ready to sell on the street." Then he looked at the floor, as if seeing such potential turn bad was just too much for him.

"His roommate was also arrested on marijuana charges," he continued. "As the old saying goes, birds of a feather flock together."

He was doing what he could to throw a wrench into my story. If the jury thought of both men as dealers, they'd be less likely to believe that Parr had made Jacob take the fall for his own crimes.

Varner concluded by telling the jury that, under South Carolina law, having that amount of marijuana was a felony. And, he explained, "You have not been called here today by the State of South Carolina to set yourselves above the defendant or tell the world he's a terrible person. That is not what a guilty verdict means. You have simply been called to hear the facts and determine whether the evidence shows, beyond a reasonable doubt, that the law was broken."

I liked that he'd put it that way. It would've put a spring in my step if not for my awareness that jurors didn't want to see defense counsel looking perky. Everything about the courtroom—the wood paneling, the high windows, the judge up on his bench—told them that the law was serious, almost holy. They had to see me respecting that if I wanted them to respect me.

As Varner gathered his papers from the lectern, I glanced up at Judge Stickman. He was looking at the clock. It was ten minutes before noon. Stickman, I remembered, didn't like to take a late lunch.

As he started turning toward the jury box, I picked up my own papers and said, "Uh, Your Honor, if I may?"

He cocked his head. "How long do you expect your opening to be, counsel?"

"I can have us out of here by five past noon, Your Honor."

He nodded, and I let out the barest hint of a sigh. I stood.

I thanked the jury for their service. I told them that impartial juries drawn from the community were the foundation of the American justice system.

Then I said, "Mr. Varner said something a minute ago that I think points out the problem here. He said that your duty, as Americans called here to find out the truth, is to determine beyond a reasonable doubt whether the evidence shows that the law was broken. But that's actually not the question in this case. I'll tell you myself that the law was broken."

I looked into the eyes of the juror at the front left, and then the woman next to him, and down the line. I told them, "The law was broken, for sure, because marijuana was found in the apartment at 624 Bouquet Street. Not ten pounds of it, but a significant amount. And that's a crime here in South Carolina. So you haven't been called here to decide whether the law was broken. It was."

I let that sink in. Then I said, "What you're here to do is listen to all the evidence and then decide who committed that crime. Who had the motive? Who had the opportunity? Who does the evidence point to?" After a second, I added, "Because I can tell you one thing: It does not point to Mr. Drayton."

I stepped out from behind the defense table and started pacing thoughtfully before the jury box.

"Here's the thing," I said. "The evidence in this case will show that Mr. Drayton wasn't on the lease for the apartment at 624 Bouquet Street. He didn't have his own apartment—matter of fact, he didn't have but one suitcase to his name—because he'd spent the whole fall semester in Germany, training with a world-renowned sharpshooting coach."

I looked at Jacob, to get the jury to look at him.

"This young man," I said, "has dedicated himself to the shooting sports since he was ten years old. At the ISSF Junior World Championships, when he was seventeen, he won a bronze medal for the United States of America. Apart from going to school, training and competing is all he does."

I turned back to the jury. "But let me get back to my point. After that semester in Germany, Mr. Drayton came home to the Lowcountry to celebrate Christmas with his parents"—I gestured to them—"and then he scrambled to find himself a furnished room in Charleston before the spring semester at Charleston College began. The room he found was in the apartment of a Mr. Kyle Parr, who'd lived there on Bouquet Street for a year and a half. It was Kyle Parr's apartment. That's fact number one." I held up my index finger to count: one.

"As Mr. Varner told you, Kyle Parr was arrested for marijuana possession the same day Mr. Drayton was. But what Mr. Varner didn't mention is that, unlike Mr. Drayton, that wasn't Mr. Parr's first drug arrest. He had a history of them. Mr. Parr, whose apartment was where the drugs in this case were found, had a criminal record of multiple offenses of marijuana possession. Unlike Mr. Drayton, who had no record at all. That's fact number two." I held up two fingers.

"And finally," I said, "there's fact number three. When the police arrived outside the apartment building in three clearly marked police cars, Mr. Parr was the only person home. When the police officers banged on the door, calling out that they had a warrant, he didn't answer. He left them out there for a whole minute, if not more. And while they stood out there waiting, he was in the apartment doing... Well, I leave it to you, ladies and gentlemen, to think about what a man who's got multiple citations and convictions for marijuana would spend his time doing if he knew law enforcement was about to enter his apartment."

We were eating a sandwich lunch in our war room when a knock came at the door. It was Varner. I stepped outside.

"I'm just checking in," he said, "on whether your client is prepared to offer any information about Mr. Parr's guests and connections."

"Uh-huh. Well, thanks for sending over those mug shots. Why don't we talk inside."

I opened the door, leaned back in, and asked if Terri and Jacob's parents would mind vacating for a moment so we could speak with the solicitor.

His father, looking mildly outraged, said, "With all due respect, Mr. Munroe, I think my input is important here."

"I appreciate that, Mr. Drayton, and we're absolutely not going to be entering into any kind of a deal without running it by you. But we do need to have this initial conversation confidentially."

That got him to move. When they were gone, Varner and I sat down. After the minimum amount of chitchat that Southern politeness required, I got to the point. "So, thanks again for those mug shots, which my client reviewed the other night. He was able to identify three of the individuals."

I looked at Jacob.

"Okay, um, yeah," he said. "So, the dude with the long, curly hair was Big Mike, and the blond guy was called Tyler. And then the one with the short, dark hair was Erik, with a K, he said. He's Kyle's brother. They all came over and vaped a few times."

"And what substance did they vape?"

"Well, they called it bud, so I assume weed—sorry, I mean marijuana."

"And did you see anything else suspicious?"

"Yeah, Big Mike once took this, like, wad of cash out from his jacket and put it on the table. And Kyle took, like, half of it and started counting it."

"Okay. And where were you at that point?"

"Getting a beer from the fridge. And then I went into my room. I just — Those guys, Big Mike especially, they kind of gave me the creeps. I stayed away from them."

"You stayed away from them." Varner was using his faintly incredulous cross-examination voice. I could tell he still didn't believe Jacob hadn't been involved in the dealing.

"Hell, yes, I did."

"Okay, so, let's think about this," I said. I needed to shut down Varner's questioning. He hadn't offered anything yet. "As I told you, Cody, my client had concerns about what Parr was doing, and he stayed out of it. He's essentially a witness to a handful of things who happened to spend about a month living in the same apartment with Parr. So my question is, what are you prepared to offer?"

"For that?" His tone was dismissive. "For that, I'm prepared to say that if your client will plead to misdemeanor possession, I'll recommend that he serve six months in the county jail and pay a $2,000 fine."

His offer didn't surprise me. I knew the MO. When I was in his shoes, I'd done it myself: play hardball until the last minute, and then suddenly get reasonable when both sides can feel the jury breathing down their necks.

And it was what I'd asked him for... before I found out that even a misdemeanor would keep Jacob out of the next Olympics.

Of course, there'd be more Olympics after that. To some folks it still might make sense to take that deal, in order to avoid a felony conviction that would keep him out of the shooting sports forever.

But I could tell Jacob didn't feel that way. He looked crushed.

"So, for now, that's what you're offering?" I asked Varner.

"For what you've provided, yes." His tone said that what we'd provided had about the same worth to him as a piece of chewing gum on the bottom of his shoe. I could tell he was a little annoyed that we hadn't jumped at his offer.

The clock on the wall said it was five minutes to one. We didn't have time to get into the other case.

"Well," I said, "my client does have some more information that I think you'd be interested in, although it's not about Mr. Parr and his compadres. Maybe we can discuss that after proceedings close today."

Varner stood up. "Yeah, maybe we can. See you in the courtroom."

About two seconds after he left, Jacob's father came back in, with Mrs. Drayton following behind, and demanded to know what was on the table.

"He's offered to take it down from a felony carrying a minimum of a year in state prison, and quite possibly a good deal longer, to a misdemeanor with six months in the county jail," I told him. "That is a significant move."

"God*dammit.*" Mr. Drayton turned on Jacob. "Boy, if you had listened to me and gone with the attorney I told you to, this would be over, and you'd be moving right the hell on with your life."

"Oz, please." Jacob's mom touched her husband's arm.

"What, Candace? He's man enough to choose his own damn attorney but not man enough to hear what I have to say?" He went back to berating Jacob. "You're grown enough to get yourself charged with a damn felony! One that carries a five-year sentence—and now you got yourself a judge who lost his, what was it, nephew, to drugs? It's too late for me to do what I could've done, so what do you think is going to happen here now?"

"I didn't *do* this," Jacob said. "I'm not guilty of any of this."

"Of course you didn't, honey," his mom said. "I believe you."

"You can believe all you want," his dad said. "You can tell that to the judge, and you know what he'll say? Everybody says they're innocent. He's heard that every day of his career."

I had to try to redirect this. "We've got about three minutes before we've got to be back in the courtroom, so if we could—"

"If we could what? Just walk my boy right down that plank?" Mr. Drayton turned back to Jacob and said, "It's a damn shame you didn't let me handle this, but if the best this lawyer of yours can do is get it down to a misdemeanor and six months, that's a damn sight better than where you started. You've got to take it. Get this over with."

Mrs. Drayton stifled a sob.

Jacob stared at his father like he was seeing him, or some part of him, for the first time. "You're telling me to go to jail for something I didn't do? And to throw away my career—because I checked, okay, and every country that hosts the Olympics has rules about athletes with criminal convictions, even misdemeanors. Rules that keep them out—"

"Oh, get off your high horse. This is why you're not cut out for business. No businessman would risk five years in the state penitentiary just to follow some pipe dream."

"High horse? Did you say my high horse? This sport is my *only* horse." Jacob turned to me. "They—the jury, I mean—can't convict me of a misdemeanor, right? Because that's not what I'm charged with. This trial, you said it's the ten-pound, four-ounce felony or nothing, right?"

As I nodded, Mrs. Drayton rushed out of the room. I guessed she didn't want to break down in front of her son.

"Okay, then," Jacob said. "Dad, Mr. Munroe's won a lot of trials before. I think he can win this one too."

"Dammit, boy! What the hell am I supposed to tell your mother?"

"Tell her you wanted me to hold my hands out for the cuffs and walk myself to jail. And tell her I said no."

22

JUNE 6, 2022

B ack in the courtroom, I expected Varner to kick off his case the normal way: by calling the lead detective to the stand. I'd pretty much slaughtered Detective Milton at the preliminary hearing, and I was looking forward to doing it again. But Varner stood up and told the judge that Milton had taken ill that morning. Instead, Varner proposed to call his second-in-command.

Stickman held a sidebar to discuss the issue. His clerk turned on a white noise machine so the jury couldn't hear what we were saying. Every sidebar got that same treatment, whether the parties were discussing a minor administrative matter or arguing about controversial evidence.

I wasn't about to cast any aspersions—like most judges, Stickman didn't care for lawyers who accused each other of nefarious behavior without good reason—but Milton's illness seemed very convenient. If he had gotten on the stand and said anything that deviated from what he'd testified to at the preliminary hearing, I could've used that past testimony against him, showing the jury that he was contradicting himself. I had a transcript of his testimony in my binder for that purpose, with the potentially useful parts highlighted.

But if someone else was on the stand in his place, I couldn't do that.

I doubted that Varner was lying to the judge. We might not be friendly anymore, but I still respected his ethics, even if he didn't feel the same way about me. Milton had probably called him that morning and claimed to be ill, to avoid a repeat of his drubbing at the prior hearing and to deprive me of one of my weapons.

In any case, there was nothing I could do about it. We went back to our tables, and the proceeding began.

Detective Hoffenmeier was tall, square-jawed, and blond. He was in uniform, and when he got to the stand, he sat with military posture. Nearly all the jurors were looking at him respectfully; I could tell from their faces that he had a head start. The exception was an older Black guy in the back row, who'd crossed his arms over his chest.

After the officer was sworn in, Varner said, "Detective Hoffenmeier, could you state for the jury the nature of your employment?"

"Yes, sir. I've been a police officer for sixteen years now with the City of Charleston Police Department. For the past nine years, I've been a detective in the narcotics/vice unit. And if you prefer, sir, you can call me Hof, like my fellow officers do. I know my name is kind of a mouthful."

Varner and several jurors chuckled. "I appreciate that, Detective," Varner said.

For the rest of his direct, Varner just called him "Detective." He knew as well as I did that although the nickname humanized the officer, making the jury warm to him, the job title was what made them respect what he had to say.

Hoffenmeier testified to the same things Milton had: the time and place of the search, the fact that procedures were followed, the locations where drugs and paraphernalia were found. He hit every point that Varner needed him to hit, and Varner used him to preempt the points he knew I was going to make.

"So, Detective, when you searched the defendant's bedroom, was he present?"

"He was not, no."

"And is there anything unusual about that?"

"Not at all, sir. When we execute a search warrant on a household or any other multitenant dwelling, very often one or more of the residents aren't there. Most folks don't spend their whole lives at home, and criminals are no different from law-abiding people in that regard."

Jacob stirred in his seat—I could tell that remark bothered him. I wrote "*CALM*" on my legal pad and tapped it so he'd look.

"And when a judge issues you a warrant to search a residence," Varner said, "what happens if you find illegal drugs, but the tenant or property owner isn't home?"

"We arrest them later, when they get home or we track them down."

"And is that what happened here?"

"Yes, it is."

"Now, when you executed the warrant in this case, on the apartment at 624 Bouquet Street, was anybody home?"

"Yes, sir. A Mr. Kyle Parr was there, who I understood to be the defendant's housemate."

"And what do you mean by housemate?"

"When I use that term, it's to indicate that they both lived there, but they each had their own bedroom. As opposed to roommates."

"Okay. And has there ever been a case in your sixteen-year career where you found contraband in one person's room, but he wasn't home, so you concluded the contraband must belong to his housemate?"

Hoffenmeier laughed. "No, sir, there hasn't. That's not the law."

Even the Black guy in the back row laughed at that one.

"No, it isn't," Varner said. "Now, if I can just jump ahead for a moment, I'm going to put an exhibit up—SC04?"

His paralegal hit a button, and a photo of the box of drugs on Jacob's desk appeared on the screen on the courtroom wall.

"Detective, do you recognize this photo?"

"Yes. Matter of fact, I took it. That there is the cardboard box of more than ten pounds of marijuana that we found in the defendant's bedroom, sitting on his desk."

"Objection, Your Honor," I said. "Facts not in evidence and lack of personal knowledge."

Stickman rotated in his chair to look at me. "How so?"

"Detective Hoffenmeier didn't weigh the box or its contents."

"Uh-huh. Granted."

Varner moved on. "Your Honor, the State moves to admit exhibit SC04."

"Granted."

Varner said, "Now, Detective, you've just testified that you found this box of marijuana in the defendant's bedroom. When you arrived at the apartment to execute the search warrant, was his bedroom door open?"

"No, it was not. It was closed and locked. We actually had to knock it down."

"I take it no key was available?"

"No. We didn't find one in our search, and the housemate, Mr. Parr, didn't provide one."

"Uh-huh. Did Mr. Parr direct your officers to search the defendant's room?"

"He did not, no."

"Did Mr. Parr facilitate your search of the defendant's room in any way?"

"No. By that point we were very nearly at the end of our search, and we'd already found a marijuana cigarette in Mr. Parr's bedroom, so he was handcuffed."

"And had Mr. Parr at any point expressed any animosity toward the defendant?"

"No, he had not."

"Had Mr. Parr even mentioned the defendant at all?"

"No. We only knew there were two men living there because the warrant informant had so stated. Mr. Parr himself hardly spoke during our search."

"So are you saying Mr. Parr let a team of police officers search practically the entire apartment and never said one word about the defendant, much less pointed them toward the defendant's room?"

"Yes, I am. That's what he did."

Varner was doing a good job of killing my argument before I could even make it. He'd already put several nails in my coffin, and he proceeded to hammer in a few more.

"Detective, did you ever consider that the box of marijuana might belong to Mr. Parr?"

"Yes, of course. That's a hypothesis we have to take into account. We don't want to arrest the wrong guy."

"Of course not. And how did you go about doing that?"

"I dusted it for prints myself at the scene, so that we could determine, essentially, whose box it was."

"And what did you find?"

"No prints, unfortunately."

"That is unfortunate," Varner agreed. "All right, then, without prints, was there any way you could figure this out?"

"Well, for instance, if we'd found rubber gloves at the scene, I might've wondered if they'd been used to transport the box. Because that could explain the lack of fingerprints."

"Did you find any such gloves?"

"No, we didn't. Not a box of them, not a pair lying around, not even dishwashing gloves under the sink."

"And did that lead you to conclude anything?"

"Yes, sir. It made it appear much less likely that the housemate, which is to say Mr. Parr, had moved the box. If he had hastily relocated it when we arrived, for instance, I would've expected to find either his fingerprints on it or a pair of gloves."

"And you didn't find either of those things?"

"No, we did not."

"You did not. Thank you."

Varner knew as well as I did that putting literally anything between Parr's hands and the box—a towel, a T-shirt, whatever was lying around—would've kept prints from being left on the surface. Their absence meant nothing.

He was looking at the lectern, shuffling through his notes. Stickman spoke up.

"Mr. Varner, is this a good time for a break, or are you about to wrap things up with this witness?"

"A break might be a good idea, Your Honor. I've got quite a few more exhibits I'd like Detective Hoffenmeier to speak on."

In the war room, Jacob asked me, "What the hell is going on?"

I asked his parents if they would mind stepping outside while we talked. They went. Terri stayed.

"I did not freaking *do* this," Jacob said. "He *knows* Kyle is a dealer. Why's he trying to— I feel like he's boxing us in! Like, we had a way out, and he's closing it!"

"What I think," I said, "is that Varner believes you know more than you do. He thinks you're holding something back, and he's trying to paint you into a corner so you spill the beans."

"But I don't! I'm not— The only thing I haven't told him at this point is that stuff from that other—from what happened on Kiawah Island!"

"Right. And have you remembered that better?"

"Yeah, I mean, I'm having thoughts. I'm—it's like I'm remembering a dream. But I still don't know if any of it is real."

"It is," Terri said. "I found the case you were talking about. Everything you said with Marianne that night matches up."

Jacob went silent for a long moment. He looked stunned, and then horrified. "Oh, God," he finally said. "Are you telling me that girl really was killed?"

Terri nodded. "A young woman from Charleston," she said, "called Melody Walters went missing over the July Fourth weekend in 2016. Her body washed up on Folly Beach a week later. The case is still unsolved."

Folly Beach was a few miles northeast of Kiawah Island.

"Oh my God. It happened, and I was there? And I didn't help her?" Jacob leaned forward in his chair until his head was on the table.

I let him be. We only had ten minutes left in the break, but I didn't want to rush this. It was a hell of a burden for him to bear.

After a minute, he sat up. "Okay," he said. "I've got to tell him this. Mr. Varner, I mean."

"Well, why don't you tell me first. Then we'll figure out how to approach him."

"Okay. Okay, that's a good idea. So, first off, Luke didn't do anything, not that I remember. My friend, I mean. It was his dad."

"And do you know his dad's name?"

"Mr. Manigault. That's what I called him. But I think I heard the girl call him Hank?"

He kept talking, but I didn't hear anything else. A bomb had gone off in my brain.

"You know what, I am so sorry," I said. "I don't feel well all of a sudden. Why don't you tell Terri the rest, and I'll step outside for just a minute."

"Are you okay?" Terri asked. I saw real concern on her face. She knew I wouldn't get up and leave at a time like this unless it was an emergency.

"I'll be fine. I just need to get some air."

I went out, shut the door, and dialed Roy's cell phone while walking toward the men's room. I hoped it was empty.

He answered just as I got there.

"Hey, Roy. How you doing?" I pushed the door open.

"Oh, fine. Aren't you in trial right now?"

"Yeah, we're on break. I just had a quick question."

"Okay, shoot."

A man in a suit was washing his hands at the sink, and I could see feet under one of the stall doors. I could not speak freely.

"You know your friend we went golfing with in, what was that, April?"

"Hank Manigault?"

"Yeah, yeah. Tell me, is he an active client of the firm right now?"

"He sure is. On top of the other stuff I was dealing with, he went and got himself sued over a slip-and-fall. Some woman was texting while she shopped and walked right past one of those Wet Floor signs. Broke her damn kneecap. Why?"

"Uh, let's talk later. But, man, how annoying. Best of luck with that."

"Thanks. And you can call tonight if you need to. I know you're in court all day."

"Okay. I'll try not to call too late. Oh, about your friend, he ever have a place on Kiawah Island?"

"Oh, yeah. Beautiful home. He sold it, I want to say, four or five years ago."

"Right. Thanks. I'll talk to you later."

We got off the phone, and I went back to the war room.

"My goodness, Leland," Terri said. "You look like you've seen a ghost."

I sat down and said, "Okay, here's the thing. Jacob, I am so sorry, but I'm going to have to refer you to another lawyer."

"*What?*" He looked utterly confused. I couldn't blame him.

"Hank Manigault is a client of my firm. You just told me he killed that girl, and you've got to share that information with the solicitor in order to get yourself a plea deal here. Under the rules—this is not my choice, believe me, but there's rules for what lawyers can and cannot do, and I cannot represent you in something that's likely to get one of my firm's clients charged with homicide."

"But—" He shook his head. "Okay, you're saying you can't represent both of us?"

"Right."

"So why not ditch him? He's not in trial right now!" Panic was rising in his voice. He all but howled, "He doesn't *need* you!"

I'd never seen him in such a bad state. I understood—he was staring down the barrel of a prison sentence and the end of the life he knew.

He'd chosen me to represent him, trusted me, and now I was walking away.

To try to talk him off the ledge, I looked him in the eye, my voice as calm as I could make it. "Listen, Jacob, here's how it works. It actually buys you some time. At least a few days, maybe a week. When we go back in there, I'll ask Stickman to let me withdraw and to grant a continuance so you've got time to find a new lawyer—"

"I don't *want* a new lawyer!" His desperation cut me to my core. I could tell he felt like I was ripping the last shred of hope out of his hands.

"Jacob, I understand, and I'm sorry. I'm *so* sorry. But I am not allowed to do this. There's no way around it. Those are the rules."

He stared at me with a look of absolute betrayal, and then he busted out in sobs.

23

JUNE 7, 2022

We got the continuance. I called a couple of great lawyers for Jacob myself, right away. But it wasn't enough. A little while after they got home from the courthouse, Jacob's mother heard a noise, ran to his room, and found him hanging in his closet. She held him up, screaming for his father, and they got him down before he died.

He was still in the hospital. I parked across the street and headed in to visit him.

It was a blazing hot day, and I was glad to get through the revolving doors and into the air-conditioning. I blinked, letting my eyes adjust to the indoor lighting. It took a minute, because I was exhausted. I hadn't slept in more than twenty-four hours. I'd been on my way to bed the previous evening when Terri called to tell me what Jacob had done. She'd heard it from a friend at the hospital.

I went to bed after that, but it was pointless. I was still awake when the sun came up.

I knew the county hospital too well. I'd visited clients there, and I'd spent agonizing hours beside Noah's bed in the ICU. If I'd had Jacob's room number, I could've gone straight there.

But I didn't, so I went to the reception desk to ask. The friendly chitchat from the lady there and the sight of her fingernails flying across her computer keyboard—each nail a different color, with fake gemstones glued on—cheered me up a little bit.

Then her fingers froze in midair, and she looked up at me, biting her lip. "Um, Mr. Munroe, I am so sorry, but… it says here on my screen that the family has specifically asked that you not be allowed to come up."

"Oh." I blinked. "Okay. I see."

"I really do apologize."

"Not your fault. Not at all."

I wished her a good day and went back to my car.

I didn't blame the Draytons for keeping me out. In their shoes, I probably would've done the same.

I sat in the driver's seat for a minute, wondering where the hell to go. I didn't want to stare at the four walls of my empty house, wondering what I could've done to prevent Jacob's suicide attempt. I also didn't want to get into any conversations.

I needed someplace with people around who would leave me alone.

It was close enough to lunch. I started the car and headed to the Shrimp City Diner.

As I walked toward the diner, I thought the couple sitting by the front window were looking at me. They turned away real quick.

Inside, it was crowded, as usual. Not the lunch rush yet—there were still plenty of seats—but getting there. I took a table and signaled a waitress for coffee.

Out of the corner of my eye, I saw somebody staring at me from a booth along the wall. I looked over, and he looked away. It was a bailiff from the courthouse across the street.

When the waitress brought my coffee, I asked for a ham and cheese sandwich with fries.

I noticed Ruiz coming in the door and raised a hand to say hello. It had been a couple months since we'd hung out, and the sight of him made me realize a lunchtime chat might be a nice distraction after all.

He stopped, gave me a micro-nod to acknowledge the greeting, and then backed out onto the sidewalk again and walked away.

The TV on the wall switched from the commercials I'd been ignoring back to the local news. A blonde woman with a microphone was standing outside the hospital.

"This is Rachel Evans, once again reporting from Basking Rock County Hospital, where doctors tell us that the vulnerable young client of local attorney Leland Munroe is now stable, but still critical. At the request of the young man's family, we are not revealing his identity at this time. However, we continue to investigate the neglect, disregard, and possible professional malpractice of Mr. Munroe, who walked off this young man's case literally in the middle of his trial up in the Charleston Court of General Sessions on Monday. That callous act, sources tell us, may very well be what drove the boy to attempt to take his own life."

The whole diner went quiet. Nobody was looking at me anymore. They were so purposefully avoiding any glance in my direction that it was worse than if they'd all stared.

Dabney Barnes had carried out his threat. But this time, I felt like I deserved it.

When the waitress brought my lunch, I said, "I'm sorry, but could I please get that to go?"

I drove home to get Squatter and brought him down to the causeway. I parked by the strip of beach, set him on the ground, and took my lunch over to one of the picnic tables. His tags jingled as we walked. He was getting old, but going to the beach still perked him up.

I fed him a piece of ham from my sandwich, then a french fry.

As I scratched him behind the ears, I said, "It's just you and me now, huh, buddy. I should've brought you on all those house visits so you could tell me which one I ought to buy."

I gave him another fry, looked out at the ocean, and said, "Or maybe I should pack it in and move back to Charleston. Give my keys back to the landlord and go. What do you think?"

Squatter had no comment. He was eating his lunch.

I ate mine, and then I gathered up the wrappers and napkins and stuck them into the bag. I knew I ought to take it to the trash can, then drive home and get some work done. Bobby's fast-tracked trial was starting in a couple of weeks, and I had a lot to do.

But I could not get up.

Squatter was digging a hole in the sand a few feet away. I could've sat there while he dug a hundred more and never felt the urge to move. Listening to the waves was all I had the energy for.

My phone rang. I knew from the sound that it was Terri. Noah had set me up with different rings for my frequent callers.

I picked up and said, "Hey."

"Leland, did I just drive past you on the causeway? On the beach?"

"Yeah, I guess. I came down here with Squatter."

"Okay, stay there. I was going home to take Buster for a walk. I'll bring him back with me. Give me ten minutes."

If it had just been me, I would've said no. But it had been a while since Squatter had seen his friend, and even longer since they'd played on the beach.

When Terri arrived, Buster bounded out of her car, and our dogs ran to the water's edge in ecstasy.

She followed, smiling, wearing a sundress in a green-and-yellow African print. The sight of her improved the day a little bit.

"Listen, Leland," she said. "I'm not here for small talk. And I'm real sorry about Jacob and that horrible news coverage, but let's not talk about that either. Because I found something. I went to see Kaylee this morning."

"Oh? Why's that?"

She tossed her beach bag onto the table, did a 360 to make sure nobody else was nearby, and sat down. "Okay, here's the thing. You got up so quick in the war room yesterday that I didn't get to finish telling you and Jacob about that case. Melody Walters was twenty-one years old, and at the time, Hank was about forty-five. And married, of course. She was his little thrill on the side."

"Uh-huh. And he... I know what Jacob said, but are you really convinced he killed her? He have any history of violence? Any domestics with his wife?"

"Oh, no. He wouldn't touch that woman. Those grocery stores he runs are owned by her family trust."

"Oh. Oh my." Roy had never mentioned that, but then again, I'd never asked. "So he'd better not get on her bad side."

"Exactly. Because *he's* not rich, his wife is. And so, here's the thing. When Melody's body was found, she was autopsied, obviously. And her pregnancy was apparent to the coroner. She'd just started to show. She was about three months along."

I stared at her.

She gave me a Mona Lisa smile—knowledge but also a hint of world-weary sadness. She wasn't done telling her story, but I knew from her face how it was going to end.

"Are you telling me… you talked to Kaylee, and—"

"I showed her a picture of Hank Manigault."

"Oh my God."

"She'd seen him with Dixie. She didn't know his name, since Dixie didn't confide in her—she kept her cards close to her chest. But Kaylee knew his face."

"Is she willing to testify to that?"

"She is."

"Well, damn."

"Mm-hmm." After a second, she added, "All I can hope is that those were the only two girls he did that to."

"Oh, God. Yeah."

I heard Squatter yip and looked over at him. He and Buster—who could have squashed him like a bug—were tussling over a wet stick. Out at sea, a sailboat was going by.

I sighed. "Does it ever *get* to you that... I mean, here we are, taking care of our dogs, doing our jobs, just... trying to live a good life, thinking we're normal, but there's actually a lot of monsters out there? Right here in town. And we *know* some of them."

She nodded. "I've got a niece who's eight years old," she said, "and last year she asked me if monsters were real. I told her yes, but not like in books. Not werewolves or any of that. I told her the only real monsters are people. I did say most people weren't—I didn't want to scare her, obviously—but some were, and I'd teach her how to avoid them."

I couldn't help but smile. Terri had never told me much about her family. Even in high school, she'd kept that side of her life to herself. "Sounds to me like you're a real good aunt."

She shrugged like she wasn't sure. "My sister actually got pretty mad at me for that. She said I was going to give Jada—that's my niece —nightmares."

"Oh, we all have nightmares. The whole world's a nightmare. At least you're teaching her what to do about it."

"Well, Mikaela's a kindergarten teacher. She wants life to be all rainbows and unicorns."

I laughed. "If it were, you and I wouldn't have jobs."

We talked a little more, and when I drove away, I had a mission. I took Squatter home, turned back around, and drove to Roy's office.

Laura looked up as I came in. Instead of saying hello, she said, "Leland, I want you to know that I've seen the news, and I don't believe one word of it. And neither does Roy."

That meant more to me than I would've expected it to. "Well, thank you. I appreciate that."

"He's in his office, if you're looking for him."

"I am. Thanks."

When I went in, Roy was at the liquor cabinet by his side window, making himself a drink. "Hey, Leland," he said. "I'd offer you something, but I know you don't drink."

"Thanks. Do you have a minute to talk?"

"Of course. Full disclosure, everybody's seen that coverage, and it's unfortunate, but I trust Dabney Barnes about as far as I can throw him. I'd like to hear your side." He brought his whiskey over to his desk, and we sat down.

He knew the gist of what was going on in both my big cases, from chatting about them at work and from reviewing the bills before they went out. I filled him in on the 2-a.m. call I'd gotten from Dabney and on Varner's misplaced certainty that Jacob had information that could help him bring down Charleston drug gangs. I told him Jacob had been hinting for a little while that he knew something about a different crime, but he hadn't told me the details. I didn't mention the hypnosis; that sort of thing was not part of Roy's reality.

"So, yesterday morning," I said, "after the plea deal Varner offered, Jacob got desperate. He finally told me what he remembered about this other crime—which was a homicide he witnessed—because he wanted me to run that by Varner to see if that could get him a better deal."

"Jacob Drayton witnessed a homicide? And he never *told* anybody?"

"Well, this was years ago. He was still in high school, and on top of that, he was so intoxicated when it happened that… I mean, it was a terrifying thing to see, and he basically convinced himself that all that alcohol must've made him remember it wrong. It's not that hard for me to understand."

"Yeah. Uh-huh, uh-huh." Roy nodded—that made some sense to him—and took a sip of his whiskey. "My goodness," he said. "Poor kid."

"And here's the crux of it," I said. "When he told me who did it—"

Roy set his whiskey down and stared at me. "Are you saying—Hank *Manigault*? That's why you called me yesterday? Are you serious?"

"Yeah, I'm afraid I am."

He shook his head and stared out the window. "Jesus Christ."

"Yeah."

"Okay, well… I'm going to need a minute to think on that. It's not like I ever thought Hank was a sterling guy, but *that*…"

"I know."

We both watched the palm tree outside his window tossing in the wind.

Then he said, "Well, I guess now I know why you had to ditch Jacob as a client. My goodness. Say no more."

"Uh-huh. But so, that's one thing. And then I just found out today, thanks to some work by my PI, that there's another conflict rearing its head, this time in Bobby Carter's case."

"Are you kidding me? Well, I guess this is a small town. Everybody's connected to everybody else."

"They are, yes. And I just… Roy, I know criminal defense attorneys aren't supposed to care about this, but I have very real reasons to believe both those men are innocent, one hundred percent. And I just, I cannot in good conscience leave them in the lurch."

"Oh." He looked at me and heaved a sigh. "Yeah, I hear where this is going."

"I don't want it to, Roy. You've done so much for me. You trained me from a pup."

He chuckled. "And you were an ornery little pup, weren't you. Back in law school, you thought you were God's gift to the legal profession."

"Did I? My God. I lost *that* idea a long time ago."

"Good thing too. No good lawyer ever had that attitude. Not for long, anyway."

We watched the palm tree for another minute. We both knew that I had to stop working for Jacob and Bobby, or stop working for Roy. Those were the rules. There was no way around them.

And we knew which path I had chosen.

24

JUNE 12, 2022

I paced outside the hospital waiting for Jacob to come out. I suppose I could have called him, but I wanted to look him in the eye when I talked to him. He deserved that much. Osborne came out first and even from here, I could see him waving his arms around as if it would make whatever he was telling his son that much better.

Jacob looked like he'd rather be back in his hospital bed.

His mom caught sight of me and I gave a little wave and she gestured for me to wait, so I stayed where I was wondering if she was going to point me out. Instead, she said something to her husband, who promptly stomped off to the parking lot. I'm guessing to get the car. Once he was out of sight, her hand signal told me to hurry, so I jogged over.

"Jacob. Mrs. Drayton." I nodded to them both unsure if Jacob would shake my hand if I offered it, so I didn't try.

"I'm glad to see you've been discharged. I was hoping to have five minutes of your time, if that's okay."

"Better make it two, Oz is bringing the car around," his mother warned before she stepped a few feet away to give us a bit of privacy.

Once I'd explained why I'd had to do what I did, Jacob was happy to have me back as his lawyer. Actually, the look of relief on both their faces said more than the words and I suspect that was mostly due to his father pushing for him to plead out. Before Jacob could change his mind, I pulled the paperwork out of my coat pocket for him to sign.

Mrs. Drayton cleared her throat and tilted her head toward the car that'd just come around the corner, so I told them both I'd be back in touch before running back to my car, as if I'd done something wrong. And well, in the court of public opinion, I had, but that was something I planned to rectify.

I had a lot of plates currently spinning and if I had any hope of keeping them all from crashing down, I needed to make sure they were all moving in the right direction.

June 13, 2022

It was nearly one in the morning, and I'd been sitting in my car outside Brandon Ludlow's apartment since ten like some sort of stalker. I'd been trying to talk to him for the better part of three days, without success. He lived on the top floor of a brick duplex on the edge of downtown. I knew the address because my son had overdosed there the previous summer. Noah had barely survived.

On my deathbed, I knew, I would still remember this place.

I was there because my mind was stuck on two things.

One of them was new. The hearing where I got to challenge the eyewitness in Bobby's case had been on Friday morning, forty anticlimactic minutes questioning the retired factory foreman who lived catty-corner from Bobbino's. I'd done what I came for, exploring the contradictions in his statements enough to find out what kind of witness he was.

He was the honest kind—as in, he believed what he was saying—but the weak point in his testimony was clear. The day after the fire, he'd told police that the man he saw fleeing the scene was "tall and slim." Two months later, after reading plenty of Fourth's news coverage and talking to the cops and the fire inspector a few more times, he pointed to a photo of Bobby Carter—all 360 pounds of him—and said, "That's the guy."

I believed he'd told the truth the day after the fire, when the memory was fresh in his mind.

So I was inclined to think he'd been right: the man who set the fire was tall and slim.

And there was one more thing.

I'd recalled how Brandon had looked at Hank Manigault that night outside Ruiz's campaign event. It hadn't made sense to me at the time —was that fear in his eyes? Why?—but now I thought maybe I understood.

I looked over at his building again. The windows of his apartment were dark. They'd been dark since I'd arrived. The whole street was dark, its few streetlights mostly obscured by palm trees.

Hank had said, when we were golfing on Kiawah Island, that he'd hired Brandon to give a helping hand to the son of a friend. Out of the goodness of his heart, in other words.

I didn't believe that anymore.

I looked at my watch. I had a meeting with Cody Varner up in Charleston at 8:30 a.m., and I needed to be in good shape for it. But I also needed to talk to Brandon because he was one of those plates.

About a half hour later, I woke with a start. A car's engine thrummed as it turned into the duplex's driveway. It shut off, the interior light came on, and I saw Brandon. He was alone.

I'd set my own interior light to the off position. I grabbed my door handle and waited. When Brandon opened his car door, I opened mine. Our doors slammed shut at the same time.

As he went up the porch steps, I reached the sidewalk in front of his house. He fumbled in the pocket of his shorts, found his keys, and jabbed them at the lock.

I heard him swearing under his breath. He tried the key again. It seemed a safe bet he was drunk.

I came quietly up the steps behind him, and the deadbolt turned. He stuck the key in the doorknob and turned that too. I could smell the drink on him now.

He was so lightly dressed I was just about sure he was unarmed, but I didn't know what he might have inside. I decided not to risk following him in.

"Hey, Brandon," I said.

He spun around in surprise, swearing.

"It's Leland," I said, holding my hands up, palms out, to show I was no threat. "Leland Munroe, Noah's dad?"

"What the hell! What are you doing here?"

"Hey, I'm sorry. I didn't mean to startle you. I just want to talk."

"Look, I told you I was sorry about Noah. I didn't even know he was taking anything. He did it in the bathroom; it's not like I was in there with him."

"I know that. I know you weren't." The next part was not easy to say, but I sensed that he needed it: "And I accept your apology."

He relaxed a little. "Okay, man. Okay."

"Can we talk for a minute," I said, "inside?"

"What about?"

"Something else."

He looked at me, then out at his dark yard, thinking. Then he laughed. "What's that saying? Like, the enemy of my enemy—"

"Is my friend?"

"Yeah, that. And you're definitely the enemy of my dad." He pushed the door all the way open. "So come on in."

He loped up the stairs, and I followed him.

His apartment was messy, but it was nicely furnished for a young man his age. I wondered whether the money had come from his father or from Hank Manigault.

He got himself a beer from the fridge, cracked it open, and then came back and sat on a black leather couch. He didn't offer me a drink. I settled myself in the matching armchair on the other side of the coffee table. I couldn't see the coffee table, but I inferred its presence from the pile of vintage *Penthouse* magazines, beer cans, and TV remotes that it supported.

After a long sip of beer, he said, "What do you want? More dirt on my dad? Because I got plenty."

"You know what, I'd like that. But can we talk about that later? Because it's real late, and that's not why I came."

His expression turned wary. "Why'd you come, then?"

"I came to talk about the fire."

Something shifted in his eyes. Now he looked haunted.

"I want you to notice," I said, "that we're not sitting in a police station or a courthouse. I'm here to talk to you in private, man-to-man."

He looked at his beer, hesitated, and took another sip. I could see flickers of shame and defensiveness and vulnerability on his face. I got the sense that if I could make him think I knew everything already, he wouldn't hold back.

To hide the holes in my knowledge, I chose my words carefully. "I know Hank Manigault is responsible for that fire."

His eyes flicked up to mine, startled, and then back down.

"He gave you a job," I said.

"Yeah, but not like—not like—"

"I know."

The flash of desperation when he'd spoken told me I was right. Hank had asked him to carry out the arson. I'd said *job* so that if I was wrong, I could pretend I'd been referring to his work in Hank's grocery stores.

He seemed to realize he was saying too much. He reeled himself back in and said, defiantly, "What even is this bullshit? Man, I need to go to sleep."

I nodded at him, saying nothing, serious. After a minute, I looked at my watch. "Yeah, it's almost that late now. She was sleeping, wasn't she."

He stood up, pointed toward the stairs, and said, "You can get out now! Just get the hell out!"

I stayed where I was. "Brandon, listen. I know you didn't know that Dixie was there."

His face spasmed. He turned around, punched the wall, and stalked into the kitchen. He stood in there with his back to me, swearing to himself.

After a minute he came back out and said, "You can't prove a damn thing. You think you can get back at my dad by putting me in jail? Good luck with that, asshole."

"Brandon, I'm not trying to put you in jail."

"Bullshit. You get the hell out of here right now. You're trespassing. I know my rights, and I know some cops too."

"Brandon, Hank knew Dixie was there. She was his girlfriend. And she'd... well, she'd become a problem for him."

He looked stunned.

"He tricked you," I said. "And what I'm trying to do is put *him* in jail. Not you."

He looked away, trying to get a hold of himself.

"If you'd known she was there," I said, "you wouldn't have done it, would you?"

He shook his head. The corners of his mouth kept spasming down, like he might bust out crying if he wasn't careful.

"Of course you wouldn't have," I said. "Whatever else you've done, I don't think you're a murderer. But Hank is."

He walked around to the back of the couch and started kicking it, rhythmically, staring at it. To avoid looking at me, I figured. "No, man," he said. "Maybe she was his girlfriend, but that doesn't... I mean, he's been helping me. I legit work for him."

"Yeah, I know. But then he told you to set that fire, and he lured her there, and he made sure she wouldn't wake up when the alarms went off."

"Why? That doesn't make sense."

I wondered if I should level with him.

I figured I had to, if I wanted him to level with me.

"She was pregnant," I said.

In his eyes, I saw the gears click into place. Realization, and then horror.

I let him digest that for a minute. Then I said, "I'm sure you know this, since your dad was the solicitor, but let me just recap for you how things work. If a man tricks you into committing a crime, and you tell that to the authorities, you tell them the truth and you give evidence, they will cut you a deal. They want to convict the bad guy, not the kid he tricked. That's what I want to happen here. *He's* the one who ought to go to prison."

He nodded slowly, almost dreamily. "You know," he said, "he told me it was an insurance thing. And I was, like, 'I'm pretty sure that's not your building, though, is it?'"

"And what'd he say?"

"Said it was a favor for a friend. For Mr. Boseman."

"Uh-huh."

For a second, I wondered if my original theory was right. Did Boseman have something going with Dixie? Was he the killer after all?

But what Brendan and Kaylee had told us meant that was wrong.

The two men were friends, though. Or associates, or whatever rich men call each other when they're playing on the same team.

Maybe Manigault had paid to remodel Dixie's apartment. Maybe that was a bribe. I supposed Brandon might help us find out.

"So, listen," I said. "For this to work right, you need a criminal defense lawyer who'll talk with the solicitor to get you a deal. And that can't be me, because I'm representing the guy who's accused of setting that fire. But I can help you find somebody. Somebody good."

He looked at me with a mix of hope and distrust.

Not many people, I realized, had ever helped this kid. I knew something about his past. His mom had been murdered when he was four years old. His younger brother—or half-brother, his stepmom's kid— was the golden child and their father's heir apparent.

Hank Manigault had told the truth about one thing: somebody had hit this kid into the rough. And maybe somebody ought to hit him back out.

I took my phone out of my pocket. "Give me your number," I said. "I'll text you mine. I can think of three lawyers right off the bat who could get this done for you. And I've got other evidence on Manigault that I'm happy to share with whoever you choose."

He winced and said, "My dad's friends with about every big lawyer in the state."

"Naw, these guys are all up in Charleston. And they're criminal *defense*. They don't know or give a crap about your dad."

"Huh." A faint smile flickered across his face. "Sounds like my kind of people," he said, and gave me his number.

25

JUNE 13, 2022

I went home, slept about three hours, and drove to Charleston. On the way, I called the three lawyers on my list. It was too early for them to answer, so I left messages. I'd gone up against every one of them at least half a dozen times as assistant solicitor, and they were the only criminal defense guys for whom, even then, I'd had the utmost respect.

I got to the French Quarter about eight, got myself a croissant and a coffee, and walked around, psyching myself up for my talk with Varner. The city was waking up, and I could smell the ocean.

Then I headed over to the solicitor's office.

Varner came and got me from the waiting room about three minutes after I'd arrived. As we walked back down the hall, he said, "I'm sorry about your client. He out of the hospital yet?"

"Yeah, he got home yesterday evening. Doing a whole lot better."

"Hell of a roller coaster for his parents."

"Oh yeah. They got way too close to about the worst thing imaginable."

"Yep."

We rounded a corner and went into his office. We were on the top floor—most of the buildings in Charleston were only four or five stories tall, and this was no exception—and when he sat down at his desk, his back was to the window. It looked like he and his office chair were floating in the sky.

"So, just as a preliminary matter," he said, "have you filed another entry of appearance? Because I didn't see it in my inbox."

I'd formally withdrawn from the case on Tuesday, and for us to make a deal now, I had to file a document to put myself back on it.

And before I could do that, Jacob had to rehire me, which he'd done last night outside the hospital.

"Yeah, no," I said. "The ECF site was down for maintenance this morning. I've got a hard copy right here." I pulled the two-page document out of my briefcase and handed it to him. "I'm going to walk it over and file it in person when we're done."

He gave me a dubious look. "Still cutting corners," he said. "I shouldn't even be talking to you until this thing is filed." He tossed the document back.

"Look, we can reschedule," I said. "The clerk of court doesn't open for filings until eight thirty, which is when you asked me to meet you, and she's two blocks away."

"Yeah, fine, fine."

"I could've gone there first, but I didn't want to waste your time."

"Sure, Leland. Great. I appreciate the consideration. Let's just get this meeting done. Listen. As far as I'm concerned, trial in this case should pick back up on Monday right where we left off. Or whenever your client gets medically cleared, which I'm assuming should be pronto. Explain to me why it shouldn't."

"You mean, apart from the fact that the drugs weren't his?"

He rolled his eyes. "Come on, Leland."

I shrugged. "Look, to the absolute best of my knowledge, that's the truth."

"Oh, please. Everybody says they're innocent. Did you forget that, somehow? Is that a side effect of going over to the dark side? Excuse me, the defense bar?"

This was getting ridiculous.

More accurately, it was getting personal.

"Look, Cody," I said. "If he *were* a dealer, he'd know enough about Kyle Parr's friends to get a better deal from you. Don't tell me you think he *wants* to go to jail."

He didn't answer. A couple of seagulls flew past the window behind him, then wheeled around toward the ocean.

Cody still had it in for me, and that was getting in the way of my ability to help Jacob. To get this job done, I was going to have to clear the decks.

I leaned back in my chair, looked at him, and said, "This isn't news to you, but I screwed up big time a few years ago. I don't know what all you heard, but I think you ought to hear it from me. You should have heard it from me back then, but..." I shook my head. "Let's just say I wasn't handling things real well."

He didn't say anything, but he kept on looking at me.

"My wife was an alcoholic," I said, "and I knew that. But because I was a workaholic and an idiot, and didn't know the first thing about addiction, I thought if I could just... keep that hidden, and break her falls—which, there were a lot of falls—that'd give her a chance to pull herself together."

He flicked his eyebrows up and down, an unspoken *wow* that conveyed how off the mark I'd been.

"Yeah, I know," I said. "That's not how it works. I found that out. But first, I did a lot of favors for local cops. A lot of you scratch my back, I scratch yours. Throw out that citation, let her off with a warning, and I'll talk to my colleague who's prosecuting your nephew or your friend or whomever and see if we can bring those charges down. Because I thought she was working on it and just needed a little more time. I thought a few nights in jail would be the end of her. So, call it careless driving instead of a DUI, and I'll see if I can get your kid a job in the solicitor's office."

He cocked his head. "Any money change hands?"

"No. Strictly quid pro quo."

"Hmm." He nodded like he was considering that. He clearly had heard otherwise. "You're lucky you didn't get disbarred. Or at least suspended."

"Yeah. I am."

He swung around in his chair and looked out the window for a second. A jet plane was drawing a white line through the air.

Then he turned back around and said, with a hint of a smile, "I have to agree, you're an idiot. But that said, you're no Tony Rosa."

I snorted with laughter. "Thanks, I guess." Rosa was a former colleague of ours now serving twenty years in federal prison for drug smuggling, among other crimes.

Cody was smiling for real now. Then he glanced at his computer and said, "Oh, hell. I got to head to court in ten minutes. Okay, unless you want to reschedule, you've got ten minutes to… I guess, pretty much save your client's life. What you got for me?"

"I've got a murder on Kiawah Island," I said, "six years ago, that my client witnessed."

"Six years ago? And he's only coming forward now?"

"He was a kid then. In high school. Let me know when you've got more than ten minutes, and I'll tell you the story." I pulled some papers out of my briefcase—articles about Melody Walters—and handed them to him.

"Oh, I remember her," he said, looking at the pictures. "That hit a lot of people real hard. And they never even had a suspect."

"Well, now you do. Or you will."

He gave a low whistle of disbelief.

"I just need something I can take back to Jacob."

"Yeah, all right. Okay."

I got up to leave, thinking I'd been dismissed when he stopped me.

"Wait." Cody made a quick call and then settled back in his chair and I did the same. "Tell me the story, now."

July 13, 2022

It was sweltering out already even though the sun had yet to rise, so I sat in my car with the a/c running until I saw headlights creeping up the hill. Turning off the engine, I climbed out as Terri's Forester pulled up alongside mine.

"Morning."

"Morning. It's a great day for an arrest," Terri sang out.

As soon as Manigault found out he was a "person of interest" in not one murder, but two, he'd gone to ground and it'd taken law enforcement weeks to track him down.

"So, what's about to happen?" Bobby joined us on the hill and was staring down at the parking lot of the seediest motel I'd ever seen. The parking lot was a sea of flashing lights. "Whoa. Is that what the front of my house looked like the night they came to arrest me?"

"Not so many cars." SLED was taking no chances on Manigault getting away, again, and we all watched in fascination as the officers advanced on the motel. One of the officers had a battering ram and was preparing to swing at one of the doors when we heard shouts.

"Don't shoot!" Something white was waved in the open doorway, probably a pillowcase, and the door opened. "He surrenders!" the person shouted again.

"Must be his lawyer," Terri stated, as the three of us watched the arrest unfold. "No one else would be foolish enough to get between Hank and a bunch of guns unless there was money involved."

I was reminded of my own trek into the Carters' house the night Rappaport showed up with the arrest warrant and I had to agree.

Soon enough Hank Manigault was escorted from the motel room in handcuffs and placed in the closest cruiser.

"Is that it? Is it over? Seems sort of..."

"Anticlimactic?" Terri finished for him, and he nodded in reply.

"I was hoping to see a chase through a junkyard and Hank getting tackled by a former linebacker or, uh, rottweiler. You know. Something climactic."

"Mmm hmm. I hear you."

The drama over, we returned to our cars and Bobby asked what happens next.

"He'll be charged and the state will build their defense. When it comes time, you'll testify to what you know." I didn't want to get into all the details as I was looking forward to getting back into my car.

Before I could say more, Bobby stuck his hand out for me to shake. "Thanks again, Leland, for everything. You believed in me while everyone else was looking to hang me." His eyes were misty and he was rapidly blinking them, so I pretended I didn't see.

"You're welcome."

Terri gave his arm a squeeze and we said our goodbyes. Bobby still had to deal with his own charges, but after talking to Ruiz, I knew the state was prepared to go easy on him, but the same couldn't be said for the IRS. That was something to deal with another day. For now, Bobby, at least, got some closure and I was happy to give it to him.

I took one last look as Manigault was taken away, hopeful that justice would be served for both Dixie and Melody.

26

SEPTEMBER 24, 2022

It was a bright blue Saturday afternoon with the first hint of autumn in the air, and I was standing in the front yard of my new house, holding Squatter in his doggie carrier and watching Noah and Jacob carry a bookshelf up the steps. Noah still had a trace of his limp —he probably always would—but he'd come up with some workarounds to keep himself stable, and Jacob was being careful not to go too fast.

This wasn't the first house I'd considered, or the second, or the third. It was a two-bedroom brick place with deep porches on the front and back and a fenced yard so Squatter could run around, and it had taken far longer than I'd ever expected to find it. Chance had been enthused about its "simple yet elegant style." I liked that well enough, but my own enthusiasm had more to do with the bullet-resistant exterior, the solid doors with peepholes instead of windows, and the reasonable price. I also liked the fact that it had a magnolia in the front, a pin oak in the back, and no shrubbery at all—that is to say, nothing for approaching burglars or other bad guys to hide behind.

Up on the porch, Noah and Jacob set the bookshelf over to the side to let the movers get past with my living room couch. Once the couch had gone inside, I went up the steps and said, "Jacob, I'm paying my own son fifty bucks and some pizza to help me move, so you have got to let me give you something too. What do you like on your pizza? You boys want some beer?"

"Mr. Munroe," he said, "I could've been in jail right now, but I'm not. So I think I ought to help you with every move for the rest of your life."

"Well, hopefully there won't be too many more of those."

"Either way, this one is on me, but I will eat some of that pizza you're offering and I like pretty much everything on pizza except pineapple."

"Smart man." I would never understand some people's fascination with fruit on pizza. Didn't belong.

"Same for me and beer would be good, too, Dad." Noah lifted his end of the bookshelf back up and they carried it into the house.

As a prosecutor, I enjoyed going to trial. There was something about standing up in the courtroom and talking through the chain of events while I watched the jurors' faces to make sure I kept them spellbound and on the state's side. As a defense attorney, while I still enjoy a good argument, I'd happily skip the trials so long as justice still gets served and my client doesn't end up doing time for something they didn't do.

Under his plea deal, Jacob had pled guilty to simple possession—the wrist-slap folks got for having a joint in their pocket—with no jail time and a fifty-dollar fine. That, his coach had confirmed, was minor enough that it wouldn't rule out the Olympics.

Jacob had been overjoyed at the news. He wouldn't have to walk away from his dreams and I'd be lying if I didn't admit to a certain level of satisfaction at seeing Osborne Drayton eat a bit of crow. Not that I was smug about it. Well, not to his face. At least, Jacob had a future now, and it was one that didn't involve getting stuck under his father's thumb, which I considered a win.

Manigault's trial, in which Jacob had agreed to testify as a witness to Melody's murder, was scheduled for next year. Most of his memories of that night, six years ago, had returned and he'd been having nightmares. So Marianne put him in touch with a therapist who took video appointments and he'd been speaking with her regularly.

Catching the murderer of a cold case, especially one that pulled at the heartstrings like Melody's, was a feather in Varner's cap and I knew he'd be eager to dig into Manigault's background. Of course, there'd be a jurisdictional pull with Ruiz and Dixie's murder but that poor girl would come first and justice would be served, thanks to both Jacob and Brandon.

Manigault, meanwhile, was in jail. Accused murderers did not typically get out on bond in South Carolina, not even if they were as highly placed and well connected as he was. Brandon was in good hands with one of the lawyers I'd recommended and once again, I'd be remiss if I didn't admit to the amount of pleasure I took at the look on Ludlow's face when his own son told him, he didn't want *his* kind of help. From the way it was described, the man looked downright apoplectic, and I'd have paid good money to see that in person.

As the boys carried the bookshelf inside, I saw Terri's Forester pull up. I waved. After shouldering the big bag she usually carried, she let Buster out, and he came bounding through the open front gate.

I said hi to him and gave him some pats, then told her, "Let's take them around back. It's got its own fence. I can't leave Squatter out front while the movers are here."

"Yeah, no, they won't even see him. They'll step on him and not even notice, poor thing."

I took her around to the backyard, unlatched the gate, and went in.

"Oh, a screened-in porch!" she said, looking at what I thought of as my back deck. "You are going to love that."

"I sure will." I set the doggie carrier down and let Squatter out to enjoy himself.

She surveyed the yard, hands on her hips, nodding approval. When I stood back up, she said, "You've got a good setup for security too. A nice defensible perimeter."

I laughed.

"Sorry," she said, smiling. "Am I being a little abnormal again?"

"No more so than me."

"Maybe not. Oh," she said, touching the strap of her shoulder bag. "I brought you a housewarming gift." She pulled out a wrapped rectangle about twelve inches by fifteen.

"Aw, you shouldn't have."

"Of course I should."

I opened it, saw bubble wrap, and peeled that away. Underneath was a framed newspaper—or not newspaper, but a printed-out page from the *Southeast Patriot* website. The headline, from a month ago, said: SECOND INDICTMENT FOR MANIGAULT: ARSON, MURDER OF DIXIE WARD.

"Damn," I said, looking at it. "Now, that's a headline."

"We do good work."

I peeled the rest of the bubble wrap away and saw the subheading—
Bobby Carter Released, Vindicated—and then the photo below it of
Bobby, me, and Marianne on the courthouse steps.

"Dammit," I said, "I cannot hang this in my house!"

"What? Why not?"

"I don't want to look up my own nostrils every day. How does he do
that? How does Dabney always find the worst photos?"

She was laughing. "No, you look fine! Anyway, even Dabney had to
admit we were right!"

"And he'll get us back for that. He already did—I mean, I look like a
freaking... What are those things called? Like some sort of hairless
capybara in a pinstripe suit."

She cracked up. "You do not! You don't! I wouldn't print out a bad
photo of you and get it *framed*!"

I smiled, watching her. I still thought I looked like a capybara, but she
seemed completely sincere.

"Okay," I said. "I'll hang it up."

"You'd better. And not in, like, the basement either."

It felt good to laugh. Given how dire things had looked for a while—
for Bobby and Jacob alike—they'd all turned out pretty well. I'd
given Bobby the names of a few tax lawyers, and I hoped he'd be able
to sort things out there without too much difficulty. He couldn't blame
his actions on his PTSD or claim he'd been misguided. Bobby knew
he'd been breaking the law and Marianne was none-to-happy about it
when she found out. Felony tax evasion in South Carolina came with
a fine of up to ten thousand and three years in prison, but I fully
expected some sort of plea deal. Of course, he'd still have to deal with
the IRS.

What all Boseman was up to was another worry. Who knew how many people were involved if he was laundering money. Plus, he's well connected and had already lawyered up. It was best to save my concerns about him for another day.

Buster trotted over and nuzzled Terri's bag for a treat. While she fed it to him, I looked out across my "defensible perimeter." I could get used to this, I thought—to spending most of my time with a woman who was proudly abnormal in a lot of the same ways I was.

"How's that niece of yours?" I said. "And your sister, the one who likes unicorns and rainbows."

"Oh, they're good. Although I don't think Mikaela'll ever stop being a little bit mad at me."

"Maybe she'll learn to appreciate your way of seeing things. You keep folks safe. She and her family live around here?"

"Not too far. Down by Bluffton."

"Yeah? Well, invite them up, maybe. I'll host a barbecue next weekend. Or whatever other weekend they can make it."

"Okay," she said, with a smile that was almost shy. "Maybe I will."

I pulled my phone out and thumbed through my contacts. "You staying for pizza?"

"Mm hmm. You know it. Skip the pineapple. Tried it once. No idea what I was thinking."

Grinning, I lifted the phone to my ear, ready to order a couple of their large deluxe pizzas, and happy that things were looking up. Noah was doing well, Jacob was headed to the Olympics, Bobby would probably owe the IRS a hell of a lot of money but he'd probably avoid prison, and I'd officially hung out my shingle away from Roy. Looking at Terri, who was now playing with the dogs, I realized that life was looking good and I was going to enjoy the moment while it lasted.

Tomorrow would be here soon enough.

END OF BURNING EVIDENCE
SMALL TOWN LAWYER BOOK 4

Defending Innocence

Influencing Justice

Interpreting Guilt

Burning Evidence

PS: Do you enjoy legal thrillers? Then keep reading for exclusive extracts from **Small Town Trial** and **Defending Innocence**.

ABOUT PETER KIRKLAND

Loved this book? Share it with a friend!

To be notified of Peter's next book release please sign up to his mailing list, at www.relaypub.com/peter-kirkland-email-sign-up.

ABOUT PETER

Peter Kirkland grew up in Beaufort, South Carolina. While he had always loved writing, his academic and debating skills made law seem like the obvious career choice. So, leaving his pen and paper behind, Peter worked as a defense attorney for many years. During this time, he saw both obviously guilty clients and a few that he felt were genuinely innocent of the crimes that they were accused of. But no matter what, Peter was always determined to give the best possible defense for his clients and he's proud to say that he won more cases than he lost.

But the more he practiced in criminal law, the more he found himself scribbling away at the end of a hard day to clear his mind and reflect on his current cases. One day, years later, he found himself absent-mindedly reading through his old journals and found he had the beginnings of a story hidden inside his notes. That the tales from the courtroom were deep and rich in characters, twists and turns, and he remembered how much he enjoyed writing before studying law. Peter began reading legal thrillers voraciously and turned the reflections from his journal into a fictional manuscript and decided to try his luck at being published.

New to the industry, Peter would love to hear from readers:

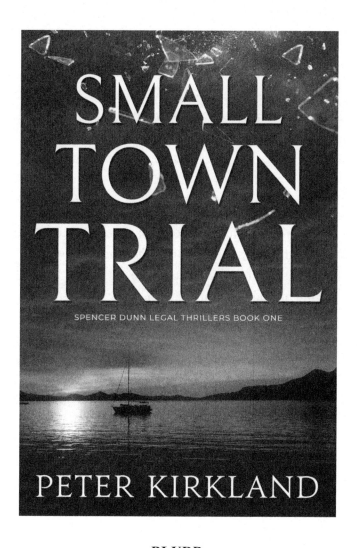

BLURB

Murder on a placid lake... Can Spencer Dunn keep his head above water?

When beloved mayor turned state senator Carlton Osborn is found dead on his boat, the local police suspect foul play. The only suspect is pregnant nineteen-year-old Amber Vega. And the only lawyer willing to take her case is Spencer Dunn. The hotshot attorney is eager to restore his reputation after a humiliating loss in court. But this case may be more than he bargained for....

Amber was caught red-handed on the boat with Osborn's body, and the police are determined to pin the murder on her. Even worse, she was having an affair with the senator, and was caught in a vicious argument with his wife. But the more Spencer digs, the less the story adds up. Something smells fishy, and it's not just Osborn's corpse!

Spencer will stop at nothing to uncover the truth, and he doesn't know the meaning of the word "quit". But if he can't unravel the mystery, prove Amber's innocence, and uncover the real killer, he might be the next one to find himself sleeping with the fishes...

Coming Soon: Sign up to my mailing list below to be the first to know when **Small Town Trial** publishes:
www.relaypub.com/peter-kirkland-email-sign-up

———

EXCERPT

Chapter One

One juror is all it takes. Every lawyer knows this, even the bad ones. Hell, *especially* the bad ones.

It was subtle but unmistakable. Juror number seven's lower lip quivered, and her eyes moistened every time I referenced the plight of the single mother: cast aside, emotionally blackmailed by a cruel ex-husband, beaten down by an unfair system. She felt it; she knew. Some of the others in the jury box seemed less sympathetic. Or maybe they were bored. It was difficult to tell. Perhaps their minds were already made up. I rested my hand on the exhibit shelf directly in front of number seven. Her own hands were shaking and tearing at a tissue in her lap as I spoke.

"So, you see, ladies and gentlemen, it is not as simple a matter as my colleagues for the prosecution would have you believe. As you were instructed when the trial began, for the crime of criminal restraint to occur, there must be both action and intent. In legalese, actus reus and mens rea."

I took a moment to look into a couple of jurors' eyes. It was hard for me to give this case my all when I thought it should never have been brought... but it had, and my client had agonized over it every day since.

"It means guilty actions and a guilty mind. The Maine family code stipulates that for what took place to be a crime, the noncustodial parent not only must take the child out of the state—that is the action —but he or she also must intend to take them somewhere where they cannot be found. In other words, the children are hidden away. That is the guilty mind, the intent. Do we have that here? Has the prosecution produced a single shred of evidence that even suggests that my client intended to conceal her children in a secret location in an attempt to deceive their father and keep them from him?"

I had no difficulty sounding sincere, at least. Shannon Maroney wanted nothing but the best for her kids, and she played by the rules. Which was more than I could say for some of my clients.

"No! We do not. We have absolutely none of that intent here. Not a scintilla. Not even a hint. First of all, my client was the rightful custodial parent when the trip north began. More importantly, these phone records," I continued, shaking the stack of papers in the air, "introduced as evidence and acknowledged by the prosecution, prove that my client notified, or attempted to notify, several people of the children's exact location, including Mr. Maroney. And we heard testimony from some of them: the girl's music teacher, several parents of school friends, Mr. Engel, the boy's karate instructor. They all knew that Ms. Maroney and the children went to Canada to visit family, and that the visit involved an unplanned excursion to the family cabin. They were also informed that Ms. Maroney's father suffered a heart attack and had to be airlifted from that remote cabin to a hospital in Ottawa. We showed you copies of those reports: the Life Flight and hospital reports. I ask you, ladies, and gentlemen. If you were going into hiding with the intent to never be found, would you tell a half dozen or so friends and acquaintances exactly where you are? And would you attempt to inform the children's father as well?"

A few of the jurors shook their heads at this, including number three, a thirtysomething man who'd spent most of the trial looking at his smartwatch.

"In fact," I continued, pointing to the prosecution's table, "we are here for only two reasons. Firstly, Ms. Maroney's travel itinerary had to be changed through no fault of her own. Hasn't that happened to all of us? Secondly, we are here because Mr. Maroney thought it would be easier—or crueler—to file a complaint than to pick up a phone and reach out to any one of those people who knew exactly where his children were. He knew the names of the parents. He knew their routines. He took the kids to music lessons and karate practice. Why not call up the music school and ask if they had heard from his ex-wife? Or any of the parents who were notified—had to be notified—that the girl's birthday party needed to be canceled? But no. Let's beat the poor woman who's stuck in the wilderness, whose father was dead for all she knew, let's drag her into court. That'll make her regret getting a divorce. That will be a nice payback. And I submit that the prosecution, by bringing this matter to trial, is only enabling that sadistic behavior."

Okay, maybe that was too much. But I was right, and I was pissed. My client was being legally assaulted by a vengeful ex-husband. And a misguided and overzealous prosecution was the weapon he chose.

Why? I had no idea. Some DAs just get a bug in their britches, I guess. Or maybe the Fathers for Equal Rights lobby were big donors. Either way, it should never have come to this.

"In conclusion, ladies and gentlemen of the jury, I'm afraid we've dragged you down here for nothing. We're wasting time that you could use for better purposes. You have been shown conclusively that, while my client did indeed take her children out of the state, Mr. Maroney was informed of the expected plans. And we have likewise demonstrated that while the plans may have changed, there was never any intent to deceive Mr. Maroney or to keep him from knowing the whereabouts of his children. We have, in fact, proven that the opposite is true." I raised the phone records again. "Ms. Maroney is innocent of this crime because there *is* no crime. Truth and reason leave you no choice but to find the defendant not guilty. Thank you for your service here today."

Whatever Perry Mason effect I hoped to create was ruined by the sound of my left hearing aid throwing feedback into the otherwise hushed courtroom. I must've brushed the stack of papers I was holding too close to my ear as I lowered them histrionically. One juror covered his own ears; another jumped in her seat, startled. I looked at the floor to conceal my red cheeks as I retreated to my seat at the defendant's table.

As was my habit, I attempted to get a furtive read of the jurors' faces as they filed out of the box and through the door to the deliberation room, hoping to get a sense of what they were thinking. Granted, for all my bluster during closing, this wasn't exactly the crime of the century, and my client would probably never face real prison time if found guilty. But this case bothered me more than most. I'd represented all kinds of clients back in New Hampshire—some innocent, many guilty—but none of them were being railroaded like Shannon Maroney.

One of the jurors stopped just before exiting and turned to look straight at me. He was pulling at his right earlobe. I wondered, did he also wear hearing aids? Or was he judging me, wondering why someone my age would have a hearing problem? It was only a matter of time before the good people of Bar Harbor learned the truth. Spencer Dunn got beat up by the son of one of his clients—an innocent man now sitting in a cell in Concord, New Hampshire, doing eight to fifteen. In retrospect, my ability to hear properly was a small price to pay for such bad lawyering. Would that get out too? Bar Harbor's newest transplant was a washed-up attorney on the run from his failures, his demons.

"What now?"

"Huh? Oh. We wait."

Shannon Maroney put her hand on my right forearm, pulling me out of my thought spiral. "Do you think they will really do it? Will they, could they, find me guilty?"

"They shouldn't. I meant what I said up there. This is one of the most ridiculous cases I've ever defended. Let's grab a coffee. The clerk will call me when the verdict is ready."

Forty-five minutes later, we were back in the courtroom watching the jurors enter and take their seats. This time, none of them looked at me or my client. That could be a bad sign. Then again, a short deliberation was usually good news for the defendant.

"Ladies and gentlemen of the jury, I understand you have reached a verdict."

"Yes, Your Honor," the forewoman replied, standing.

"And your decision is unanimous?"

"Yes, Your Honor."

Unanimous. My gut fluttered at the word. No matter how large or small the case, the impending verdict always evoked a nervous reaction. It's an experience shared by most trial attorneys. But I've often felt that the suspense hits me harder than most. Maybe I just take these things too personally.

"Excellent. Please hand the verdict to the clerk."

The clerk took the sheet and gave it to the judge, who scanned it quickly and snapped it back to the clerk without any hint of what it contained. I made a mental note never to play poker with Judge Dickenson.

"Please read the verdict, madam clerk."

"In the case of the State of Maine versus Shannon Jean Maroney, the court finds the defendant not guilty of the crime of Criminal Restraint by Parent, as defined by section three-zero-three of the Maine Family Code."

"Thank you, clerk, and thank you for your service, members of the jury. Please remain seated. This matter is not yet closed."

Not yet closed?

"I wish to offer my remarks on this matter, which we have all been a party to these last few days."

Judge Dickenson's tone was serious. This was the first case I'd argued before the man—hell, the first case I had in the whole state of Maine. But I could tell a lecture was coming.

"Ms. Greathouse, Mr. Carter, far be it for me to suggest frivolousness on the part of the Hancock County prosecutor's office. I like to believe the best of our public servants."

"I'm sorry, Your Honor?" The man at the prosecution table shot to his feet.

"Sit down, Mr. Carter. I'm not looking for a rebuttal. Now, since we have what I believe was the correct verdict in this matter... It was very obvious that Mr. Maroney—are you in the gallery, sir? Yes, you, Mr. Maroney. I'm talking about you. Mr. Maroney, as an aggrieved ex-husband, clearly embellished the circumstances of his children's supposed disappearance at the hands of his former wife. He made remarkably little effort to find them. One wonders if he was even trying to find his kids at all. I agree with defense counsel. This complaint smacks of retribution and a misuse of the law. I am also inclined to admonish the prosecution for bringing us to this point."

"Thank you, Your Honor," I said.

"Sit down, Mr. Dunn. As I was saying, Ms. Greathouse and Mr. Carter, I would be remiss if I did not take this opportunity to reacquaint you with our mediation process. This matter could have been adjudicated with much less fanfare and, I would add, less jeopardy to a mother who has demonstrated a willingness and desire to do the right thing for both her children and the law."

————

Coming Soon: Sign up to my mailing list below to be the first to know when **Small Town Trial** publishes:
www.relaypub.com/peter-kirkland-email-sign-up

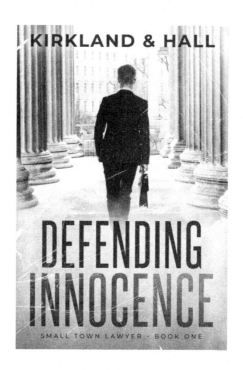

BLURB

An innocent client harbors dark secrets...

Defense attorney Leland Monroe lost it all: his big-city job, his reputation and, worst of all, his loving wife. Now he's back in his hometown to hit restart and repair the relationship with his troubled son. But the past is always present in a small town.

Leland returns to find his high school sweetheart hasn't had the easiest of lives—especially now that her son faces a death sentence for murdering his father. Yet what appears to be an open and shut case is anything but. As Leland digs deeper to uncover a truth even his client is determined to keep buried, a tangled web of corruption weaves its way throughout his once tranquil hometown.

Leland soon realizes it's not just his innocent young client's life that's at stake—powerful forces surface to threaten the precious few loved ones he has left.

Grab your copy of *Defending Innocence* (Small Town Lawyer Book One) from www.relaypub.com/blog/authors/peter-kirkland

EXCERPT

Chapter One:
Monday, June 10, 2019

The Ocean View Diner, where I was waiting for my fried shrimp basket, was a dump with a view of nothing but the courthouse parking lot. It was already shabby when I was in high school, living on fries and coffee while I brainstormed the college application essays that were my ticket out. Much to the surprise of folks in my hometown, I'd made it to law school and beyond. I owned more than a dozen suits. I had tan for summers in the office, navy for opening statements to the jury, charcoal for talking to the media on the Charleston courthouse steps. My kid had admired me at an age when it was almost unnatural to think your dad was anything but a loser. I was a law-and-order guy trying to make the world safer. I'd thought I might run for office.

I nodded to the bailiff who walked through the door giving him a cordial "howdy", but he looked right through me, as he walked past. We'd certainly seen enough of each other in the courthouse, and I tried not to take offense at the slight but there's only so much a man can put up with when it comes to small town judgment.

They say pride goeth before a fall.

I'd seen enough, in my past life representing the great state of South Carolina, to know a man could have it a lot worse. The amount of depravity and human misery that had flowed across my desk made me know I ought to be grateful for what I still had left. My son, in other words, and my license to practice. I'd nearly lost both. The accident that took my wife had nearly killed him too, and even if he still hadn't entirely recovered from it, he'd come farther than anyone expected at the time, but Noah was incredibly angry all the time. Mostly at me but I tried not to let it get to me.

Like water off a duck's back, the little things ought not to have bothered me at all. It shouldn't have mattered that the locals at the next table had stopped talking when I walked in, apparently suspicious of anyone who wasn't a regular. Which I wasn't yet, since it'd been barely six months since I dragged my sorry ass back from the big city. Getting to be a regular took years.

A better man would not have been annoyed by the smell of rancid grease or the creak of ancient ceiling fans. It was even hotter in here than in the June glare outside, and a good man would've sympathized with my waitress, who was stuck here all day and probably never even got to sit down.

But I was not that man. I did say "Thank you kindly" when she dropped my order on the table and sloshed another dose of coffee in my cup, but I was irrationally annoyed that no one had ever fixed the menu sign on the wall between the cash register and the kitchen. The word "cheeseburger" was still missing its first R. When my friends and I were sixteen-year-old jackasses, we thought it was hilarious to order a "cheese booger." Now it was just pathetic that I was back. Especially since the reason I wasn't in the new '50s-style diner on the next corner—the popular lunch place for judges, local politicians, and successful attorneys—was that I couldn't afford it. Here, in exchange for tolerating the broken AC and worn-out furniture, I got decent shrimp at prices that were fifteen or twenty years behind the times.

The folks at the next table had gotten back to jawing, though at a lower volume on account of my being unfamiliar, I supposed. Between crunches of my dinner, I caught the gist: a body had washed ashore a little ways down the coast, where tourists rented beach houses. Maybe I shouldn't have eavesdropped. But although I wasn't a prosecutor anymore, I was probably never going to lose the habit of keeping a close eye on every local crime.

"Bunch of them Yankees was playing volleyball on the beach," the man said. "You know, girls in their bikinis, one of them thousand-dollar gas grills fired up on the deck." His voice held a mix of humor and scorn. "They were having themselves just a perfect vacation. And then this *corpse* washes up! This, I swear to you, decomposing *corpse* crashes the party!"

The table erupted with guffaws.

"So what'd they do?" a man said. "Hop in the Subarus and hightail it back to New York or wherever?"

"No, the thing is—and I heard this from my cousin, you know, the one working for the sheriff? The thing is, they thought a gator got him! Thought they had a gator in the water! And I'll be damned if they weren't pissing themselves like little girls, trying to get everybody back out of the water. Couple of them was so scared they started puking!"

They all lost it. One of them was so entertained he slammed a hand on the table, rattling the silverware. As the laughter started fading, one of them wondered aloud who the dead man might be.

"Aw, don't matter none," the storyteller said. "We ain't missing nobody."

I felt a sourness in my gut. I couldn't go a day here without being reminded why I'd left. In Basking Rock, compassion for your fellow man was strictly circumscribed. Tourists got none. The wrong kind of people, whatever that meant, got none. Your family and lifelong friends could do no wrong, and everybody else could go straight to hell.

I signaled the waitress and asked for a doggie bag. Might as well finish eating at home, away from present company. She scowled, probably thinking I was switching to takeout to avoid leaving a tip. I scrounged through my wallet, sure I'd had a few ones in there and grudgingly set down a five knowing I was leaving more than necessary. Making any kind of enemy was not my style. You never knew who might help you out one day, if you'd taken care not to get on their bad side. More to the point, I knew from friends who worked in health code enforcement that there were few things stupider than making enemies of the folks who make your food.

———

I'd parked my Chevy outside. It used to be the beater, until the nice car was totaled in the accident. When I fired it up, the engine light came on again. I kept right on ignoring it. I'd yet to find a local mechanic I could trust. The one I knew of had been a bully back in high school, and from what I'd heard, age had only refined his techniques. If he thought you'd gotten too big for your britches—which I certainly had, what with my law degree and my former big-city career —he took his rage out on your wallet.

The Chevy heroically made it home once again. I parked beside the clump of fan palms that were starting to block the driveway. I needed to get them pruned, and to fix the wobbly porch railing that would've been a lawsuit waiting to happen if we ever had visitors. I needed a haircut. My geriatric Yorkie, Squatter, who limped to the door to greet me, needed a trip to the vet. The to-do list never stopped growing, and checking anything off it required money I no longer had.

I tossed the mail on the table and scratched the dog on the head. He'd come with the house—the landlord said he'd been abandoned by the previous tenants, and I couldn't bring myself to dump him at the pound. As he wagged his tail, I called out to my son. "Noah?"

All I could hear was the breeze outside and Squatter's nails scrabbling on the tile. I was no scientist—my major, long ago when I thought I was smart, was US history—but I knew physics did not allow a house to be that quiet if it contained a teenage boy. It looked like I'd be eating another dinner alone. I'd texted Noah when I got to the diner, to see if he wanted anything, but he hadn't answered. I never knew where he was lately, unless he was at a doctor's appointment I'd driven him to myself.

After feeding Squatter I pulled up a chair, took a bite of now-cold shrimp, and flipped through the mail. The monthly health insurance bill—nearly thirteen hundred bucks just for the two of us—went into the small pile of things I couldn't get out of paying. Noah's physical therapy bills did too; as long as he still needed PT, I couldn't risk getting blacklisted there.

And he was going to need it for a good while yet, to have a shot at something like the life he'd been hoping for. We were both still hanging on to the thread of hope that he could get back into the shape that had earned him a baseball scholarship to USC in Columbia. The accident had cost him that, but he was determined to try again.

Or so he'd said at first. Lately he'd gotten depressed with how long it was taking, and how much fun he saw his high-school buddies having on Instagram. They'd gone to college and moved on with their lives. He'd started making new friends here, but to my dismay, they were not what you'd call college bound. College didn't seem to have occurred to them. One worked in a fast-food joint, and another didn't seem to work much at all.

I heard gravel crunching in the driveway. Even without the odd rhythm his limp gave him, I knew it had to be Noah; our little bungalow was an okay place to eat and sleep but too small to be much of a gathering place. I stuffed the bills into my battered briefcase. He didn't need to know we were struggling.

Squatter raced to the door to celebrate Noah's return and accompanied him back to the kitchen in a state of high canine excitement. Noah looked a little glum, or bored, as usual. Without bothering to say hi, he poured himself some tea from the fridge, sat down in the chair next to mine, and took one of my shrimp.

"I would've brought you some," I said. "I texted you from the diner."

He shrugged. "I didn't see it in time," he said, feeding the crispy tail to Squatter.

"That's a shame," I said. "What were you so busy doing?"

He glared at me. That look was a one-two punch every time. He had his mother's eyes, so it felt like the hostility was coming from both of them.

I knew I should back off, but I was never good at drawing the line in the right place. "Hanging out with Jackson again?"

He took another shrimp, got up, and went into the living room. At fourteen, Noah had perfected the art of sullen teenager. Now at nineteen, he'd turned it into a lost art as he immersed himself in the depression and apathy that comes with having your life turned completely upside down.

———

Grab your copy of *Defending Innocence* (Small Town Lawyer Book One) from www.relaypub.com/blog/authors/peter-kirkland

Printed in Great Britain
by Amazon

40422130R00185